memoirs

of a

dilettante

volume one

helena
hann-basquiat

 dilettante publishing

Memoirs of a Dilettante Volume One

ISBN 13: 978-0-9940419-1-3
ISBN 10: 0-9940419-1-8

Published in Canada by Dilettante Publishing

caveat emptor

Most of what follows is true. Well, sort of.

Okay, *some* of what follows is true. There. That's better.

Except where I've exaggerated, embellished, romanticized or out-and-out made stuff up. Whether for the sake of narrative, or because the bitter pill of truth is always easier to swallow with a candy coating of pretty lies, I may have blurred the lines between truth and fiction.

Consider this a cowardly confession; I find it easier to tell certain autobiographical tales if they are dressed up in another set of clothes. While I will never reveal what is word for word and what is complete fabrication, I will leave it up to you to decide just how much (if any) you are prepared to swallow.

My hope is that you will be entertained, and if you are moved to laughter, tears or anger by my words, does it really matter what is fact and what is flourish? If you want to read "I got up, I drank my coffee, I got dressed, I went to work, I had lunch, I worked some more, I went home, I wrote a bit, I had some Chinese takeout, I went to bed, I got up the next morning and did it all again," then you've come to the wrong place, darlings. What follows is life turned up to full volume, in HD full technicolour – remixed and re-mastered – Life (the extended dance remix). So put such pedestrian labels like fiction and non-fiction (as if there really, truly is such an animal outside of a science textbook) out of your head, grab a couple white chocolate macamadamia nut cookies and some chocolate milk (or your favourite non-dairy alternative if you're lactose intolerant) and sit back and enjoy the ride, darlings. Be sure to keep your hands and feet inside the vehicle at all times, and if you find yourself occasionally slipping into the archaic cockney accent of a certain Dickensian street urchin, don't be alarmed – the Countess tends to have that effect on everybody.

With great affection and much gratitude, I remain

Your favourite dilettante,

Helena Hann-Basquiat

dramatis personae

Helena Hann-Basquiat

Powers: Alliteration.
Post-modern ironic self-detachment.
The ability to shamelessly insert the word 'darling' into almost any sentence.
Stops conversations when she enters the room with her stunning good looks.
Vanity on a prodigious scale – off the charts. When her vanity powers are activated, there is really no defense possible.

Strengths: Can tolerate a superhuman amount of bullshit – no, really – it's astounding. Is incredibly adaptable, and can blend in to any situation seamlessly. Uncanny knowledge of dated pop culture references, particularly anything related to '80s Brit Pop or the films of John Hughes – she can pretty much act out all of *Ferris Bueller's Day Off*.

Weaknesses: Musicians. Vodka and citrus fruits, particularly pink grapefruit. Sad songs sung by tragic singers. If the aforementioned singer is dead, and the circumstances of their death were heartbreaking (say, for instance, accidental drowning, just to pick something random) she has the tendency to slip into a deep melancholy and may become completely dysfunctional and maudlin for hours at end. Inability to comprehend modern trends such as 'twerking' or 'LOL-cats' due to an atrophied pop culture muscle caused by a self-inflicted injury that nobody around here seems willing to talk about. Sometimes commits social suicide by acting out all of *Ferris Bueller's Day Off* much to the annoyance of others and great embarrassment of the Countess Penelope of Arcadia.

Eyes: Yes, of course she has eyes (oh – not to be insensitive to the eyeless).

Hair: Red. No, Brunette. But with ginger highlights. Sometimes a dark chestnut. But today it's blonde.

Height: 5'9", plus add another two inches with heels.

Age: You'll have to read and do the math.

Profession: Dilettante. Duties include writing on a myriad of subjects in a variety of forms, formats and fashions; exploring any and all artistic avenues that strike her fancy, including, but not limited to: painting, music, sculpture, film, acting, fire-eating, and the making of semi-pornographic balloon animals (a cottage industry with a small but profitable niche market). And, of course, she does have a nine-to-five where she works for a talent agency, placing would-be actors (or just people who want to be a small part of the movies) in background roles for various movie and television productions. But that is only how she collects a paycheck, that's not who she is.

Bio: Born at a very young age in the small village of Bichon-Frisse near the France/Switzerland border, she is the daughter of a part-time cello teacher and a painter — well, her mother painted nails at the Happy Time Nail Salon — so that's sort of painting. And that bit about her father being a part-time cello teacher, that was not so much of a lie as a typo — it should read Jell-O teacher — he taught Home Economics three days a week at the local high school, and really was only called upon for his culinary expertise in the medium of Jell-O.

Due to a congenital personality defect, she kept on the move for most of her life, lest someone pin her down like a butterfly in a glass box. She is constantly changing her appearance to avoid being recognized by people who may have seen her awkward performance as Audrey in her 8th grade production of *Little Shop of Horrors*, a debacle from which she has never truly recovered.

To make up for a crippling sense of high self-esteem, she dabbles in whatever she can get her hands into in order to fail spectacularly at something. And so, she's written cookbooks, ten volumes of horrible poetry that she then bound herself in leather she tanned poorly from cows she raised herself and then slaughtered because she was bored with farming, all while listening ironically to *Meat Is Murder* by The Smiths. She hopes one day Morrissey will forgive her.

She has an entire portfolio of macaroni art that she's never shown anyone, because she doesn't think that the general populous or, "the great unwashed masses" as she calls them, would understand the statement she was trying to make with them.

She was completely self-educated in a private institute in the Catskills where she majored in Pop Culture and Unpopular Music. She wrote her doctorate thesis on the films of John Hughes, and awarded herself a doctorate, though it's not generally recognized.

Her most current abandoned project was a rock-opera based on the life of Cecil B. DeMille, but now she's working on a one woman play loosely based on The Who's 1979 concert in Cincinnati, Ohio during which eleven people were killed during a stampede. Her choice to market it as a sci-fi thriller, and the fact that neither The Who, nor their music, nor in fact, Cincinnati feature in the play is a bit of a conundrum at this point, as is the fact that the plot is pretty much ripped off of an old *X-files* episode. Don't look for this to surface any time soon.

The Countess Penelope of Arcadia

AKA: Penny, The Countess, The Countess Arcade, Penny Arcade

Powers: Neologism – she can make up words like nothing you've ever experienced, and then, by sheer force of will, insert them into popular usage. Then, when made up words fail her, she has the ability to gratuitously use the word 'fuck'

without causing offense. She can mimic any accent known to man or woman and yet still have them end up morphing after a little while into a Dickensian street-urchin voice that bears more than a passing resemblance to that horrid accent Dick Van Dyke affects in *Mary Poppins*. Inhuman ability to get under your skin in the best possible way – her power to charm is unstoppable, and is useful for imposing her will on others.

Strengths: Penny is a chameleon, and uses her skills of reinvention to shock and disarm as the situation demands. She is a master of deductive reasoning and the art of misdirection. Penny possesses the universe's only fully functional Spontaneity Drive, which, when activated, causes her to act out in some random manner, such as jumping up on a lunch counter and singing an impromptu version of some '80s hair metal song, thus deflecting any harm that may come her way onto unsuspecting passersby. Another fun fact: the Spontaneity Drive is fuelled by coffee, which is relatively inexpensive, however, the Countess prefers Shade Grown, Fair Trade coffee, preferably something in a dark roast.

Weaknesses: Her grasp of recent history and her insistence that Al Gore is the greatest villain of the modern age gives her something of a blind spot, and, when teased about this, gets all flustered and over-defensive. Her affection for physical media, for example, can be exploited to your advantage and amusement. Unlike Helena, the Countess has a near fatal allergy to bullshit, and will break out in a rash of tantrums, ill-advised throwing, dropping, or kicking whatever may be at hand, and the most creative and diverse cursing you've ever heard. If you experience Penny in the midst of an allergic reaction, please do not try to intervene. Seek immediate assistance, or provide an anti-allergic agent, which usually comes in the form of ice cream.

Eyes: Blue (Purple with contacts)

Hair: Black. Or pink. Or black and pink. Or blue. Or black and blue. Or orange. Or black and orange (Hallowe'en, usually).

Height: Taller than she'd like. Not that she minds being tall, but for the longest time she was taller than all the boys in her class, and no one wanted to dance with her. Not that she wanted them to. God forbid.

Age: She never gives her actual age -- she likes to keep people guessing.

Profession: Student (mostly). Has worked as a barista, a waitress, a film extra, a line cook, and then there was that summer she wore a giant stuffed head to work as the mascot of a local video store (even though that thing was air conditioned, she still came home smelling like the inside of a gym bag every night).

Bio: Without spoiling what you're about to read, all you need to know is that Penny is Helena's niece, and that she's a university student. She was born in the small town of Arcadia during the early years of Clinton's reign (Jean Chretien had just become PM of Canada with his opposition being the Bloc Quebecois – a political party whose main goal was to divide the nation. Across the pond, John Major sat at Ten Downing Street desperately trying to keep the Pound from bottoming out. Is it any wonder her sense of identity is fluid, or that she retreats into fantasy from time to time? The world she grew up in was – and continues to be – strange, frightening, and full of uncertainty).

To say that the Countess Penelope of Arcadia has a flair for the dramatic would be an understatement of elephantine proportions. As a child, she once staged a group protest at her daycare, convincing all the other toddlers to throw their dirty diapers at the teacher while they chanted "More Cookies, No Naps!" They called her La Revolucionista and sent in the C.I.A. (Children's Intermediary Assistant) to take her out. They have a picture of her up on the wall of that day, a stern look on her little face, fist in the air, her other arm draped over the shoulder of a child that bears a striking resemblance to an infantile Nikita Khrushchev.

After reading *Alice in Wonderland* during a particularly bad citric acid trip, Penny developed a penchant for dressing in outlandish striped socks and crinolines, and enjoys turning her hair into sculptured works of art that require a scholarly knowledge of both Salvador Dali and Dr. Seuss to understand and/or appreciate.

Then you'll blink, and Penny will appear as if she were suddenly an extra on the cast of Friends, maybe sitting on a comfy sofa in the background sipping a latte while laughing at something witty her extra friends just said. Blink again and she's lounging around in sweats and oversized t-shirts around the house, and then blink again and she's cleaned up in a cocktail dress and looks like a runway model just so she can go to the store.

It's as if her entire closet is a costume shop for a production company that did *Hairspray* and *Death of a Salesman* last month, *The Wizard of Oz* and *Waiting for Godot* this month, and is gearing up to do *The Velveteen Rabbit, Macbeth* and *The Rocky Horror Show*.

If you want to know why she does these things, go out with her sometime when she's dressed all in black like some Goth princess and listen to her laugh in pure joy as she receives dirty looks from little old ladies and different kinds of dirty looks from little old men. She's fascinated with people, and loves watching their reactions. She is a true student of cultural anthropology, and if she does things to elicit extreme reactions, why, she'll tell you that it was purely for academic reasons, and not because she is an incorrigible urchin who just loves causing trouble.

a note about the notes

These memoirs have been annotated for your pleasure. Sometimes the notes are to explain some esoteric bit of pop culture that I've referenced, and sometimes it's commentary as to what was going on in my mind at the time. You can treat this like the commentary on a DVD (or Blu-Ray if you're all up to date with your physical media) and ignore it as you will, but you might just enjoy what your favourite dilettante has added for your increased enjoyment.

couche-tard
and the jumping asians

When I stepped off the bus in Montreal, sidekick in tow, en route to see a band you've never heard of, (and really, that's your loss) the very last thing I expected was to be hugged by a young man in a dress – though, in retrospect, after all that followed, it was really not all that strange. No stranger than the sordid tale of Couche-Tard and the Jumping Asians, which, if I manage to avoid unnecessary digressions, I may end up telling. So, please, do read on.

The first thing you need to remember when visiting *La Belle Province*[1] is that it is absolutely crucial that you distinguish the pronunciation of your 'B' sounds versus your 'P' sounds. You don't want to end up like my protégée, the young Countess Penelope of Arcadia, expecting a hot chocolate, and ending up with hot tuna latte. She gave the waitress an undignified sneer as she exclaimed, *"Il y a un poisson dans ma boisson!"*[2] and stormed out to one of the half dozen sex shops we'd passed along the way to purchase a bull whip with which to punish the offending waitress.

Returning twenty minutes later with a shocked expression and sans bullwhip, she instead flicked her gloved hand with a riding crop she said she'd purchased from something she called the

---

[1] Quebec is sometimes called this – the beautiful province.
[2] There's a fish in my drink!

couche-tard, and at the time I let it pass, but later I'd have cause to question just exactly what a couche-tard was, and what exactly it had to do with jumping Asians. Right then I just watched with amusement as my indignant novitiate peeled a layer of paint off the well-meaning waitress, who by this time had developed an expression on her face not unlike that of a Rembrandt aficionado at a Jackson Pollack exhibit.[3]

"What is the meaning of this?" The attendant Countess demanded.

"*Que veux-tu dire?* Uh... zat iz, what do you mean? Zis iz what you ordered. Ze hot fish. Le poisson chaud." The bewildered beverage mistress blundered her way around the English language with a Parisian accent for some reason, even though we were in Montreal. What can I say? I'm an unreliable narrator.[4] An unreliable narrator with an unusually unconventional yet somehow appealing penchant for alliterative prose, so really, in the end, the taking of the occasional liberty is forgivable, n'est-ce pas?

"Not le poisson, you couche-tard! Le boisson! Le boisson!" Penny was the first to use the phrase thusly, and hence brought it into current usage, much like those uneducated but genteel writers who popularized the bastardized word "thusly" through sheer force of will, or like those poor grammatically impaired souls who insist that "hopefully" is indeed a real word.[5] Sad, deluded fools, to be sure, and both the Countess and I would say a prayer for them at the Notre Dame after we finished our respective hot beverages, being sure to leave not a penny *pourboire*,[6] but I am getting ahead of myself.

---

[3]Rembrandt was one of what are now referred to as "The Dutch Masters", and created paintings of a life-like quality. Jackson Pollack splashed paint on large canvasses. There are those who would say that art is in the eye of the beholder, darlings, but usually those people are unskilled and envious of those with actual talent.

[4]This is a title I wear with pride, darlings. How very post-modern of me, I know, but being an unreliable narrator is not just being a poor storyteller. On the contrary, playing with the conventions of storytelling and disassembling the traditional modes of writing is not a kamikaze task. There actually is a skill involved in mixing fact with fiction and making your reader guess which is which. It is yet another skill to boldly tell your reader "this is fiction" and then ask them to play along anyway.

[5]Neither "hopefully" nor "thusly" are real words, darlings. Sorry to break it to you.

[6]What the French call a "tip" – literally meaning "for drinks". As in, what you leave your waitress will get spent getting them drunk after work.

It was about this time that the Countess Arcade and I went searching for a soothing balm – one that could not be found in the potions and lotions section of the aforementioned sex shops along the red light district of the Saint Laurent – and found ourselves, unlikely as it may seem if you hadn't just read the last paragraph, on the steps of the Basilique Notre Dame de Montréal.

Did we step inside? Yes, we did, and I am delighted to report, dear reader, that neither myself, nor my chaste and virtuous acolyte were subjected to any of the filthy violations purported to occur at the hands of the clergy in such places. Protective though I am of my young charge, I could tell that this came as almost a disappointment (along with the fact that I did not, in fact, burst into flames upon entering the Basilica – a fact that lost her five dollars, and, of course, the right to sing the "I was right and you were wrong" song), and so I assured her that if she wished to be violated by a stranger, we could always march right back up Saint Laurent[7], where the promise of defilement beckoned like – to be à propos –a whore. I just told her to count me out – if my cohort wanted to indulge in that kind of smutty behaviour, she was on her own.

"It's not that I don't want you to see naked, sweaty men, dear," I assured her, "it's just that I don't want to be there when it happens. Now, be a good girl and keep up – I believe there are still yet some sex shops that we have not yet frequented – you may ogle the preposterously prominent plastic penises of the storefront mannequins should that be to your liking."

So it was that there, on the very steps of Notre Dame[8], that we were accosted by the jumping Asians. (Remember the jumping Asians? This is a story about jumping Asians, darling – do try to keep up).

---

[7] Home of Montreal's "Red Light District". Strip clubs directly adjacent to other strip clubs. Then there's the strip club across the street. Oh, and then if you're tired of the strip clubs you can always visit another strip club.

[8] For those of you who are picturing gargoyles, hunchbacks, and Demi Moore as a gypsy, you're thinking Paris. What the hell is the matter with you? Montreal's Basilica was built between the years 1824-1843, and is one of the largest churches in North America. God needs a big expensive house, don't you know? Whatever, it is an architectural marvel, a true thing of beauty.

We were just stepping out of the cathedral, when four, maybe five stringy Asian students approached us, and without warning, thrust a camera into my hands.

Now, if you're thinking that the next words out of their mouths were "You take-a peecha" à la Mickey Rooney in *Breakfast at Tiffany's*, or whatever Charlie Chan Hollywood Chinese stereotype you want to cite, then you are a racist bastard.

In actuality, they asked us if we spoke English (I know, right?) and if we could take a picture of them. A pretty simple request, sure, until they added "but it's a bit complicated..."

"Complicated?" I asked, a bit warily.

"Yes," their glorious leader said, taking a little red book[9] out of his pocket. "We need a picture of us jumping off these steps."

I considered this for a moment, and as I considered this, I also considered the possible outcomes of jumping on the steps of the cathedral. I didn't consider, however, not even for a moment, why these five (or was it six?) Asians required this photograph.

"I don't know," I hesitated, "what if you fall? That's pretty far to fall."

"Don't be such a couche-tard, Helena," Penny chided, "take the bloody picture."

Penny, while neither British, nor an orphan (nor indeed, it bears mentioning, an actual Countess), nonetheless occasionally adopts the affectations of a Dickensian street urchin[10], which is, one might argue, in direct contrast to her pretension of being a Countess. Somehow, though, the marvelous girl pulls off each flawlessly, and without a pinch of effort.

I was still waffling, however, when one of the Asians, a particularly zen-like girl who looked like Lucy Liu (if Lucy Liu had been a philosophy major and had no idea what a Hatori Hanso[11] sword was) looked me in the eyes and said "A mountain isn't far to fall when you've fallen from the moon," and then performed the

---

[9]Glorious leader/little red book – a reference to Chairman Mao Tse-Tung, Communist Leader of China from 1943-1976, and his book of quotations, which every good party member carried. Come on – didn't they teach you anything in history class?

[10]I could give you a brief history of Victorian London and the writing of Charles Dickens here, darlings, but honestly – if I say Tiny Tim will that suffice as an explanation?

[11]Lucy Liu/Hatori Hanso sword – A reference to the actress and her role in Quentin Tarantino's *Kill Bill*. This philosophy major kept her wits about her, and didn't lose her head. The same could not be said for O-Ren Ishii, I'm afraid.

standing Lotus position (and not the one advertised by the exotic dancer with the unlikely name of Miso Honey at that club on Saint Laurent).

What could I do? I took the picture.

Now, previously, I had mentioned that we were in Montreal in order to see a band you'd never heard of, and while this has little or nothing to do with the jumping Asians, nor the couche-tard, to be completely fair, it bears mentioning, and if you follow the threads carefully, I promise, despite my reputation as an unreliable narrator, that it may all make sense in the end. However, I feel it only fair to add one caveat, and that is that the story is not all that well woven, and that if you pull too hard on any loose threads, it may very well unravel – my sincerest apologies in advance.

We were there to see Marillion perform their album *Brave* from beginning to end – which is, I should mention, a pretty big deal. While I could gush and bubble about the band, this album in particular, I'll simply take a moment to say that the show was an incredible experience, akin to driving a 1961 Ferrari 250GT California Spyder through the streets of Chicago. (I have it on the good authority of a close personal friend of mine that this car is, as he likes to say, "so choice." I can only assume that is a positive endorsement).[12]

Brave is what the cool kids call a 'concept album', or what the hippies might call a 'rock opera', and it tells the story of a runaway girl who is found wandering on a bridge by the local constabulary, and brought in off the streets for her own good. After some investigation, it is discovered that the girl comes from a dysfunctional home, dad's molesting her, (revealed in the cleverly-penned *Alone Again in the Lap of Luxury*) and she's been wandering the streets, crashing in less than savoury places with less than well-meaning friends, and in the end, despite being dragged back home, she ends up leaving again and finishing what she had set out to do when she was found by the police. In the finale, the narrator berates those closest to her for hurting the very one that they should have protected, and then (in a way that Penny insisted was très passive aggressive), she says, in effect, that jumping off a bridge isn't so bad

---

[12]Mr. Ferris Bueller, ladies and gentlemen.

when you've been through what she's been through – metaphorically falling from the moon.

Now, if you experienced a vague frisson of déjà vu just now, don't be alarmed – it was completely manufactured by yours truly. One of the tell-tale signs of an unreliable narrator (or bad writer, you decide) is that they will alter events to fit the story, and bring everything full circle.

Does that make the story any less true?

The answer is a resounding "Yes."

Where was I? Oh yes – somewhere around here:

"Don't be such a couche-tard, Helena," Penny chided, "Take the bloody picture."

Which I did, and it was fine, and nobody got hurt, and we got into a heated discussion about people who put on ridiculous affectations when they insert foreign words into their conversations – you know, the Latino chef who speaks perfect English until they say the word jalapeño, and then they pronounce it with so much accent that you need subtitles. Yes, we get it, you're Latino. But even though I use French words on a regular basis, like rendezvous, je ne sais quoi, menage a trois (well, maybe not on a regular basis), and I'm fairly confident that I'm pronouncing them with enough French in them as to make them sound French, I don't feel the need to roll my 'R's or stop wearing deodorant while I'm saying them. I know not to pronounce the 'S's at the end of a word, but that doesn't make me feel the need to dress all in black, chain smoke, and watch a Jerry Lewis[13] film marathon (why do the French find him funny? I don't know). I know enough of Spanish to know you don't pronounce tortilla to rhyme with more filler, and I'm fairly confident I can correctly use the word *presque isle*[14] in a sentence. After all, I'm not American. Ask an average American to say that word, and you're going to hear something that rhymes with fo'shizzle.

---

[13]Jerry Lewis is a beloved American comedian whose slapstick humour and crazy voices were highly influential on people like Jim Carrey and Eddie Murphy. Slapstick is a comedic aesthetic that has gone out of fashion for the most part, as we are far too cynical to enjoy the old pie-in-the-face gag, and prefer our comedy to be more subtle. Except for the French, apparently.

[14]Literally, almost an island. A peninsula (think Florida) only being attached to land by a small strip of land.

It was about this point, if I recall correctly, which I always do, that a group of college students walked up to us, and without any warning, a young man who kind of looked like Lucy Liu (if Lucy Liu were a white dude with hipster glasses wearing what was supposed to be a dress but looked more like a big apron of the sort that Jean Stapleton might have worn on *All In the Family*)[15] put his arm around me while one of his friends took a picture. I didn't even have time to wonder why. I just took it in stride.

At this point, I'd like to thank Lucy Liu for not just one, but two cameos in this story. Big round of applause for Lucy Liu, dear readers.

Which brings us, by the by, to the couche-tard. No, really, it does. All that bit about language and pronunciation and Lucy Liu was just a distraction, and perhaps a bit of a segue to talk about how words – slang words, foreign words, mash-up words – are adopted into popular usage.

"What did you call me?" I asked, suddenly realizing that this was not the first time I had heard or seen the phrase couche-tard that day.

"Couche-tard," Penny said without missing a beat. "It's a thing now."

"Since when?" I asked cautiously, not wanting to sound like somehow I wasn't up on current trends.

"Since now," the Countess shrugged. "I saw it on a sign, it sounded offensive, but, you know, in a harmless way. I called you couche-tard, and you've obviously taken it as the insult it was intended to be, ergo – it's a thing now."

"Couche-tard?" I asked, unsure.

"Well, yeah, I mean, douche bag's played out, ennit?" The Dickensian urchin was back in her voice. "And retard, well, thass just hurtful, and not at all PC. So..."

"Couche-tard."

"Right. Couche-tard."

---

[15] Jean Stapleton played Edith Bunker on *All In The Family* – think Marge Simpson for the 1970s.

"But what's it even mean, Penny? I mean, you can't very well go around calling people names when you don't even know what you're calling them."

Could you? Is that a thing one can do?

"That's the fing," Penny smirked, affecting an even heavier urchin accent, and took a bite of a pastry, spraying flaky golden crumbs down the front of her. "It don't mean nuffink. It's like, Sleep-Late, or Late-Night or sommat. Just sounds offensive."

"Wait a minute," I said, doing a double-take. "Just – just hang on just a second. When did you get a pastry?"

"When you were going on about jalapeños and Jenny Saquois and stuff."

"Je ne sais quoi. It means I don't know," I corrected her.

"Well, if you don't know what it means, I'd be careful using it if I were you – some of the people around here can be pretty touchy about their language, if you know what I mean."

"I know what it means," I said, feeling like I'd just stepped into a John Hughes film[16] for a moment. "It means 'I don't know what', as in, it's indescribable. There are no words to describe that 'it' that you're trying to describe."

"I don't know gov'ner," the Countess Penelope of Arcadia-cum-street urchin teased, "thass a lot o' words, that is."

"You sound like Dick Van Dyke in *Mary Poppins*, you know that? Anyway, where'd you get the pastry?"

She pointed down the street, and that's when I saw it – and it was winking at me, the smarmy bastard! Like it knew something I didn't.

"Huh," I said. There really wasn't more to be said. "Well, did you at least get me something?"

Penny shook her head sheepishly. "Sorry."

So I called her a couche-tard.[17]

Apparently, this is a thing now.

---

[16]John Hughes 1950-2009 – made some of the definitive adolescent films. *Sixteen Candles, The Breakfast Club, Pretty In Pink, Ferris Bueller's Day Off.*

[17]In some places of the world, it's Mac's, in others it's Winks (which is the only one that makes sense to me, darlings), but it's actually the corporate name of one of the largest convenience store chains in the world, so to prevent them from suing me, I'm using the picture I took of their logo rather than a stock photo of their logo. Who thought Couche-Tard was a good name? Honestly!

this just in: "there are no more original ideas," declares stephanie meyer

$\mathcal{F}$resh off her plundering and watering down of Anne Rice[1], Stephanie Meyer secretly confesses that she always wished that she'd written *The Body Snatchers* instead of Jack Finney.[2] Me, too, love. Me, too. Only I didn't have the audacity to actually do it, and more fool me. Had I known that one could get away with what is only one step below outright plagiarism, you can bet your indignant-how-dare-she-criticize-Stephanie-Meyer-like-OMG-IKR? ass that by now I would have somehow turned *The Communist Manifesto*[3] into a coming-of-age romantic teen drama featuring a love triangle between Karl Marx, Friedrich Engels and the princess Anastasia (again with the taking of liberties, I know).[4]

---

[1]Author of *Interview With A Vampire* and the rest of the Vampire Chronicles, Anne Rice popularized the idea of a brooding vampire that misses his humanity. Where Ms. Rice's characters delved into existentialism and philosophical musings on the soul and the nature of evil, Ms. Meyer, well, the less said about that the better.

[2]Of course she didn't actually *say* this, darlings, but I think she sent a pretty clear message by writing a book that is essentially borrows Mr. Finney's plot.

[3]Please don't make me give you a history lesson. Exactly what do you think *The Communist Manifesto* is about, darlings? It's a treatise on the history of class struggles, and puts forth the notion that corrupt capitalism would be replaced by socialism and then communism. Not much of a love story, but then, neither was *Twilight*.

[4]Seeing as Marx died in 1883 and Engels died in 1895 and Anastasia wasn't even born until 1901 – but why let facts get in the way of a good trashy love triangle?

Hell, I could have made it a trilogy, because, as my dear confidante, the Countess of Arcadia likes to say, "It's all about the trilogy, bitches!"

Book One: Bourgeois, the story of the palace life of the princess Anastasia, a timid, awkward, shy yet brave and independent girl of an indeterminate age, skin type or hair colour who doesn't know who she wants to be, and finds herself at home both surrounded by luxury, but also, running barefoot through the fields with her stable-boy, the handsome and usually shirtless Freddy.

Book Two: Proletariat, in which we see the devotion of Karl, a bookish, scrawny young man, who wears glasses, and is Anastasia's math tutor (work with me here). Anastasia is drawn to his nerdy mystique and his ideas of, you know, being true to yourself, and your people, and other abstract and harmless ideas that, at the same time, sound deep and wise. Also, when he takes his glasses off, he is transformed, not unlike the transformation of Clark Kent to Superman, into an Adonis of Robert Pattinson-esque stature.

Book Three: Communist, in which the princess finally has to make a choice between the two men who love her – the ruggedly handsome Freddy, or the shy but brilliant Karl, who reveals that he is also secretly a vampire.

Okay, I know what you're thinking – you're thinking *Really, Helena? You're going to follow in the footsteps of every other Internet malcontent and rag on poor Stephanie Meyer? That just reeks of sour grapes. Also, hey, great idea for a trilogy, when does **that** come out?*

Perhaps. But it's not really about poor (and really, darling, there's nothing poor about her) Stephanie, is it? When it comes right down to it, it's just a slap in the face to anyone who wants, nay demands more from their entertainment. Is it really too much to ask for just a *soupçon* of originality?

I am referring, of course, to the upcoming film *The Host*, based on the novel of the same name, which somehow got published without anyone raising any red flags about the recycled plot line. I mean it's not like it's some random, unknown cult film that she plundered hoping no one would notice. It was a book, and then a movie, then a remake, then another remake called *Body Snatchers*, and then *The Invasion*. In case you have no idea what I'm talking about, here's a side-by-side comparison for you:

From Wikipedia: *Invasion of the Body Snatchers*: The story depicts an extraterrestrial invasion in a small California town. The invaders replace human beings with duplicates that appear identical on the surface but are devoid of any emotion or individuality. A local doctor uncovers what is happening and tries to stop them.[5]

From IMDB: The Host: When an unseen enemy threatens mankind by taking over their bodies and erasing their memories, Melanie will risk everything to protect the people she cares most about, proving that love can conquer all in a dangerous new world.[6]

I mean, goddammit, I've seen every variation and version ever captured on cinematic celluloid, and I'll be double-damned if I'm going to watch one of my favourite frightening moments from childhood (and indeed, a lifelong recurring nightmare) be watered down into a poorly written love story exploring not issues of paranoia and isolation coupled with the dangers of conformity at any cost, but rather, issues of body image and a reminder of how wonderful it is to have a body (I'm not making this shit up)[7] complete with a love song by Taylor Swift or whoever.

But Helena, you argue, *nothing is new, and not even that is new. People have been recycling stories for generations! Even Harry Potter is just Star Wars, which is just The Hidden Fortress.*

My point exactly, and also, well done on the Kurosawa[8] reference. Maybe it's not that writers have lost their imaginations,

---

[5] http://en.wikipedia.org/wiki/Invasion_of_the_Body_Snatchers#Plot
[6] http://www.imdb.com/title/tt1517260/plotsummary
[7] http://en.wikipedia.org/wiki/The_Host_(novel)#Major_themes – I really wish I were making this up – but sadly I'm not.
[8] Akira Kurosawa was a Japanese director who made epic films that influenced all of the Hollywood greats. *The Hidden Fortress* was cited as one of the major influences for *Star Wars* by Mr. George Lucas himself. You may have never seen a Kurosawa film, but you've surely seen films that have either been influenced by one, or are, in fact, a Western re-imagining of one. Seven Samurai became *The Magnificent Seven*, a western starring Yul Brenner about seven hired guns who fight on behalf of a small village that is being pillaged by bandits. And if you haven't seen that, but the plot

it's just that they know something that we are not willing to admit – that we really haven't changed that much from when we were bossy little babies, demanding to be read the same damn story again and again and again. We don't want something new. All evidence would suggest that we don't even necessarily want something good, and I guess that's where Stephanie Meyer comes in. We want what's comfortable, predictable and familiar, and we don't want any subtle agendas or hidden meanings, because that's just not good entertainment, and as Kurt Cobain allegedly said in a rarely publicized interview with *Vogue* magazine, "Here we are now, darlings, entertain us."[9]

Or maybe it's not plagiarism, or lack of imagination – maybe there really are just no more original ideas.

Whatever. Get me my agent on the phone. I've got a trilogy to pitch, bitches!

---

sounds familiar, close your eyes and try to imagine the voice of Kevin Spacey as a giant grasshopper and you'll realize I've just described the plot of *A Bug's Life*.
[9] I could be mistaken, but I believe this was in the same issue where that crazy French philosopher René Descartes coined the phrase "I think, therefore, I am, darlings."

sister i'm a poet...[1]
or something

"**P**oor old Morrissey,"[2] the seemingly ancient Countess Penelope of Arcadia sighed from behind a newspaper that was not, I assure you, *The Daily Mail*,[3] but was a rag, nonetheless. Her air of loss far extended her brutal youth, but that's Penny for you – all affectations and melodrama. Even her manner of speaking this morning, and the cadence of her accent suggested that Arcadia was somehow in the vicinity of Manchester.

"What's this, love?"I asked trepidatiously (yes, it's a real word, look it up, you lazy bastards).

"Well," she sighed again, billowing the newsprint out in front of her like a mainsail, "it says here that Morrissey isn't going to be

---

[1]Sister I'm a Poet is a song by Morrissey

[2]This whole story hinges on you knowing who Morrissey is, so, really -- lead singer of The Smiths, part of the Manchester music scene, famous outspoken vegetarian and asexual. (Much speculation has been made regarding Morrissey's sexuality, and the fact that he has never weighed in one way or the other has only given him more allure). He has refused to tour in Canada, much to my chagrin, due to the fact that seal hunting is still practiced in the far far north where there is nothing else to do – I'm not sure if he expects people there to farm ice or something but never mind. He's a handsome devil with a golden voice, that's really all you need to know. Oh, and the vegetarianism, too.

[3]*The Daily Mail* is a British tabloid. Make your own judgements, as I'll not risk a libel lawsuit – you know – the kind *The Daily Mail* is often charged with.

able to finish his tour —too many health problems. S'a bloody shame, thass wot that is, ennit?"

Well, actually, I was a bit relieved, and I told her so. The way she was acting, I had thought she was going to say he was dead, and I do not look forward to ever hearing that news. The day after that happens, you will find me locked in my room with my Smiths L.P.s and a Texas Mickey[4] of Grey Goose alternately singing *Reel Around The Fountain* and *Miserable Lie*[5] repeatedly and poorly (but passionately), and I will not come out – absolutely will not emerge until someone can convince me that he was not, in fact the last of the famous international playboys[6], and that someone better than Brandon Flowers from The Killers[7] will eventually be discovered, and that this yet-to-be discovered singer will not mind that I enjoy a nice thick steak from time to time (sorry, Moz).[8]

"I mean, the cow's dead, it's not like it's going to mind me eating it after it's dead," I thought, apparently out loud.

"That's messed up," Penny said, and buried her snooty little pseudo-aristocratic snout deeper in her dingy little dishrag of a paper.

"You know what else is dead?" I declared, tearing the paper out from in front of her face. "Print media. There, I said it!"

The Countess Arcade gasped and recoiled as if I'd slapped her across the face. "Take it back, Helena! Take it back!"

"I'm sorry," I replied resolutely, "but it's true. This just in: Print media passed away quietly, after a long illness brought on by inconvenience and obsolescence. It was preceded by the Radio Star, who, you'll remember, was the victim of murder most foul at the hands of Video, which was the subject of the now-famous documentary by the Buggles in 1981.[9] In lieu of flowers, the family

---

[4]Canadian slang for a very large bottle of booze – 3000ml/101oz – it's custom to give these as prizes at Stag and Doe (bachelor/bachelorette) parties. The name comes from the notion that "everything's bigger in Texas."
[5]Smiths songs. Duh, right?
[6]*Last of the Famous International Playboys* is the title of a Morrissey song.
[7]Mr. Flowers owes a great deal to Morrissey as far as influences go.
[8]See previous note about vegetarianism. Moz is a nickname for Morrissey.
[9]*Video Killed the Radio Star* by The Buggles was the first video to be broadcast on MTV in 1981. Why Video was never convicted of this crime remains a mystery.

of print media just urges its few remaining fans to buy as many CDs, Blu-Rays, and other physical forms of media so that this same sad fate doesn't.... oh wait, I'm getting something handed to me just now – physical media is also dead."

"It's not dead," Penny pouted, "it's pining for the fjords."

"Don't even..." I started, but Penny was resolute in seeing this played out. So go ahead. Go watch the video. I'll wait.[10]

There. We good? Okay, then, where were we? Ah yes:

"It's not pining, Penelope, it's passed on."

"Whatever," the Countess sneered, sticking out her tongue at me in an most un-Countess-like fashion. "You just wait and see. Print media is just biding its time – resting up for the final battle. Just wait until the zombie apocalypse happens and your precious Interweb is gone, and see how quickly you come running back to good old print media. You just better hope print media takes you back, Helena, or else you'll be out in the cold, holding your useless tiny little electronic device – which, by the way, I mean both figuratively and literally. Just see how much protection against the elements your little iPod provides you versus print media. Me, I'll be wrapped up in copies of the *Globe & Mail*,[11]burning pages of *Infinite Jest*[12]to keep warm – and believe me, Helena, that will keep me warm for a very, very, very, very..."

"Yes, I get it, Penny, it's a very large..."

"..Very, very, very long time."

"Are you done?" I inquired impatiently.

"Yes. Wait, no! I also think Al Gore should be charged with crimes against humanity."

"Okay," I said, knowing I would regret allowing this train of thought. "Pray tell, my love. What for?"

---

[10]Penny is referring to the famous dead parrot sketch from Monty Python's Flying Circus. If you haven't seen it, or even if you have, you should really stop what you're doing right now and look it up on You Tube. There's nothing funnier than the idea of a Norwegian Blue parrot (not that there is such a thing) pining for the fjords of Norway.
[11]Canadian newspaper with the largest circulation in the country. Occasionally just the mouthpiece of the Right, but you didn't hear that from me.
[12]A mammoth satirical novel by David Foster Wallace that is adored by hipsters everywhere. It really is a long, long, long book.

"Well, global warming, for one," she started, and when I tried to interject, she waved me off. "But I know, I know, that's a whole other conversation."

"The man received a Nobel Prize,[13] darling, I'd hardly say he..."

"TUT TUT!" She stopped me, and my eyes widened in disbelief. "The man invents global warming, and you're defending him, Helena, honestly! Sometimes I have no idea why we're friends."

I had no reply for this. This wasn't the first time the Countess had regaled me with her confused interpretation of modern history.

"And then," she continued, pointing her finger angrily at me, "he does something unthinkable, and creates what will likely be remembered as the most vile, useless, world destroying invention of the 20th century!"

"Now, Penny, I really don't think anyone's going to say that about the electric car..."[14]

"The Internet, Helena! I'm talking about the Internet and you know I'm talking about the Internet!"[15]

"Easy, darling, your angry old cat lady is showing. Besides, even if Al Gore did create the Internet (and I'm not conceding that he did, love), that's no reason for you to vent volumes of vitriol at me like some vapid..., um..."

"Valkyrie?" Penny suggested. "I could be a valkyrie, Helena. Oh, can't I be a valkyrie?"

"Yes, love," I allowed, "you can be whatever you like."

"I didn't find Tom Cruise terribly convincing in that film, though, did you?"[16]

---

[13]Yes, that really happened. And isn't that an inconvenient truth?

[14]Look up a company called Fisker Automotive sometime. Oh, Al Gore, what were you thinking?

[15]To set the record straight, Al Gore never even said that he invented the Internet. He made an off-hand comment in an interview where he said that he took the initiative in creating the Internet, which turned into the urban legend that the Countess and I enjoy laughing about. We've extended it to pretty much anything. For example, just the other day, the Countess said that the whole reason that Al Gore invented the Rice Krispy was to mix them with marshmallows and butter to create squares. I countered with something to the effect that the whole reason Al Gore invented marshmallows was to melt them and mix in Rice Krispies. The possibilities are endless, darlings.

[16]Tom Cruise film *Valkyrie*, in which he plays a German Colonel trying to save Germany from Hitler.

"Now, now, don't be a bitch, Penny, Tom Cruise is a wonderful actor, with an incredible range, who just disappears into his roles, and..."

And I'm sorry, but the Countess and I burst into tears of laughter at that point, and we may have lost the plot for a moment or two.

What was I saying? Oh yes, I was telling Penny that it's like what Morrissey says in *Sister I'm A Poet*, when he sings "is evil just something you are, or something you do?" and that...

What? Oh no, I'm pretty sure that's what I was telling Penny before we lapsed into Tom Cruise ridicule, but then, I've been told that I'm fairly unreliable as a narrator, so what do I know?

At any rate, the question hangs in the air as to whether any of us can actually be whatever we want to be, or if it is only our actions that make us what we are. Like if a person says they're a poet, but then never write any poetry, or those pathetic couche-tards who hang around music stores and call themselves musicians, as if they could just declare it to be true and will it into being so.

"I take it back, Penny," I retracted. "You can't be anything like – or rather, you can, but you've got to actually do it, and not just talk about it. If you want to be a painter, then paint. If you want to be a singer, then sing, if you want to be a writer, then dammit, Penny, you've got to write!"

"And if I want to be a valkyrie?" The Countess Penelope of Arcadia, by way of Valhalla, asked ambitiously.

"Well, then, by Odin, you just, um, do whatever the hell it is that valkyries[17] do." I declared passionately and yet a bit unsure, which is a strange combination, I realize.

"Well, I know they...,"she began tentatively, "I mean, they're in operas, right? They come in at the end, right before the fat lady, I think."

---

[17]In Norse mythology, Valkyries are like the angels of Death, choosing who will die in battle and taking them off to their reward in the halls of Valhalla. They are female, and serve as the bar wenches of Valhalla, serving the fallen warriors mead as they await Ragnarok, the final battle to end all battles.I'm sure you've heard Wagner's famous "Ride of the Valkyries" from his opera Die Walküre, if only in that old Bugs Bunny cartoon, "What's Opera, Doc?"

"I don't know, darling– look it up on the Internet," I suggested, and she scowled back at me.

"I'll find a book, thanks."

the elusive
mccuban sandwich

"You know," I said to the boy behind the McDonald's counter, "it seems unfair that there is not a McCuban sandwich simply because the word poblano doesn't fit well into a catchy TV jingle."

His name tag read 'Luis' but everyone called him Paco because every day for lunch he ate fish tacos that his mom packed in a brown paper bag.

I know this because I asked him "Why does everyone call you Paco?" and when he replied with a confused look on his face that nobody called him Paco, I ignored him completely and called him Paco, while at the same time creating a quick fictional anecdotal history for him starring his poor immigrant mother, who woke up at 5 am every morning to make fresh tortillas for Paco and his seven brothers and sisters.

Later, Countess Penelope (you remember Penny – thin, waifish type, likes to dress alternately like a hipster of the Bright Eyes/Death Cab For Cutie/Decemberists variety, or, contrariwise, like something out of Lewis Carroll's[1] worst nightmare) would create a grander, Dickensian history for Paco that involved an

---

[1] Lewis Carroll wrote *Alice's Adventures in Wonderland*, and *Through the Looking Glass*.

alcoholic mother, a pederast pimp of a father, fourteen siblings floating on a door across ninety miles of shark infested water (only three of whom would arrive with both life and limb intact), and then something involving the use of an Arab Strap.[2]

And speaking of Dickensian, that was a very, very, very long sentence, darlings.

We had arrived in sunny Miami two hours previously, and had been sweating along South Beach ever since, so when Penny declared, anything but *sotto voce*,[3] that she was starving, and couldn't we just get something to eat already, I recanted my quest for the perfect Cuban sandwich in favour of getting out of the sun. We had passed several restaurants, cafes, and assorted *panaderias*[4] that advertised Cuban sandwiches, but none of them had just what I was looking for.

"And why, pray tell, do we need to find a Cuban sandwich?" The Countess inquired impatiently.

"My dear Penny," I chided, "don't be so obtuse." I had recently watched *The Shawshank Redemption*,[5] and 'obtuse' had been officially added to my top ten all-time favourite words. "When we were in that shitty little dive in Philadelphia, what did we order?"

Well, in all fairness, I ordered a Philly Cheesesteak[6] sandwich, but Penny, distracted into a distemper by the dubious dinginess of the dining facilities, deigned only to order toast, which was, she declared indelicately, all she dared desire in such a desperately

---

[2] A sexual device made of leather and a metal ring that is placed around the penis and testicles. Hey, you asked.

[3] Lower voice – used in theatre and music to draw attention or for emphasis.

[4] Spanish for bakery.

[5] Andy Dufresne, protagonist of this excellent story, is a former accountant in prison for a crime he truly didn't commit, despite the evidence against him. When the evidence is found that would exonerate Andy, he presents it to the warden, who is using Andy's accounting skills to embezzle from the prison, and so has no interest in seeing Andy go free. When the warden dismisses the evidence, Andy asks him how he can be so obtuse, which lands Andy in solitary.

[6] A Philly Cheesesteak sandwich is chipped steak, grilled onions and peppers – all of which is then covered in cheese. The worst Philly Cheesesteak I have ever eaten was in Philadelphia. Go figure.

disgusting diner. However, at my insistence, she did at least add Philadelphia Cream Cheese to her toast.

"Yes, yes," Penny moaned, "and while we were waiting at the Buffalo airport, you insisted we have Buffalo wings – even though we've had them, like, a zillion times before..."

"And in Montreal?" I prodded.

"You had me walk through the red light district in fishnets just so you could have a Montreal Smoked Meat sandwich from Schwartz's – yes, I get it. But why a Cuban sandwich, Helena? Why here?"

"Look around, you, Penny. There are more Cubans here than anywhere on earth. Well, except maybe Tampa. So when I say Miami, you just think Cuba – ergo, Cuban sandwich."

"Whatever you say," The Countess Arcade sighed, exhausted from the heat on her too-pale skin.

"Yes," I agreed. "Whatever I say. And I say we are on the hunt for the perfect Cuban sandwich."

"Okay, as long as it's not pork. My people don't do well with pork," decreed The Countess Penelope of Arcadia, as if Arcadia were somehow a suburb of Tel-Aviv.

"Your people?" I asked, incredulously. "But you're not..."

"Yes, my people," Penny insisted. "Vegetarians."

Mea culpa, dear readers, *mea maxima culpa*.[7] I had recently introduced my dear young associate to the music of my youth, and she had fallen, like so many a young maid, for a certain Mancunian with a reputation of being outspoken, particularly on the matter of vegetarianism and animal rights, and had immediately declared herself a vegetarian. However, this all occurred last Thursday, and while I really had no issue listening to *Meat Is Murder*[8] repeatedly for the past few days, I was doing my best to hold my tongue when she made sweeping statements about my barbaric eating habits, as if she hadn't just eaten an entire ten taco family dinner from Taco Bell the week before on a dare. (Although I guess an argument could be

---

[7] Latin for "My bad." No, really. I'm no Catholic, but I first heard this phrase in *The Exorcist*. Great flick.

[8] A Smiths album.

made that there was no actual meat consumed during that exercise in gluttony).

"Fine," I said, clenching my teeth a little. "We'll go somewhere where you can get a salad or something, okay?"

"We could go to McDonald's," she said cheerfully. "They have good salads! Ooh! Or a Filet-o-Fish."

I stared at her and waited for the moment to dawn on her that fish might not be on the list of Morrissey-approved foods.

"What?" She asked, eyes bugging out at me in annoyance. "Fish don't have faces, Helena. It's not the same thing. Lots of vegetarians eat fish."

And so, without further debate, we found ourselves in the line-up at McDonald's. It wasn't long before we became the centre of inevitable, yet unwanted attention. It didn't help that Penny was dressed in military green khaki shorts and an admittedly adorable matching khaki waistcoat over a red t-shirt with an ill-advised (I told her it was a bad idea, considering) portrait of Che Guevara,[9] complete with ankle high oxblood Doc Martens and a similarly bloody beret to boot.

Perhaps it was the spirit of *la revolución* that compelled Penny, all hundred and three pounds of her, to leap over the McDonald's counter and grab Luis by the polyester labels and scream something about her not caring how many back alley blow jobs he'd had to give to work his way up to the McDonald's counter, and if he thought that he could just stand there and deny her mistress' request, then he was madder than those fat cat *gringo pendejos* who thought that they could keep Cuba under their oppressive boot heel.

Then she jumped up on the counter, pumped her fist in the air and yelled, "Viva la Cuba Libre! Viva Castro! Viva La Vida Loca!" Then, for some reason yet-to-be adequately explained to me (and believe me, I've asked her since), she launched into an impromptu

---

[9] Oh hey! It's that guy from the Rage Against the Machine T-shirts! Yes, yes, that's exactly who that is. He was a major figure in the Cuban Revolution before he went into the T-shirt business.

rendition of *We're Not Gonna Take It*,[10] complete with the opening dialogue where the dad asks what the kid wants to do with his life, and the kid responds "I wanna rock!"

Luis looked at me in utter bewilderment, and apologized again that they didn't have a McCuban sandwich, but then suggested that he knew a good place get one. After all, he beamed, he'd lived in Miami his whole life (a fact which shattered both my and Penny's fictional histories for the dear boy), and he knew all the best places.

"That's really very nice of you," I said, having to shout a little over Penny's off-key singing, as a girl no older than the Countess, but with the distinction of having the word MANAGER pinned to her lapel tried to talk her down off the counter. "But you see, we're here now, and my dear friend has clearly had too much sun (she's very delicate), and if you could just make me a Cuban sandwich, I'd very much appreciate it, and I'm sure you have the ingredients on hand. You just take a thinly filleted chicken breast, and top it with a roasted poblano pepper, some Raclette if you have it, but if not, then whatever cheese you have will... what?"

Luis looked blankly at me, went to speak, and then saw something in my face that caused him to hesitate. After an awkward pause that could not be called silence as it was filled with the wailing Countess of Arcadia on her third refrain of the only Twisted Sister song I could name, even under duress, Luis finally said:

"But miss, that is not a Cuban sandwich. A Cuban sandwich is made with roasted pork, Swiss cheese and pickles. Plus, it's on the best bread you ever had, miss– better than anything we serve here."

"No," I said, shaking my head. "No nononono, that's not right. I know what a Cuban sandwich is. Penny, get down off of there and come do your thing with Luis again, dear – he's trying to tell me I'm wrong, and we both know that I cannot be wrong."

"You can be," Penny said, jumping down off the counter with one final fist pump, "and frequently are."

---

[10] A horrible, if catchy cock-rock song from the 80's by a band called Twisted Sister. This anthem is thankfully all that remains of them in pop culture.

Annoyed, I shot Penny a look that said I would deal with her insolence later, and then told Luis again that I knew what a Cuban sandwich was, that I had eaten a Cuban sandwich before.

"Remember that cafe in Napa, Penny?"

"Yes, I remember," she said, losing patience with me. "I had chewy chorizo and eggs, you had a chicken poblano sandwich, and you kept making goo goo eyes at our waiter, and if I can remember his name I'll die a happy, if hungry young woman."

"No, I had a Cuban sandwich," I retorted, "I distinctly remember. And I do not make goo goo eyes. Never have, and never will."

"No, no, no," Penny corrected. "You had The Cuban, yes, but all their sandwiches had names. The Italian Stallion, The Snooty Frenchman, Der BullzenSchnitzel. But The Cuban was a chicken poblano sandwich, which you raved about the whole rest of the trip. Apparently you're not the only one who doesn't know what a Cuban sandwich is."

I turned to Luis.

"So you're saying that there's no poblano or chicken in a Cuban sandwich?"

Luis shook his head."Sounds like you want a chicken poblano sandwich, miss."

"Really?" I asked, nonplussed.

Luis nodded, insisting that he'd lived here all his life, and therefore, was a reputable authority on the matter of what goes in a Cuban sandwich. He then also reminded me that I was holding up the line.

"Huh," I said, feeling foolish. "Well, can you make me one of those?"

"No, miss, I'm sorry, we cannot," Luis shook his head said, "but I think the 1909 Café over on Bird Road has something like that."

"Well, all right," I said, tugging the Countess Penelope's khaki-clad arm out of the fast -food disappointment, "let's go get one of those, then!"

amanda palmer's eyebrows

"Got nuffink," said the Countess Penelope of Arcadia. "Go fish."

"What's this?" I asked, showing her the card I'd drawn.

It was the Joker, but someone (Penny, *J'accuse!*) had glued a picture of Heath Ledger on it. "You're supposed to take the Jokers out."

"Not so, my love," said Penny with a grin. "It's like a bonus set, right? 'Cause there's only two."

"So who's on the other Joker? Nicholson? Romero? Hamill?"[1]

"Bite your tongue, Helena my sweet. It's annova Heaff, ennit? And the rule is, if you collect bofe Heaffs, you win. Blimey 'n such."

"Okay, whatever, but can you just drop the cockney for the moment, you're doin' me 'ead in." She pouted and I dropped her a wink so she knew I wasn't being cruel.

"Well, at least I can affect a proper cockney – not like your poor attempt at Liverpool scouser – it's less convincing than Neil Gaiman's[2] American accent."

---

[1] That would be Jack Nicholson, Cesar Romero and Mark Hamill, who, along with Heath Ledger, played The Joker in one form of Batman or another.
[2] Neil Gaiman is the best-selling author of *Sandman*, which you must surely already know, darlings, but you never know. He is, incidentally, also married to Amanda Palmer, whose eyebrows (or lack thereof) is the subject of this tale (well... sort of).

I pounded my fist to my chest, miming being hit by an arrow, but somehow, the wound was not fatal. Like Gloria Gaynor before me, I would survive. (God, someone hand me the Monistat, 'cause that reference was, well, not so fresh).[3]

"Okay Countess, you win. The cockney urchin can stay. It's your turn, by the way."

"Brilliant!" She beamed. "Got any Heaffs?"

I sighed, tossing all my cards in her face. "You are an urchin!"

The Countess giggled and then stood up and did an awkward looking victory dance, and then declared, completely out of the blue that she was thinking of shaving her eyebrows like Amanda Palmer.[4]

"Don't do it, Penny," I advised, leaving it at that.

She stopped her dance and looked at me defiantly. "And just why not?" She dropped the cockney accent at this point, because frankly, it's easier to speak it than it is to write it. If you insist on continuing to read Penny's dialogue in a cockney accent, by all means, be my guest, but just know that you would be wrong to do so, because at this point, Penny really did drop the cockney accent. Really. Trust me.

"Don't presume to tell me what to do, Helena. I am a strong, independent woman, and I will find beauty in my own way, and not according to some misogynist ad man's..."

"And I'm all in support of that," I interrupted what promised to be a lengthy diatribe involving references to restrictive undergarments, woman on woman cannibalism metaphors,

---

[3] *I Will Survive* was a hit for Gloria Gaynor in 1978, so, yeah...

[4] Amanda Palmer is an independent musician who affects a very Brechtian stage presence, and her music has been described as punk-cabaret. (Particularly her work in the duo The Dresden Dolls). She finds herself the subject of much public scrutiny due to her outspokenness, her feminism, her sexuality, her politics, but then, others focus on such superficial things as her personal hygiene and the fact that she shaves her eyebrows off and then draws them back on. Because that is certainly newsworthy.

gratuitous use of the word 'phallocentric', and (and I'm just guessing here) about a 90% chance of the sacred name of Tori Amos[5] being invoked. "But let me ask you a question, Penny – how's your burger?"

I was referring, of course, to Penny's brief and hasty foray into the world of vegetarianism, which lasted only as long as her appetite could be sated by salads and other sundries lacking the savoury, saliva-soliciting scent and sizzle of a succulent steak. Or, as the Countess herself summed up so succinctly:

"I think couscous is French for 'shit pebbles'. I'll take my burger, thanks. Morrissey will just have to forgive me, and really, if he can forgive Jesus,[6] I think he can find it in his English heart to cut me some slack on my carnivorous-nesus."

"Carnivorous-nesus?" I asked dubiously.

"Yeah. It's a word," insisted the Countess Penelope of Arcadia, late of Who-ville.[7]"See also: Roast Beast; Diffendoofer; Sala-ma-goox; Fiffer-feffer-feff, or kwigger (although I'd be careful about who you use that around, just between you and me). Besides, I've heard you use the word 'thusly'[8], and that's as pretentious, made-up and couche-tardy as any of the crazy stuff Spike Lee makes up during interviews."[9]

---

[5]Tori Amos is a singer/songwriter and piano player who is famous for speaking her mind about dirty sex and masturbating in church and abuse and all kinds of other things that men find terribly intimidating. Three hundred years ago she would have probably been burned as a witch (oh, did I mention she's also a witch?) but now she's a feminist icon. She's also famous for her professional friendship with Neil Gaiman, who you might have just previously read, is married to Amanda Palmer. Is her inclusion here a coincidence, darlings? You decide.

[6]Morrissey has a song on one of his more recent (and wonderful, darlings – the man really does get better with age!) albums called *I Have Forgiven Jesus*.

[7]Who-ville is the creation of Dr. Seuss, who, like Penny, had a real penchant for neologism. Seriously, why am I explaining who Dr. Seuss is? What kind of childhood did you have if you don't know Dr. Seuss? Oh, I'm sorry – was that insensitive of me? Well, it's never too late – go read *The Cat in the Hat* – still a classic.

[8]Still not a word.

[9]Spike Lee is an African-American film director with a tendency to make inflammatory racial comments about white people. If you substituted the word "black" every time he uses the word "white", you could close your eyes and just imagine the pointy white hood he could be wearing.

"Wow," I say, not sure what to make of that, though I am aware of the *Django Unchained*[10] reactionary piece she is referring to. "So, the eyebrows, then?"

"Well, I don't know," the usually anything but hesitant Penelope hesitated.

"You know who else shaved their eyebrows, Penny?" I asked, preparing to launch into my own diatribe. "Bob Geldof."

"Who?"

"My point exactly. Bob Geldof shaved off his eyebrows for *The Wall*[11] and the next thing you know he's doing Live Aid and then disappears off the face of the earth entirely, never to be heard from again. Coincidence or correlation?"

But Helena, you say, *that's not true. In fact didn't he cause some shit not that long ago by calling Russell Brand a cunt on live television?*[12]

"NEVER. TO BE HEARD FROM. AGAIN," I repeated, apparently out loud and in all caps, because Penny replied with:

"Yeah I know. You just said that. Helena, who are you talking to? And why are you using really awkward and improper punctuation? You sound like someone doing an impression of a bad Shatner impersonator doing a half-way decent Christopher Walken as performed by Kevin Spacey."

"Um, wow, that was pretty specific. What was I saying?"

"Bob Geldof. Oh, wait isn't he the guy who single-handedly ended world hunger? Or was it just Africa? Hey Helena, did you know that Ethiopia is in Africa? And Egypt too? Spike Lee doesn't think that white people know that Egypt is in Africa, and that..."

"You're really going to do this?" I tried interrupting.

---

[10] Spike Lee was really not impressed with Quentin Tarantino's film set during the slavery era (despite the fact that he refused to see it, and was basing his opinion on, well, who knows?) Jamie Foxx, the film's star, responded by calling Lee's comments "shady" and "irresponsible."

[11] Bob Geldolf played the character Pink in the movie version of Pink Floyd's *The Wall*, where he played a burned out rock star who, at one point, shaves off his eyebrows. His band, The Boomtown Rats, achieved some level of success with their hit *I Don't Like Mondays*, and he was instrumental in Live Aid – a music festival to raise money for the starving children of Ethiopia. But of course, you knew all this already, darlings.

[12] NME Music Awards, 2006 – look it up on YouTube, you lazy gits!

"...And that black people think that Cleopatra was white because of Elizabeth Taylor..."[13]

"Oh God, kill me now," I muttered.

"Which is ridiculous, of course. It would be like saying that Chinese people think that Mickey Rooney is Chinese because of *Breakfast at Tiffany's*."

Seriously, another **Breakfast at Tiffany's** *reference?* You ask. *Pretty soon you're going to have to start paying Truman Capote royalties.*

Yeah, but he's dead, so...

He's not dead, he's pining.

Don't start with me.

"You've never even seen that movie, Penny," I reminded her.

"Well, no, but you're always making reference to it, so..."

"Well that's because it's a classic, darling. But that's beside the point."

"Don't you hate people that say *besides* the point?" Penny snickered, and I nodded.[14]

"I do, darling, I really do. But that is also not the point."

"Oh I'm sorry. What is the point, then? Because I just know that somewhere in here you had a point coming."

"The point," I replied, ignoring the snarkiness of my usually sweet if sometimes sycophantic sidekick, "is that much as there is more to you than your mind-blowing collection of stripy socks and unsurpassed skill with eyeliner – really, my dear, you look truly outrageous today –there's more to Amanda Palmer than her frequently publicly naked body, her bisexuality, her husband, or, indeed, her eyebrows. The fact that anybody anywhere is talking about her eyebrows at all, is, well... disappointing.

---

[13]Interview with *Esquire Magazine*, 1992 – you didn't think I was making this up, did you?

[14]See also: suposably, irregardless, I couldn't care less, nonplussed, ironic, bemused, pristine... look, the point is, learn how to speak, darlings. If you aren't 100% sure on what a word means, don't use it. Trying to use complex words is like walking into a music shop without knowing how to play the piano and then sitting down and banging away anyway.

"My mind quails, I mean absolutely ka-wails at how people will focus on all the wrong things and discuss them to death, missing out on the fact that she's an artistic revolutionary, challenging the very nature of the relationship between fans and artists. So I guess what I'm saying Penny is that if you want to be inspired by Amanda Palmer, then be inspired by her music. Be inspired by her attitude, or be inspired by the poetry and honesty of her lyrics. Go listen to her talk on TED[15], and see what she's really all about, rather than just dwelling unnecessarily on her facial doodling."

"Um, okay," the Countess replied amicably. "About the nudity..."

"Oh here we go," I rolled my eyes.

"Do you think that the nudity is to draw attention away from her eyebrows?"

"No," I answered, chuckling a bit at the very idea. "I think she just, you know, enjoys nudity."

"Who doesn't?" Penelope allowed. "You want to go get tattoos?"

I considered for a moment. "Yeah, alright."

---

[15]TED (Technology, Entertainment, Design) is an annual conference run by a non-profit organization called the Sapling Foundation and is dedicated to "ideas worth spreading". Amanda Palmer gave a talk about sharing and the "Art of Asking".

march thirty-second,
twenty-thirteen

H i, I'm Helena, and I don't like people invading my personal space and blah blahblah it's disrespectful...

Shhh... hey, it's Penny, and while Helena is washing the Snidely Whiplash[1] moustache off her face (hah! Good luck with that, I used a Sharpie!) I thought I'd hi-jack her memoirs for a moment to set the record straight on a couple of things. But don't say anything to her, 'cause she really hates it when I touch her stuff.

Yes, It's April Fool's Day, and I tend to go a little crazy sometimes, particularly on this day. Did you know that in France, the victim of an April Fool's prank is called *un poisson d'Avril?* (That's April fish, just so you know). I don't know why that is, but I also read somewhere that certain species of clown fish will spontaneously change sex in order to maintain balance in the school. Now that would be quite the April Fool's prank.

But anyhow, I just wanted to give you a heads up that you shouldn't believe everything Helena says about me. I'm not nearly

---

[1]Snidely Whiplash, cartoon villain with a long black curly moustache, bane of Dudley Do-Right's existence, and frequent kidnapper of Nell. Not ringing any bells? Well, then, look it up on the Internet, darlings; that's what it's for.

as crazy as she... okay, I'm not gonna lie, I am kinda crazy, but I certainly have never referred to myself as The Countess Penelope of Arcadia or whatever – Penny's fine.

And I do have normal clothes. I just enjoy making a statement if I know that I am going to be out in public.

Also, I do like to talk about normal things – I like boys. In fact, my perfect boy would be a cross between Sam Winchester from Supernatural and Hawkeye from the Avengers – well, really just Jeremy Renner in pretty much anything, right? Oh, and he'd have the voice and swagger of Morrissey. He should probably be closer to my age, though, 'cause all those guys are nearly old enough to be my dad, so...

Or, well, they would be, anyhow. My dad died a few years ago; my mum, too. Stupid car crash. There one day and gone the next. But don't go thinking that's why I'm crazy, because I was crazy long before that. Since then I've been staying with my Aunt Helena, which has been cool, 'cause she doesn't treat me like a victim, or analyze my behaviour, or whatever. And I'm okay, I guess. I mean, it's never going to be okay, okay, but time wounds all heels, right?

Anyway, I better get going – Aunt Helena hates April Fool's Day. When I was little, she told me that, just like how there's no thirteenth floor in high-rises, all sensible people should just skip over April Fool's Day by referring to it as March Thirty-Second, and then just skip right on to April Second.

But I say that's no fun!

See you in the funny papers!

MWAH!

Penny

cummerbund bandersnatch
and the girl with the wet spot

It's not often I find myself in McDonald's, but (or perhaps because) every time I do, I am subjected to something bizarre, disgusting, or otherwise out-of-the-ordinary (though if this is the norm, one could argue...)

Anyway, believe it or not, my recent trip to Miami notwithstanding, me and mine are usually not the cause of these McDonaldland mishaps (though admittedly, when we are, it is always... memorable). In this case, the fault lay entirely with Cummerbund Bandersnatch and The Girl With the Wet Spot.

Penny and I had been up late the night before watching the second series of the BBC's *Sherlock*,[1] which led to meandering, maudlin conversations, mispronunciations, and copious consumption of cocktails into the wee small hours. So when the sunlight struck me, and my head (feeling anything but small or wee) reeled, and my stomach cried out for greasy, sloppy sustenance,

---

[1] In case you're not familiar, this is a modern re-telling of the actual Sherlock Holmes stories, as opposed to the American show *Elementary*, which uses Sir Arthur Conan Doyle's characters but is not based on his wonderful stories. Incidentally, *Elementary* stars Lucy Liu, who was kind enough to appear in *Couche-Tard and the Jumping Asians*.

there was only one possible solution – that of the golden-arched variety. Now, I don't know what people did before the Egg McMuffin, but nothing soaks up too much vodka like the breakfast fit, not for a king, but rather for his floppy-shoe-wearing court jester Ronald.

McBreakfast was not a hard sell on Penny, and even though I lost the rock-paper-scissors battle for who would retrieve our repast, the lovely and merciful Countess agreed to come with me, I suspect more out of pity than duty, but one cannot judge or complain if the result is the same.

I must have nodded off on the drive there, because when Penny poked me to tell me that we had arrived, I sat up, startled, and blurted the words Cummerbund Bandersnatch! I then proceeded to surreptitiously wipe an undignified stream of drool from the corner of my mouth.

"Not that again," Penny smirked. But more on that later. Explanations would have to wait – everything would have to wait – as everything else suddenly became superfluous to the immediate moment, which required all of our attention and inner fortitude to come through intact.

It would have been nice to be given a warning; to have a moment to prepare, but just then, we were trying to process what we were seeing, and at the same time, trying to maintain a certain degree of composure so as to not give away that we thought that anything was amiss. It was like turning a corner and walking into a brick wall, or like opening a door on a sex crime involving a beloved relative. My initial internalized response was revulsion, with a touch of incredulity, with perhaps a pinch of confusion, which then led to a dangerous and insatiable curiosity. My inner monologue went something like this:

*Oh my God, that's disgusting! Did she honestly...I mean, there's no way that is what I think it is, is there? Although, I suppose it... how old **is** she? She's not... that is, she's not wearing a helmet – oh, jeez, Helena, that's cruel. But what other explanation could there be? She's acting like there's nothing out* *of the ordinary, and here she is, a girl – nay, a young woman (she's at least Penny's age), and she's quite obviously peed her pants.[2]*

In retrospect, now that I've had some time to consider it, and I have a touch more mental clarity about me, our encounter with The Girl With the Wet Spot (as it has come to be known) only lasted for about four minutes – about the length of time it took Penny and I to order our McMuffin meals, pay the cashier, and step aside to allow people behind us (who were also doing their very best not to look even remotely in the direction of The Girl With the Wet Spot) to order their breakfast. However, when one is trying not to stare at a young girl's crotch for fear of being publicly shamed, four minutes can seem like a very long time. Especially since every instinct in my body screamed out for me to stare, to solve the mystery, and my internal curiosity kept involuntarily drawing my eyes toward the wet patch that darkened her skin tight sweatpants right at the V where her legs came together. If I was to avoid jail time, (or at the very least a sea of unwanted raised eyebrows), I had to remain vigilant, and keep my eyes moving anywhere but in the vicinity of The Girl With the Wet Spot, even if my overcompensated eye and head movement seemed unnatural. Then there was the matter of protocol and etiquette – what to do in this situation? Should I say something? Perhaps she wasn't even aware...

Fortunately, I was spared more speculation by Penelope, the wise and quick-thinking Countess of Arcadia, who, sensing that I was likely about to do something embarrassing, grabbed me by the crook of my arm, and dragged my hung-over posterior back to the car.

"And just what the hell was that?" Penny snapped when we got back in the car, though at first I took it as mutual shock and commiseration, until I took a second look at her face.

"I know, I know," I said, shaking my head. "How crazy was that, right? Was I staring? Oh, God, I was staring, wasn't I?"

---

[2]This phrase must be real popular for some reason. In the stats of my blog, this phrase "obviously peed her pants" was a search phrase that drew people to my blog. Who knew?

"Well, of course you were staring," Penny declared. "You were meant to be staring! Everyone in there was meant to be staring. And when you weren't staring, you were doing your best to be obviously not staring, which was her plan all along."

"I'm sorry," I said, rubbing my throbbing temples, and then reaching into the brown paper bag for my McMuffin of glory, "you lost me."

"Precisely," Penny said with a confident smile. "Misdirection, Helena. Misdirection."

"I doanforrooo," I said with a mouthful of McMuffin, then swallowed and repeated myself.

"Well, see if you can follow me around the room, Helena. And do try to keep up, you know I hate repeating myself."

"Who are you?" I asked, stunned to the point of mild awe.

Without missing a beat, the Countess Penelope of Arcadia, late of Baker Street,[3] continued.

"Behind us and to the left, the unhappy mother who snuck out of the house after getting her baby back to sleep in the crook of her lazy husband's arm, nursing her flavourless coffee as if it's the finest espresso on the planet. By the size of the bags under her eyes, I'd say it's been two, no, three weeks since she's had more than four hours sleep a night. She's come to McDonald's in the clothes she slept in, for indeed, she fell asleep in them, and still has some regurgitated baby formula on her right shoulder that she doesn't even know is there.

"And then behind us in line, on their way to the breakfast of shame, the couple that, by their silence, and by their complete and utter lack of physical contact (even accidental) tells me that they likely don't even know each other's last names. They're also both wearing wristbands, the kind they give you at clubs for re-entry, and this screams one-night stand.

"And then there's little Suzy on the Playland slide, monopolizing the..."

---

[3]221B Baker Street is the fictional home of Sir Arthur Conan Doyle's Sherlock Holmes. I went searching for it one time in London – technically it doesn't really exist, though there is a Sherlock Holmes gift shop and memorabilia store there where it should be. I just saved you a flight to London and a boring tube ride to a place where there's really nothing else of interest. You're welcome, darlings.

"Just leave little Suzy out of this," I interrupted, "and tell me what this has to do with The Girl With the Wet Spot."

"I'm getting there," Penny conceded, "I just want to make sure that you were paying attention, and that you didn't miss the obvious."

"Which is?" I asked, as it was obviously not obvious to me.

"There was something missing," Penny began. "Something that, if what you and everyone in the establishment presumed had occurred, should have been there, but was not, in fact, present."

"And that is?"

"Urine," Penny stated firmly. "Piss. Pee. Golden Arches."

"I don't actually think that last one..." I started, trying not to laugh.

"Fine," Penny said, disappointed that her attempt at neologism fell flat, "withdrawn."

"And besides," I said, thinking that my argument was pretty cut and dried, "there kinda was pee, Penelope."

"Then where was the smell?" Penny asked, and I knew she had me there. "If that girl peed herself, then I will eat your Deerstalker."[4]

"But I don't even own a..."

"TUT-TUT!" Penny cried, putting a finger to my lips. "Let's see what else you remember. Do you remember what The Girl With the Wet Spot ordered?"

I thought for a moment. Did she order at all? I didn't think so, and I told Penny so.

"And her friend," Penny continued. "Did you see what she ordered?"

"What friend?" I asked. "The girl standing in front of her? Were they together? I didn't even notice..."

"You weren't supposed to," Penny said, making an impatient *let's go, carry on* motion with her hand, and then asked: "And what did she order?"

"A bagel sandwich." I said, without really thinking too much about it. "And the significance of this is?"

---

[4] A deerstalker hat has a front and back brim, and it traditionally associated with Sherlock Holmes.

"And what was on her bagel sandwich, Helena? Please, details are important."

"I dunno, Penny, I'm not exactly my best this morning, can you just tell me what you're driving at?"

"She had a bacon and egg breakfast bagel, Helena. And where do bagels come from?"

"I don't know, Penny. New York?"[5]

"Oh Helena," the Countess of Arcadia sighed in her trademark aristo fashion, "how difficult must it be to be so ignorant."

"Hey! Now listen, here, you..."

"Poland, Helena. And what do we know about the Poles?"

"Um, Vaclav Havel, Solidarity Movement[6], Polish Sausage..." I couldn't think of anything else on the spot.

"Ah, Vaclav Havel is Czech[7], Helena, but thanks for playing. You also missed it entirely – Poland has a large Jewish population, and in fact, it was a Jewish baker who, in the 1600s, invented the..."

"... Jammie Dodger!"[8] I said, winding her up.

"The Bagel, Helena, and you know it's the bagel."

"So you're saying that you think this girl is Jewish? Because she's ordering a bagel? I like bagels. So what's your point?"

"I know, Helena, I do not think. For I have deduced it. It's quite obvious, actually."

"It is?" This was news to me. I was lost at sea by this point.

"Yes, of course," Penny stated with an air of smarty-pants-iness (yes, this is a word now). "I have it all figured out. One need

---

[5] In North America, most people would either say New York or Montreal – these are the two most popular bagel destinations. Acolytes of the sacred bagel make pilgrimages to these two cities to pay homage to one of the two sects of Bagelism – either the smaller, sweeter, slightly crunchy Montreal bagel, or the larger, softer, saltier New York variety. But like most religions, this tradition did not originate here, but was brought from the old country. Read on, you'll see.

[6] The first non-communist trade union formed by the shipyard workers in Gdansk, Poland – I think I must have been thinking of Lech Wałęsa but couldn't think of his name at the time.

[7] Vaclav Havel was actually a Czech playwright and essayist and eventually politician, whose dissidence influenced the overthrow of Soviet rule in the Czechoslovakia. He eventually became President first of Czechoslovakia, and then was the first President of the Czech Republic. What can I say? I was pretty hung over at the time.

[8] What do you mean you don't know what a Jammy Dodger is? Two shortbread cookies with raspberry jam in the middle!

only look at the details. Not only is she Jewish, but she is a Jewess with a secret. You saw her, Helena, tell me what you remember."

"Well, I…"

"Oh, never mind. You remember nothing. Our girl (not The Girl With the Wet Spot, the other one) has a secret bacon addiction, and as addicts are wont to do, she has drawn her poor friend into being her confederate in culinary conspiracy."

"Nice." I said. Hey, credit where credit is due, I always say.

"Thank you, Helena. Now, it is commonly known that the secret bacon consumer often has to cook their bacon away from the public eye, and, due to the potent smell, will sometimes keep a change of clothes handy. Bacon users will have little bacon hovels where they go to 'fry-up' to use the vernacular of the bacon crowd, and then there's usually a 'clean room' where they go and wash up, change their clothes, spray on something aromatic, and come down from their bacon high. But this girl – this girl has gotten sloppy, though she thinks that she's been so clever, all the while sneakily sucking traces of bacon grease from her fingers. Did you see the drops of grease on her jumper from the splash-back of the frying pan?"

"That could be from anything," I said dismissively.

"It could be," Penny admitted, "if you didn't notice the bits of white powder under her fingernails that one might attribute to habitual cocaine use, but not this girl, no, her addiction is much more… carnal.[9] That white power is baking soda from putting out the occasional grease fires that happen when the bacon abuser is in a state of euphoria and leaves the frying pan unattended."

"So why wasn't she at one of these notorious bacon dens?" I challenged. "Why was she at McDonald's when she could be tripping the fat fantastic elsewhere?"

Penny sighed and shook a finger in my face matter-of-factly. "The reason they were at McDonald's is because they ruined their morning batch of bacon, of course, as someone had blown the whistle on their little bacon frying operation, and the girl's rabbi was on to them. When they got the knock on the door and saw it was her rabbi, come to extol upon them the virtues of kosher living,

---

[9]There really is nothing like a bacon fiend. We pass them all the time down at the subway station, begging for change "for a bit o' skin" they'll say – 'skin' being short slang for 'pig-skin' of course. Bloody savages.

they'd had to quickly abandon the frying bacon and hastily dump the frying pan, bacon and all, into a sink of soapy water and flee the house through the back door with the rabbi hot on their trail. McDonald's was just the most convenient place."

"So you think that when they threw the frying pan in the water, the soapy water splashed the other girl, and she just didn't have time change before running away?" I ventured.

"You'd like it if it were just that simple, wouldn't you Helena? No, there's something more devious afoot."

"Did you just use the word afoot?" I asked the Countess.

"Yes," she replied, unfazed. "Get over it."

"Whatever," I waved her off, and took a large and unladylike bite of my McMuffin.

Ignoring me, she continued, scratching her head with her straw.

"There was something deliberate about that wet spot. It kept the eyes of bystanders occupied. While you were busy trying not to look at the wet patch, your eyes went everywhere else in an effort to hide your discomfort – which is exactly what The Girl With the Wet Patch wanted – what our obviously unorthodox bacon fiend brought her for. Misdirection."

"You mean the girl with the wet bandersnatch, don't you?"

"You're not going to let that go, are you?" Penny sighed.

"Never," I agreed.

The previous evening, while watching *Sherlock*, Penny confessed her undying love for the actor who portrays Sherlock Holmes, a man with the incredibly unfortunate and ultimately unintelligible name of Benedict Cumberbatch. Only she had consumed her limit of three vodka and cranberries by that point and Penny (who I assure you is of legal drinking age but who is, I also assure you, a lightweight) insisted that his name was Cummerbund Bandersnatch, which I said sounded like a dirty euphemism for something bad involving female genitalia, as in, 'She should have been wearing a cummerbund to, you know, cover her bandersnatch'.

Or perhaps it was some sort of mystical beast as thought up by Lewis Carroll:

Beware the Jabberwock, my son!
The jaws that bite, the claws that catch!
Beware the Jubjub bird, and shun
The Cummerbund Bandersnatch.[10]

And at two o'clock in the morning, when talk turns to Lewis Carroll, and then devolves into half-remembered snippets of nonsensical verse or shouts of *O frabjous day! Callooh! Callay!* It is decidedly time to turn in before the re-enactments begin.

"So you think she did it on purpose?" I asked, accepting for the time being Penelope's premise on The Girl With the Wet Spot.

"Oh, without a doubt," Penny replied without a doubt. "Brilliant, really. Made the other girl – our illustrious bacon fiend – nigh invisible."

"Well, you don't want an angry rabbi catching you with a mouth full of bacon, I'll bet," I speculated, having no idea what I was talking about, to be honest.

"Nope," Penny agreed, finally settling into her McMuffin.

"The true measure of a friend, and all that," I said vaguely.

We sat quietly for a moment, contemplating the absurdity of it. Finally, Penny asked:

"Would you do that for me? Would you pour a drink in your lap as a distraction for me?"

"Darling," I said without hesitation, "I would pee my pants for real for you."

Penny looked at me lovingly and then replied, "You're disgusting."

---

[10]Paraphrased from *Through the Looking Glass*, by Lewis Carroll, 1871

fiona apple and the saga of the great staples suppression of 13

"So let me get this straight," the Countess Penelope of Arcadia began incredulously, "you're saying that Fiona Apple[1] got refused service at Staples?"

"No," I said, biting my lip, "that's not what I said at all."

"Well good," Penny – you remember Penny – opinionated, impulsive, doesn't listen very well and tends to speak over top of you from time to time – stated, "because I see no reason why an office supply store would have cause to discriminate against poor Fiona Apple. She's completely inoffensive (I mean, other than that whole *Criminal* video[2], but we've all tried our best to put that behind us, haven't we?) and besides, shouldn't she have people who run

---

[1]Fiona Apple is a musician who has absolutely nothing to do with this story, other than the fact that she shares a first name with the comic book artist Fiona Staples, and her last name with a giant computer company you may have heard of. When the events lampooned in this story were taking place, using the search words 'Fiona Staples' called up all kinds of interesting things, which led to Penny's feigned confusion for the sake of humour. For instance, Fiona Apple, Staples, Applebee's, etc..

[2]Early in Fiona's career, she made the choice to be in a video of one of her songs, Criminal, directed by Mark Romanek. The singer has since expressed remorse and dislike for the video, and received flack for its exploitative sexuality. Silly, really, because the song is all about expressing remorse for using sexuality to get what you want. Unfortunately, it kind of hurt her reputation and mainstream pop's ability to take her seriously, which is too bad, really, as she's a hell of a songwriter.

those kinds of errands for her? She's, like, a totally famous musician, and stuff."

Before things spiralled further and further out of control, I knew that I was going to have to reel this in and get back to the matter at hand. But first, I felt I would be my remiss in my duties as a mentor to the young and impressionable Countess if I did not set the record straight on a couple of matters.

"Okay, first off, I think that your perception of the rock star lifestyle is highly exaggerated, and second, even if there are some musicians with entourages that fulfill even the most bizarre or outlandish demands, and for whom a trip to Staples would be a welcome reprieve from their egotistical employer, I happen to know for a fact that Fiona Apple is not one of those types."

"Yes, yes," Penny waved me off, "I'm sure she's lovely. But even the nicest people can sometimes lose their shit, and obviously she did something to upset the poor people at Staples – or was it Applebee's? See, now you've got me confused."

Speechless, I grabbed Penny by the hand and dragged her out the door, hopped in Penny's new yellow VW Beetle (Happy Birthday, Penny!), and proceeded directly (Do not pass GO, do not collect $200)[3] to my favourite comic book store, where they greet me by name and don't talk down to me or make assumptions about me, or what I like to read, just because I happen to have a vagina.

"Helena!" The voice of Dave greeted me as I walked in the door. I say 'the voice of Dave' because Dave was nowhere to be seen, as usual. Dave is a disembodied voice that consistently senses my presence and disappears without a trace. Penny says she thinks he has a crush on me, but that he's hideously disfigured and so he hides whenever I come in to the store.

"Helena," James, the clerk nodded to me, and then raised his pork pie hat to Penny. "Countess."

---

[3] A reference to my favourite board game, Monopoly, by Parker Brothers. Hours of enjoyment, and the catalyst for many hair-pulling fights between me and my sister. The closest I've ever come to committing homicide is over a Monopoly game.

Penelope blushed and shot me a look and then corrected James. "Penny's fine."

It was impossible to take Penny seriously sometimes. At least I hadn't given her any time to prepare a wardrobe, and so she was thrust upon the world in most un-Countess-like fashion in mismatched striped stockings and a knee length sweater – excellent lounging around the house clothes to be sure, but in public she resembled a runway model gone wrong, and I suddenly found myself wondering if (and hoping that) she had something else on under the sweater.

"So, Helena," James said, in a way that told me I was suddenly being asked to weigh in on some heated discussion, "Damien Wayne – really dead, or just a marketing ploy?"

James was referring, of course, to the recent 'death' of Bruce Wayne's fictional son at the hands of his clone, (oh, for God's sake, go read the spoilers)[4] and the ramifications thereof.

"Morrison says he's dead," I replied, "What DC does with it after Grant leaves the book is out of his hands, but I respect his intentions."

"Yes, but death in Morrison's writing is never really about dying – it's symbolic, it's transformation, it's..."

"Well, we'll just have to wait and see, darling," I interrupted him, not really wanting to get into a lengthy debate just then. James could be a scholar on all things Grant Morrison,[5] that is, if they actually handed out degrees in that kind of thing (and, you know, someday they just might!) "I'm actually looking for the new issue of *Saga*."

---

[4] In the comic book *Batman Incorporated* V.2, issue 8, Damien Wayne, acting Robin and son of Bruce Wayne, dies at the hands of The Heretic, who is, himself, actually a clone of Damien. Only in comic books, darlings! Isn't it wonderful?

[5] Grant Morrison is a Scottish writer who was part of the British (I know, let it go...) Invasion of comics in the mid-'80s who brought comics to mature audiences. He's written legendary runs on Animal Man, X-Men, Doom Patrol, as well as his own character created epic Invisibles. Most recently he had one of the most popular if somewhat divisive and controversial runs with Batman – giving him a son, 'killing' Batman, bringing him back, having Bruce Wayne become publicly 'involved' with Batman, and then killing his son. Oh, and somewhere in there, the Queen saw fit to make him a Member of the Most Excellent Order of the British Empire (MBE).

"You and everyone else," James said, a trifle contemptuously, and pointed to the wall, where there were a few copies left.

"Why?" Penny asked. "What's the big deal?"

Heads turned in a synchronized pivot so pronounced that Penny suddenly found herself the subject of unwanted scrutiny, and looked to me for help.

"She hasn't heard," I apologized for her, "she's not on Twitter."

"Helena, please," Penny protested. "You're embarrassing me. You know how I feel about the Interweb."

Penny held fast to the opinion that the Internet was going to be the downfall of civilization, and that someday, mankind would look back on the folly of their ways and curse the wretched name of Al Gore the way that the name of Oppenheimer[6] is used as a boogeyman among Japanese children and their parents, ie. "Eat your sashimi, or the Oppenheimer will come to your window and quote the Bhagavad Gita to you until your brain explodes". (I don't know if that's even a real thing, but Penny insists that in the original, Japanese version of *The Ring*,[7] the video that you're not supposed to watch or else you die is just a loop of U.S. nuclear tests and the voice of Oppenheimer repeating "I am become Death, the Destroyer of Worlds" over and over again).

"Fascist homophobes over at Apple," James spat indignantly. "Well, at least it's driven more people into the store to buy a floppy copy. They're selling like hotcakes."

"Um, excuse me," Penny interjected, "but when's the last time you bought a – what did you say? A hotcake?"

"Not now, Penny," I said, rolling my eyes. Penny could be kind of critical when it came to archaisms. She was a total hypocrite

---

[6]Robert Oppenheimer, developed the first atomic bomb, and who, upon seeing it tested, reacted by quoting the Bhagavad Gita bit about Death.

[7]*The Ring* was an American remake of a Japanese horror movie *Ringu* about a cursed VHS tape (shudder!) that, when watched, ended in the viewer's death. Pretty creepy flick with a fantastically dark twist ending, if you haven't seen it, it's worth it just so you know what people are talking about when they make reference to it.

about it, but she liked catching other people using them and making them feel totally uncomfortable.

"Foine," said the Countess Arcade, a bit of the Dickensian street urchin creeping in, "I'll be'ave meself I will. Wass this about the *Saga* fing, then? An' wass it got ta do wiff Fioner Appo?"

Faces stared blankly at Penny, and so, in a huff, she dropped the urchin act and, exasperated, said: "All right, all right! I can tell you're all dying to tell me all about Fiona Apple, and *Saga*, and how this somehow all relates to a crazy encounter in Staples, so please..."

"What's she on about, then?" asked James, affecting his own faux cockney accent, absorbed from many a Doctor Who marathon (which I am not too proud to say that I have attended after my many polite refusals were no longer accepted).

"Oh sure," Penny pouted, "It's okay for him to..."

"Hush," I said to Penny and turned back to James. "I was trying to tell her this morning about how Apple was refusing to publish Brian K. Vaughan[8] and Fiona Staples'[9] latest issue of *Saga* on iTunes and comiXology, but I think she only caught the tag words[10] and so now for some reason she thinks Fiona Apple had some sort of altercation at a Staples."

"Seriously?" James asked first me, and then Penny.

"What?" Penny exclaimed. "With her I only ever catch every third word!"

"It's a travesty," James continued, "a [edited for content] travesty. I thought we were living in the 21st century."

"What?" Penny asked, anxiously. "You're being so cryptic! What's the big deal?"

---

[8]Brian K. Vaughan is an American comic book writer famous for *Y The Last Man* (which Stephen King called the best graphic novel he'd ever read) and *Ex Machina*, and now *Saga* (I won't mention his involvement in a certain television show that has become a literal FOUR LETTER WORD in my mind – you may remember it – it involved a plane crash on a mysterious island – the less said about it the better, darlings.

[9]Fiona Staples is a relative newcomer to the world of comics – and she's Canadian!

[10]This was my indictment of the entire Internet community, darlings. Everyone was reading the tag words and nobody was really hearing what was really going on. There were writers and other celebrities (some rather famous ones who I will not mention here, and I'm sure they're embarrassed enough) who were calling for boycotts and calling Apple and comiXology all kinds of inflammatory things based on the Internet's buzz on this.

James reached behind the counter and came back with a book, which he handed to Penny.

"Here," he said in an unconsciously hushed tone, as if he were handing her a sacred text. "This is a collection of the first six issues of *Saga*. It's like *Star Wars* meets *Romeo & Juliet* through the eyes of the Marquis de Sade. It's science fiction, it's a love story, it's beautifully perverse and perversely beautiful. It's got robot sex, it's got magic, it's got eviscerated ghosts, lie-detecting cats, bounty hunters, giant testicles, spaceships, and love overcoming the obstacles of hatred – it's... it's... uh! I just can't say enough about this book, Countess. You read this, and then, if you don't understand why I say I love this book and why it hurts like a personal wound that those douche-bags..."

"Couche-tards," Penny corrected. "It's the new thing. Couche-tards is the new douche-bags."

"Huh?" James asked, looking at me. I shrugged and nodded.

"Well, anyway, ask your mom here..."

"Oh, I'm not her..." I began.

"Oh, she's not my..." Penny protested simultaneously.

"Whatever," James ignored us, and pressed the book into Penny's hands. "That's the first six issues, and I'm sure we've got issues seven through eleven on the shelf, and then with today's issue you'll be up to date. You go read that and then you go see what those rat bastards are saying. Those petty, puritanical pissheads!"

"Well look at you!" I laughed. "Get down with your alliterative self."

(Note to reader: Yeah, I made that last bit up. James, while a fascinating guy, really isn't clever enough to intentionally use alliteration. Carry on).

So we paid for our books and Penny went home, and dove right into *Saga*. I tried to ask her what she thought a few times, but she was, as she put it, NOT TO BE DETERRED from finishing. Finally, she came up for air, declared she loved it, and then made a disgusted face – one she usually reserved for when she knows she's going to have to do something she doesn't enjoy, like cleaning the bathroom, or watching *It's a Wonderful Life*[11] with me at Christmas time.

"Do I have to do it, Helena?" She pleaded with me. "Can't you just give me the gist?"

"The gist? You mean, like I tried to do this morning? Not a chance, Miss 'With her I only ever catch every third word.' No, you march yourself right up to your room and don't come out until you've read at least three editorials and four– no, five tweets about Apple's decision not to publish issue twelve[12]– and I'll know if you're faking, dear!"

I always know when someone's faking. So, when a half an hour later I heard the indignant vulgar cry of the Countess Penelope of Arcadia, I knew that she was not faking, and had indeed discovered (as you have as well by now, I can only hope) that censorship is still alive and well, despite rumours of its long-awaited demise.

"WHAT THE RIGHTEOUS [edited for content]?" Penny screamed in disbelief. "Seriously?"

"I'm afraid so," I said, poking my nose into Penny's room.

"But why this issue?" Penny asked. "Because of the dick? I mean, it's not like this is the first time there's been explicitly sexual material in this book – not even the first homosexual material..."

"Yes, but that was girl on girl..." I explained, as if that excused everything.

"Pretty explicit girl on girl, if I recall."

"Well, my dear, lesson learned for today – it's a man's man's man's man's world, and while objectification of the female form has long been man's second favourite sport (masturbation being the first, and you can see where those two go – you'll pardon the pun – hand in hand), one gratuitous stiff cock and the sirens go off. I

---

[11] Classic Frank Capra film starring Jimmy Stewart as a man who thinks he's lost everything and makes a wish that he was never born... seriously, you've never seen this? Clarence the Angel? Not ringing any bells? That's too bad, because, you know, every time a bell rings an angel gets his wings.

[12] The buzz around the Internet was that due to explicit homosexual content (a male performing fellatio on another male in a TV screen the size of a postage stamp) that Apple had decided not to publish it in digital format for download in the comiXology app. Screams of censorship and homophobia and hypocrisy abounded.

hope you'll forgive my cynicism, but sometimes it almost seems that it's best just not to upset the apple cart."

"Was that a dig?" Penny asked.

"Not too subtle, I hope."

"It's bullshit," Penny decided. "We should do something about it."

"Well, we can just be like every other Internet junkie and complain about it," I suggested.

"Yeah," Penny sighed. "But there's got to be something we can do. You know, to show people how awesome this book is. I mean, they're only afraid of it because they don't understand the beauty of it. There should be somewhere everybody could go to check out *Saga* for themselves."

"Oh, there is, Penny," I replied, turning and winking at you, the reader, "There is."[13]

"Oh, you're shameless, Helena," Penny teased.

"Can I do one more?" I asked.

Penny sighed. "I suppose." I clapped with joy, and said:

"The latest Fiona Apple release[14] is also wonderful!"

(Note to reader: since I wrote this, comiXology and Apple have clarified, that is, er, rescinded, er, backpedalled...)[15]

---

[13]Go to your local comic book store, or else download Saga #1 for free from Comixology.com

[14]Her last album (and she has a penchant for wordy titles) is *The Idler Wheel is wiser than the Driver of the Screw, and Whipping Cords will serve you more than Ropes will ever do.* It really is excellent, darlings.

[15]Both comiXology and Apple clarified that it was merely a release time issue and had nothing to do with the sexual depiction. People all over the Internet shook their heads dubiously, and the most vocal retractors, ahem, swallowed their words.

plans

" April is the cruellest month," T.S. Eliot said[1], and the way I'm feeling, I'm inclined to believe him. I've been thinking a lot lately about the plans we make, and how fragile and out of control life can be when we try to see those plans through. To paraphrase the prophet of NYC, Mr. Woody Allen, God laughs while you make plans. Or, as J.W. Lennon (another prophet of NYC by way of Liverpool) once wrote, "Life is what happens to you while you're busy making other plans."[2]

Anyway, that's the preamble, and I'll keep it brief – like the poesy of a ring. April is apparently National Poetry Month[3], and I'd be neglecting my reputation as the consummate dilettante if I did not at least contribute a haiku. (Bless me, darlings!).

So, without further ado, here is something I call "Plans"

———————————————

paper boats at sea

———————————————

[1]The Waste Land, 1922
[2]Beautiful Boy (Darling Boy) by John Lennon, 1980
[3]Since 1999 it's been celebrated in Canada. Who knew?

wish them well then say good-bye

find them washed ashore

_____

'til next time

XO

HH-B

gotta catch 'em all! (the modern young woman's guide to choosing friends)

H i there! Penny here! I just wanted to take a moment to discuss something truly important to me, and that is the difficult task of choosing friends. Life is short, and the people you surround yourself with will not only help mould you into the person that you will become and be remembered as, but they reflect who you are as a person. So you don't want to be surrounding yourself with the wrong people. No, you have to have strict criteria for who will form your inner circle.

The first thing that you need to know is that gays are all the rage right now, so you're going to want to get yourself a gay friend. I mean, if you don't have a gay friend, you're, like, nobody. People are going to accuse you of being a homophobe.

And when I say gay friend, I mean, the gayer the better. You don't want some 'Pass As Straight' gay friend like Neil Patrick Harris, you want a flaming, effeminate gay friend like Kurt from *Glee*,[1] so that everybody knows that you have a gay friend. That

---

[1] A musical television show that I wish I had no knowledge of. Sadly, I do. Kurt, played by Chris Colfer, is every gay stereotype one can possibly imagine. If he were wearing blackface to portray an African American, people would be booing and rioting in the streets – but to play gay as a caricature is apparently okay.

way, if someone makes a homophobic statement around you, you can react with righteous indignation and say, "Hey, my best friend is gay!" You can also use this with racist comments, i.e. my best friend is African American, Asian, etc... But more on that later.

Now, I know what you're thinking – how will I choose a gay friend? Aren't there so many different types of people? You'd think so, but if all the feed on Tumblr[2] by all the teenage girls right now promoting all their slash fiction[3] is any indication, it's that every gay person is exactly the same. It's like they're not even people at all! Gay men are all very body conscious and fit, love singing and dancing, are hilarious, and have excellent fashion sense. Gay women are artistic, introspective, outspoken, and usually have no sense of fashion – you probably don't want to hang out too much with lesbians, for fear of being accused of being one. I mean, c'mon, you like the gays, you just, you know, don't love them.

So go on! What are you waiting for? Go out and get yourself a gay! Gotta catch 'em all![4]

The next thing that every modern young woman needs is a black friend. Having a black friend is like getting to be in a rap video every day. You can get away with calling them bitch, and if you're really lucky, and you endear yourself to them, you just might get to experience the sheer joy and utter ecstasy of being referred to by them as their home-girl, or, if you are truly lucky (and so very few are, and ain't that a shame?) as their nigga. Oh my gosh, I can't believe I just typed that... I feel like such a bad-ass. I feel like I should have said 'N-word' but now that it's out there, it's just such a RUSH![5]

---

[2]Tumblr is to social media what McDonald's is to restaurants. From what I can tell, it's mostly teenage girls posting short animations and memes ad nauseum. Like Facebook, only more obnoxious. The world is so connected for the first time in history, and we use that technology to spam each other with nonsense and call each other names. Human Race FTW! (Yes, that was completely intentional, darlings. It's called irony).
[3]Slash fiction (fan fiction where all the popular characters of your favourite show are written as gay) is all the rage on Tumblr.
[4]This was the catch phrase for Pokemon, the video game where the goal was (you guessed it) to collect them all.
[5]Are you offended yet? You should be. Penny is one hell of a satirist.

Having a black friend gives you street cred. Just make sure that you learn the right gang signs from the wrong gang signs, and be sure to always say 'Peace Out' when you're saying good-bye. This won't be a problem for you to learn, because every black person is in a gang, and they all enjoy gangsta rap, bustin' caps, and slapping bitches. Every black man is a gansta pimp, and every black girl is a booty-licious ho.[6] It's like they're not even people at all!

The one thing I've learned from Spike Lee movies and BET is that there is nothing better, no feeling more rewarding, than the righteousness of being oppressed. So make sure to get yourself a black friend so that you can feel oppressed by proxy. If you're with your black friend and someone calls them a racial slur, you can open a can of whoop-ass on their face, get all up in their grill, and release all that pent-up righteous rage that you, as a young urban privileged white girl like me, cannot legitimately lay claim to. Make sure to practice the Black Person Head Swivel, that every black person does while saying, "Excuse me? What did you just call me?"

So go on! What are you waiting for? Go out and get yourself a black! Gotta catch 'em all!

Now, if you can't find a black friend, in a pinch, a Latino will do. Latinos differ only slightly from blacks in that they are in different gangs, their music contains more horns, and they speak Mexican.[7]

Every Latino can dance, so, you know, they can teach you to dance. And every Latino has a grandmother who lives with them and will make you fresh tortillas when you drop by to visit. So there are many reasons to... oh shit, here comes Helena!

---

[6]This can't all be blamed on 'The White Man'. What message do you send when you show up at an awards ceremony with scantily clad women on leashes (I'm looking at you, Snoop Dogg).

[7]A recent poll by *I'm Making This Up Right Now* magazine showed that 37% of Americans refer to all Latinos as Mexicans, and think that the language they speak is Mexican. Seriously, though, you've heard some couche-tard refer to a Latino as a Mexican, or say something like 'I don't speak Mexican'.

"Hello Penny Arcade," I said, kissing the top of her head as I snooped a peak at the laptop screen. "What are you doing on my computer?"

"Um, nothing," the Countess of Arcadia replied sheepishly, arousing my suspicion. "Just reading your memoirs, which, you know, you haven't been writing for a few days now."

"I've been busy," I protested, "and besides, it looks like you've been trying to fill in for me – what's that you've written then? C'mon, let's see. Hand it over."

"Now, Helena," Penny cooed, waving her hand like a windshield wiper slowly from one side to the other, "you don't need to see what Penny has written."

I looked sternly at the Countess of Arcadia, which would seem to be somewhere in the vicinity of Tatooine, and motioned again for my laptop.

"Do you know what happened to the last person who tried to use the Jedi Mind Trick[8] on me?" I asked rhetorically as I began to read Penny's Guide to Choosing Friends.

"Um, no disintegrations?"[9] Penny pleaded, perhaps hoping that emulating Empire could calm my caustic choler.

"Oh, Penny, you're killing me!" I said, after reading only the first two paragraphs.

"Now, Helena," Penny protested, "I was making a point. It's satire!"

"I can see that," I said, laughing a bit, "but aren't you worried about people being offended, darling? Not everybody is as fluent in sarcasm as you and I, love."

---

[8]Okay, seriously, how in-depth do I need to go here? Do I need to make you aware of the existence of a little movie called *Star Wars*, or give you a history of the Jedi, and their various powers, or are we all on the same page here. Tatooine was the name of the planet Luke and Obi Wan were on when Sir Alec Guinness first showed the world the Jedi Mind Trick by telling two weak minded stormtroopers that 'These aren't the droids you're looking for.' while waving his hand in a subtle display of his mental powers. The funny thing – they totally were the droids they were looking for.

[9]Another *Star Wars* reference this close together? Risky, I know, but I like to live dangerously. This, of course, is what Darth Vader says to Boba Fett before he sends him and the other bounty hunters out after Han Solo (which was really only a trap to draw in Luke Skywalker).

"Fuck 'em." the Countess said, eloquently shrugging as she did. "Those couche-tard twits are too busy daydreaming about Martin Freeman and Cummerbund Bandersnatch[10] to even realize that I'm making fun of them."

Penny had recently declared, while inebriated, that she had a rather large and undying crush on the actor who portrays Sherlock Holmes in the BBC series.

"Seriously?" I asked. "You know the man's real name, but you're going to continue calling him by your drunkenly mistaken pet name?"

"I am," Penelope declared. "You used it as something to mock me with, and I am reclaiming it as a badge of courage. You know, kind of like the N-word."

I shook my head in mock disbelief, though really, nothing Penny did was beyond belief.

"Tell me you didn't just say that."

"Sorry," Penny said, reaching for the laptop. "No can do. Now give it back, I want to finish."

"I don't think so," I said, closing the laptop and moving it away from her. "You've already done enough damage – think of the angry e-mails I'm going to get."

"Oh, get over yourself, Helena! Nobody reads this shit anyway! And besides, I didn't even get to Asians yet! Don't you think that the world deserves to know why everyone needs to have a generic Asian friend? I had this whole bit about the pronunciation and proper usage of the words *manga, anime* and *hentai,* and how all Asian men are secretly pedophiles, and..."

"You know, we're going to have to end this like an after school special if you keep it up," I sighed.

Penny shrugged. "I'm game if you are. Cue the Depeche Mode song[11] in the background. Now, you go first, okay?"

---

[10] You may remember them as Watson and Sherlock Holmes from BBC's *Sherlock.*
[11] The Depeche Mode song in question is, of course *People are People,* with its lyrics espousing equality and inclusivity.

"Fine," I sighed, and then turned to face the imaginary camera that is you, dear reader. "Hi, I'm Helena..."

"And I'm Penny," said the Countess Penelope of Arcadia, which is in the neighbourhood of I'm so gonna kill her when this is done, "and we'd like to talk to you about racism, homophobia, and other general couche-tardiness."

"Really?" I asked, aside and off camera.

"Yes, really," Penny insisted. "The more I use it, the more likely it is to catch on."

"Alright," I said, and surrendered the floor back to the Countess.

"Ahem," Penelope continued. "As I was saying, you shouldn't choose your friends based on who (or is it whom– Helena, is it who or whom?)"

"I don't know," I offered. "Finish the sentence."

"You shouldn't choose your friends based on whom they insert their penis into..."

"WHAT THE..." I choked in all caps.

"Whatever," Penny sighed, unfazed. "So which is it?"

"Who," I said, finally catching my breath.

"Really?" Penny asked, unsure. "Because I was sounding it out in my head – 'Excuse me, but, whom did you insert your penis into? You inserted your penis into who?'–and I can't figure out which is more grammatically correct."

"I'm sorry, Penny," I said, confused, "but what does this have to do with penises, and the insertion thereof into persons unknown?"

"AHA!" Snapped Penny, grinning from ear to ear (though not literally, because that just sounds painful). "My point exactly."

Penny then composed herself and turned back to the camera (again, that's you – do try to keep up), and said, "Choosing friends is a really important thing – but choosing friends as status symbols is just insulting and demeaning. Do you realize how stupid you sound when you say *OMG, I wish I had a gay friend?* As if they were a commodity to collect, so you could feel better about yourself. Do you hate yourself so much? Are you so uninteresting that the only way that you can make yourself more interesting is by clinging to someone else? *Oh hi, I'm Tracy, and I'm kinda boring, I just go on Tumblr and ship the ships and mock fandoms[12] all day, and don't contribute anything original or interesting to the world, but hey! I've got a gay friend! I don't know anything about them other than the fact that they're gay, and being gay is their entire identity, and..."*

"Okay!" I interrupted, before Penny started into deep sarcastic territory that would require a translator and defeat the purpose of the After School Special style ending we were trying to go for. "What Penny is trying so very hard to say, darlings, is that people are people, whether they be gay or straight, black, white, brown, yellow, purple or plaid, and that (and oh, God help me I'm about to paraphrase Batman) it's not what they are on the outside – not what group they belong to, what colour of skin or social status, or whatever superficial tags you want to apply to people – but rather what they do that defines them."[13]

"Yeah," said the Countess of Arcadia, channelling any number of 1980's sitcom actors on a PBS telethon, "So dig deeper, and find the treasure beneath – and you'll find you'll both be richer for the experience."

"Are you talking about fisting?" I asked, deliberately trying to break Penny's composure so you can all see what a freakazoid she really is.

"Eww, Helena! Disgusting! Here I was trying to give a nice, moral lesson to the people, and you had to go all low brow."

---

[12]'Ship the ships'. Sadly, this is a real phrase used by teenage girls, wherein a 'ship' by definition is no longer a sea-faring vessel, but rather a fictional relationship in either very crappy teen fiction (think Twilight) or on a TV show or movie. 'Shipping' a certain 'ship' is akin to supporting that relationship – fictional or otherwise. Back to the slash-fiction element, it is very popular to 'ship' non-existent gay relationships (like, say, for example, between Watson and Holmes, or Iron Man and Captain America) because hey, gay is the new black, and if you don't 'ship' these 'ships' you're a bigot! Fandoms are just what you think they are. Fans of a certain show, etc...

[13]In Batman Begins, Bruce Wayne's childhood friend Rachel (played in this film by ex-Mrs. Tom Cruise Katie Holmes) catches him all wet after going for a dip in a hotel pool with a couple of models, and he comes off looking very childish and shallow. He tries to excuse his behaviour to Rachel by saying that he's more on the inside. Rachel responds by saying that it's not what he is on the inside that counts – it's what he does that defines him. Later, as Batman, he repeats this phrase back to her to a) show her that he took what she said to heart, and b) to reveal his identity to her. What to take away from this: It's what you do that defines you. Also, Scientologists are fucking nuts.

"Well, now you know how I roll. And knowledge is power."[14] I said, knowing exactly what I'd just done.

"Oh, Helena, you suck! You know that I was trying to work that in. You stole it from me," Penny pouted.

"Oh, fine, you big baby, you say it."

"No," Penny sighed, "No, you've ruined it. Good-night everyone! Tune in next time, when you'll hear Helena say:

I don't know, there's just something about Jack White[15] *that makes me want to be a nineteen-year-old girl in a Go-Go cage again.*

"I've never said that," I protested, "and I never will."

"Oh, you will," Penny laughed like a cartoon villain and rubbed her hands together deviously. "You will."

---

[14]This slogan 'Knowledge is Power' has been used by every self-help infomercial imaginable, but I always attribute it to PBS' *School House Rock*, where cartoons tried to teach kids history and politics etc. with the tag line 'And now you know – and knowledge is power!' Of course, you all know that the quote is actually attributable to Sir Francis Bacon from his 1597 *Meditationes Sacrae.*

[15]That would be Jack White of The White Stripes, The Raconteurs and The Dead Weather, and yes... yes he does... (But I never said that... yet).

accidental portrait
of jacob moon

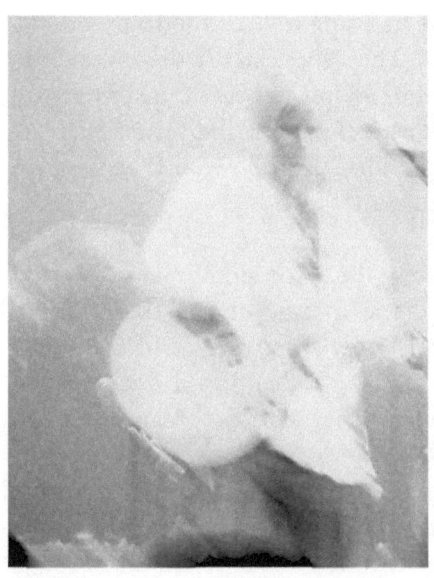

Some accidental artistic photography I found while Penny and I were perusing through photos of our trip to Montreal – you may remember Montreal as the site of the Couche-Tard and the Jumping Asians. Anyhow, this was the talented opening act, Mr. Jacob Moon[1] (which Penny said sounded like a stage name if ever she heard one, and, well, wouldn't she just know, but whatever). I do have a soft spot for guitar players, darlings (oh, get your minds out of the gutter!), and I do declare, this was one impressive performance.

He actually played Kayleigh/Lavender[2], which was just delightful, and Penny and I just about burst with excitement.

---

[1]Really talented indie musician, you should check him out at www.jacobmoon.com
[2]The only Marillion song that ever made it to the charts in North America.

cheyenne wyoming and the accidental plagiarist - part one

Q few years ago, some friends in Napa invited me to come and stay with them for a while. They suggested I drive out, but, knowing myself well enough to know that if I started out across the country I'd likely get side-tracked, like the time I was out chasing my uncle's new droids and ended up following Obi-Wan on some damn fool idealistic crusade...[1] but wait....

See, my mind wanders, darlings, and sometimes even I can't keep the plot straight. So imagine me driving across the country, with all the distractions and possible side-trips, and you can understand why that might not be the best idea. No, I decided that if I was to get to Napa and enjoy the world's greatest Cuban sandwich,[2] I was going to have to fly.

So, the plan was, that I would fly out to Napa, spend a week with my friends out there, visiting wineries, eating clam chowder in San Francisco, and searching for Ewoks in Muir Woods[3] (but that's

---

[1]Yes, it's another *Star Wars* reference, darlings. This is why Luke's Uncle Owen didn't want him hanging out with Obi Wan.

[2]Imagine my surprise when, on a trip to Miami, I learned that what I'd been eating and enjoying as a Cuban sandwich was not one at all.

[3]Muir Woods National Park is just north of San Francisco in Marin County – there's a great little town called Mill Valley that has a wonderful little French bakery where you

a tale for another day), and then I'd rent a car and drive back across the country, when I could let the capricious whimsy of adventure have its way with me with complete abandon. Never in my wildest or most mundane dreams would I have imagined that complete abandon would mean being trapped for six weeks in Cheyenne, Wyoming, home of the worst Chinese food[4] in the universe, and not much else.

In retrospect, I can identify the exact moment when everything went wrong, though at the time, a little innocent flirting with the man at the car rental office seemed completely harmless. If anything, I was hoping that a little batting of the eyes, a perfectly timed laugh while instigating what appeared to be accidental physical contact would help me achieve the best possible rental rate available. And when accompanied by a shamefully low cut blouse showcasing Thing One and Thing Two in all their bountiful glory, why, I was setting my sights on an upgrade to a convertible, which, as everyone knows, is the only way to go on a summer road trip. I'm not ashamed to say that I can always count on my double-Ds to dazzle the XYs into a state susceptible to suggestion. What I didn't count upon, darlings, is just how powerful an effect I was having on Mr. 'Did I Not Offer You The Damage Waiver? No I'm Sure I Offered You The Damage Waiver', because while he was ogling my tempestuous ta-tas, he clearly didn't offer me the damage waiver, or I wouldn't have gotten stuck for six weeks in Cheyenne, Wyoming, home of the keepers of the traditional Cowboy code of Hopalong Cassidy, and not a whole lot else.[5]

I drove into town at sunset, LCD Soundsystem blaring on the radio, all windblown hair and dark sunglasses, looking like Janet Leigh on the run. I hit the first motel I could find that didn't

---

can get a brie and Canadian bacon omelette served with freshly made croissants and other wonderful pastries. It also has great little book stores, clothing stores, and a fantastic record store, where you might just catch a glimpse of someone famous doing some record shopping. But that's Mill Valley. Muir Woods is home to giant redwoods, and it just happens to be where they filmed the Endor scenes from *Return of the Jedi*.

[4] Honestly. I ordered it once, it cost me $50, and I threw 90% of it out as completely inedible.

[5] The Cheyenne Frontier Days Old West Museum is located at 4610 N. Carey Ave in Cheyenne Wyoming and is open 9 to 5 seven days a week for your old west enjoyment.

remind me of the infamous Bates Motel[6] (and believe me, darlings, there were a few I passed over), and checked in. I wasn't planning on staying more than the night, as Cheyenne wasn't exactly on my itinerary, just a place to stop and consider my next direction – did I continue east through Nebraska, or pop on down to Denver, following in the footsteps of Sal Paradise on his way to see Dean Moriarty et al. on his own Beatnik trip across America, only, I realize, in reverse.[7]

With the salt from the flats of Utah still lingering in my nose and throat, I was thirsty for something in the way of a citrus drink, preferably grapefruit-y and heavily spiked with Grey Goose. I asked the disinterested clerk behind the counter of the motel where a girl might wet her whistle (and yes, I said it just like that, as I considered the best way to get his attention would be to use what I presumed was the vernacular in Cheyenne, Wyoming, home of the F.E. Warren Air Force base and the Peacekeeper Missile,[8] but sweet little else), and he looked up briefly from his copy of Guns & Ammo[9] (I'm not making this up!) and suggested that I might get a drink at The Den, and, after looking me up and down like a lion might a gazelle, he reiterated that, "Yep, The Den's the place fer you."

Not knowing exactly how to receive that recommendation, I would later reflect that the man who bore a passing resemblance to Wilford Brimley[10] was making a judgement of my moral character, and would remember to be offended. In any case, as things would

---

[6]Janet Leigh played Marion Crane in the 1960 film Psycho, where she met her fate while on the run with money she stole from her employer at the infamous Bates Motel.

[7]Sal Paradise is the main character (and fictional version of Jack Kerouac) in *On the Road* – the seminal novel of the Beat Generation. Sal travelled East to West. I did the reverse.

[8]You ever wonder where all those weapons of mass destruction were held during the Cold War? Wonder no more. But don't worry, darlings – Dubya (That'd be George W. Bush) started inactivating the Peacekeepers in 2002, and the last one was inactivated in 2005.

[9]A magazine dedicated to – you guessed it – guns and ammunition. On an interesting side note, my favourite Beatles song takes its name from an ad John Lennon allegedly saw in a copy of this magazine – it said: Happiness is a Warm Gun.

[10]You may remember him as the guy from the Quaker Oats commercials, or perhaps doing awareness campaigns for the American Diabetes Association.

play out, his estimation of me would turn out to be not that far off the mark.

I would love to tell you that The Den was a family establishment, whose decor did not rely heavily on black lights, neon tubes and day-glo paint. I would really prefer to tell you that the waitresses were friendly, polite and professional, and definitely not topless. I would also very much like to tell you that I would never in a million years find myself in a state of aforementioned toplessness, nine sheets to the wind, while a stranger who (a drunken argument could be made, in the right light) looked passably like John Cusack circa. *Say Anything*[11] (complete with boom-box, if memory serves me, and, well, please indulge me) did body shots off of my magnificently misappropriated mammaries. Furthermore, I would desperately like to tell you that I did not (italics and underscore understood, and therefore unnecessary) in fact, wake up in some strange motel room beside a man who no longer resembled John Cusack so much as John Belushi,[12] and I would also like to add that I am not being generous with that comparison (but in fact, I am). I would love to tell you all these things, dear reader, but sadly, I cannot. Like the song says, it could have been the whiskey, it might have been the gin....[13]

Ah, who am I kidding? It was the tequila. Always the tequila! Jose Cuervo, you son of a bitch!

I quietly crept out of the den of shame and was fortunate to find that I was not far from the so-called Gentlemen's club – quite literally stumbling distance – and went in search of my car, treading carefully to avoid tripping over my dignity, self-respect, good sense or my sense of self-preservation, all of which I'd quite obviously dropped the night before somewhere between countless lemon wedges, salt shakers and shots of liquid fire. My head was ten sizes

---

[11]Iconic late '80s movie directed by Cameron Crowe. John Cusack standing outside the love of his life's window with a boom box in a sweet if somewhat stalker-ish attempt to woo her.
[12]Ex-SNL alumni, deceased. The shorter, pudgier Blues Brother, not to be confused with his brother Jim Belushi, who is nowhere near as funny as his late brother.
[13]The song in question is *Wasn't That A Party* written by Tom Paxton, but made famous by a Canadian band called The Irish Rovers.

too big, and the so-called Magic City of the Plains[14] had an agave coloured blur that was playing hell with my equilibrium. So when I couldn't find my rental car right away, I didn't immediately panic. I merely chalked it up to being completely shit-faced the night before, and, in fact, not yet hung-over, truth be told.

I didn't panic until I realized that not only could I not find my car, but neither could I find my purse, and therefore, my wallet, all identification, my lucky cigarette case (I quit long ago, darlings, but as any fan of film noir will tell you, you never know when a cigarette case will come in handy – it may even save your life), and, of course, my car keys.

I seem to recall voicing a virtual vichyssoise of verbose vulgarities at various volumes, vomiting, and then I recall very little else, as I suddenly found myself prostrate and passed out on the pavement.

When I awoke, a figure stood over me, the sun forming a corona around her like an angelic halo. I thought perhaps I'd died and gone to heaven, until I heard her voice. A grating, definitely not angelic voice that reminded me of cats in heat, and screaming babies, and Patsy Cline.[15]

"Hi," the voice said, "I'm Cheyenne."

I had all but erased that foul memory from my mind, darlings, until the phone rang last night and the voice on the line brought it all flooding back.

"Helena?" A voice I hoped I'd never hear again said. "Hey, honey, guess who's in town?"

I froze, suddenly remembering promises of repayment, of debts owed, and like a regretful knight who swore fealty to a king

---

[14]A nickname for Cheyenne, Wyoming.
[15]Singer of the famous country song *Crazy*, which has been covered by everyone. There's just something about her voice that makes me want to stick knitting needles in my ears. But that's just me – I realize I'm in the minority on this one.

out of desperation, thoughts of falling on my sword to avoid making good on past promises fluttered through my mind, only to vanish just as quickly.

"It's me, silly! Cheyenne!"Cheyenne was her stage name, because, well, for obvious reasons. "You remember, Cheyenne. From Wyoming?"

"Darling!" I said, trying to muster as much enthusiasm as possible and hoping that I'd pulled it off. "How are you? It's been so long!"

"I know, right?" Cheyenne agreed, like we were long lost BFFs from childhood. And, just like someone with that familial bond, she felt no hesitation in letting me know that she was in town, and that she needed a place to stay, and would I mind putting her up for a couple of days? That is, you know, if it wasn't any trouble.

There was so much unspoken in that small statement – so much looming over my head, that I can't even get into just now. Give me a moment.

"Oh, it's no trouble at all, darling," I heard myself say, as if having an out-of-body experience. "You come and stay as long as you need to."

And that was how Cheyenne Wyoming (yes, she's a clever girl with the picking of the stage name) and, by extension, the Accidental Plagiarist, came to live with me.

The Countess Penelope of Arcadia was not amused.

cheyenne wyoming and the accidental plagiarist - part two

The first time it happened it was just weird – like maybe it was a joke, like he was putting us on.

Penny had been bopping around the house all morning humming the surf guitar riff from *Brand New Cadillac* by The Clash,[1] and while she was getting on my nerves, I really had no one to blame but myself. I had recently bequeathed to her my ten crates of records, and had made a point to pull out *London Calling* and insist she give it a listen loudly and with great enthusiasm.

Wow, Helena, you say, *that's very generous of you to part with your record collection like that.*

Don't start with me.

The fact is, the records were piled up in my spare room/studio/office/would-be boudoir, and two weeks ago I had to clear them out to make room for Cheyenne and (surprise!) her boyfriend, Chuck. Or Chet. Or Chewie. You know, I don't think I

---

[1]Brand New Cadillac was originally a 12-bar blues song by Vince Taylor, recorded in the late '50s. The Clash wasn't even the first group to cover it, but it's the version I like best. London Calling is on my top ten must own albums.

actually know his name because I've never heard Cheyenne call him the same thing twice, which leads me to believe that maybe she doesn't know his name, either. Oh, and in case you missed it in there, yes, I said two weeks. It had been two weeks since Cheyenne and the Accidental Plagiarist showed up on my doorstep intent on staying for a couple days as a visit, which then turned into needing a place to stay until they can find something nice of their own.

Chet/Chuck/Chewie is a guitar player struggling to make his way in the club scene, or maybe join a band. Currently he was sitting in what was once the room where I went to channel my inner goddess (I went through a crazy transcendental meditative yoga phase[2] darlings, you'll just have to forgive me) playing the guitar riff from *Brand New Cadillac*– the same riff the Countess had been humming for the past three hours – precisely, I suspect, because she knew it was getting on my nerves.

"Hey that's pretty good, Chester," said Penny. "Sounds just like it."

"Sounds like what?" he asked, without a trace of irony.

"Um, the song you're playing. It's The Clash, yeah?"

"I don't think so," he replied after mulling it over. "I just made it up."

Penny looked at him and then broke into nervous laughter and then suddenly stopped when he didn't join her.

"No, seriously, dude," said Penny, channelling her inner surfer, "It's The Clash. I've been listening to it for the last week and I've been humming that particular tune all morning, so I know you didn't just make it up. Helena, back me up here!"

I poked my head in and said, "It's not even The Clash's song, either – it's a cover."

"Really?" Chet asked. "I could've sworn I made it up! I had it stuck in my head and just had to get it out but, I couldn't remember hearing it anywhere before." His face showed no sign of guile or deception, and he conceded that he sometimes got confused and forgot stuff innocently enough to convince us that it was a

---

[2]So did The Beatles, and we still love them, right?

complete fluke, which is how we began referring to him (never to his face, of course) as the Accidental Plagiarist.

"Um, yeah. It's called *Brand New Cadillac*. Here I'll throw it on again so you can hear it. Helena won't mind, will you Helena?"

"Not at all," I said, grinding my teeth and going to grab some headphones and listen to something else, anything else – not that I don't love The Clash, darlings, because I do. I wept openly for three days straight when Joe Strummer died, and when I die, I want his cover of *Redemption Song*[3] to be played at my funeral, but a girl needs some variety! So I reached for the iPod and programmed in an eclectic mix of Britpop, New Wave and '70s glam rock, because hey, I love to boogie.[4]

After Cheyenne and Charlie left for work (which is to say that Cheyenne went to dance the modern hootchiecoochie and Charlie went to watch her – which was kind of the problem, but we'll get to that later), Penelope cornered me, as she'd been trying to do every day for the past two weeks but somehow I had always managed to avoid her, and again demanded to know why they were still here. And so I told her.

"Let me give you a piece of advice, Penny. Never sign anything without reading it..."

(Insert flashback segue sound effects here).[5]

Cheyenne picked me up out of the dirt, took me to a diner around the corner and fed me pancakes, which she swore were the best things for me in my state. I never wanted to eat anything less my entire life, and as I chewed each bite slower than the last, I secretly wished there were a way to get the pancakes from my plate into my stomach without them having to travel via my mouth.

---

[3] Joe Strummer (singer for The Clash) recorded a duet of Bob Marley's *Redemption Song* with Johnny Cash. It'll bring tears to your eyes, darlings.
[4] So does T-Rex, a glam rock band from the '70s whose track *I Love To Boogie* I was referencing.
[5] This can either be a harp, some sort of weird, wavering synth-chords, or, I like to think of the noise the TARDIS makes when it appears or disappears. You make your own bloody sound effects; I can't do everything for you!

I was a blubbering, panicking, it's-the-end-of-the-world-as-we-know-it-and-I-feel-anything-but-fine mess by the time Cheyenne tucked me into her bed at two o'clock in the afternoon, keeping me well stocked with Gatorade and sitting by my side and holding my hair while I threw up. In between bouts of vomiting, I confessed to her that I'd lost everything, and that I was far away from home, and that I had no money and nowhere to go – pretty much all the things that you never confess to a stranger when you're in a vulnerable situation, but I wasn't thinking clearly. Clearly, I wasn't thinking. So, being vulnerable, I let Cheyenne take care of me, and make decisions for me, which was, I now realize, the worst thing I could have done. At the time, though, it just felt good to let go of the steering wheel, if only for a moment.

Cheyenne stroked my hair as I fell asleep, telling me that it would all look better tomorrow, once I'd had a chance to rest and recover. I tried to protest that I should at least call the police and file a report, but she told me it could wait. I've lost track of all the mistakes I'd made thus far, but let's just say this one ranked pretty high on the list.

Of course, I didn't realize that until the next day, when I called the police, and had to explain to them that I had no ID, no passport, nothing, in fact, to lend any credence to my tale of woe, or, indeed, to prove I was who I said I was, and that my rental car, which of course I could not prove existed in the first place, had been stolen. Invisible car, invisible purse, invisible passport – what could I expect but for the Cheyenne equivalent of Chief Wiggum[6] to tell me not to get my hopes up. With the way I looked and the company I was keeping (it's a crying shame that strippers just don't command the respect of law enforcement that they deserve) it's a wonder he didn't lock me up on suspicion of any number of crimes, not the least of all being Canadian without a permit. Because let me tell you, darlings, when Officer Friendly learned that not only was I from out of town, but that I was also a foreigner without papers, why, his Homeland Security alarm went off all bells and klaxons

---

[6]The bumbling Chief of Police from *The Simpsons*, who was known to type things up sceptically on his invisible typewriter.

and whistles, and I swear I could almost hear the word Al Qaeda repeating over and over again in the back of his mind. So before I found myself in lockup being water-boarded by a glorified security guard with delusions of heroism, I broke down and cried. I bawled like a little baby, and, in between hitches of hyperventilation, I begged for mercy and understanding and compassion, which, by the look on poor Barney Fife's[7] face, I was going to be granted.

"Oh, gosh, ma'am," he said, suddenly treating me like a lady."Don't cry, now. It's not the end of the world. We'll get this sorted out. First things first, we should call your rental car company and let them know what's happened. Now, I ain't gonna lie to you, it's not gonna be pretty, but these things do happen, dear – that's why there's insurance and damage waivers and such. You'll see, sweetheart – everything's going to be right as rain, you just wait and see."

But everything was not going to be right as rain, because when the fax came through of my rental contract, it clearly showed that, while I had signed in all the right spots, I had clearly not paid attention to what I was signing, because one of the paragraphs (which Mr. Oh, I'm So Clever To Cover My Ass So I Don't Get Fired Or Sued Or Worse was kind enough to highlight and draw attention to) detailed the Damage Waiver and Extended Coverage, which covered me against loss due to theft or damages over $5000. Which (as the fax clearly showed) I had declined, even though it would have only cost me an additional $10 per day.

Furthermore, it was not going to be right as rain, because when the car did turn up a couple of days later (they never did find my purse or any of its contents), it had been taken for a joyride and damaged beyond repair. Or, I should say, it may as well have been beyond repair, because the estimate I got from the garage that the Sheriff recommended to me was just shy of $7000.

"But where am I going to get $7000?" I cried in horror when I got the news. Cheyenne had gone with me, and had been letting me stay with her, for which I was incredibly grateful, and swore to one day return her kindness.

---

[7] Deputy Sheriff from Mayberry on *The Andy Griffith Show*.

"Oh, don't worry, hon," she drawled, "it looks bad now, but we'll figure it out."

At this point, Penny interrupted me. I welcomed it, because I wasn't quite sure how to launch into the awful third act of this sordid play.

"Why didn't you just call mum?" She asked, and I confess I blanched a bit at the mention of my sister, Penny's mother.

"Oh, Penny," I sighed, "I just couldn't. Do you remember this time at all? When your crazy aunt Helena disappeared for two months, and then, when I came back and nobody would talk about it?"

Penny nodded. "I was still in high school, but I'd just broken up with Danny Thibeault– remember him? Gag! I was pretty wrapped up in myself. I spent an entire month looking like a melting wax sculpture, so, yeah, I remember Mum and Dad arguing about it, but not any details. Just stuff about you being flighty and irresponsible and reckless, and not a good role model for dear Penelope and blah blah blah... And then, after Mum and Dad died and I came to live with you... well, I just never thought to ask where you'd been."

Okay, I'm sorry, dear readers, but I have to admit that I got a bit teary over that, and had to take a few deep breaths before I explained myself.

"Penny, you have to understand that your mother and I were always the best of friends, but in a lot of ways, I think we both envied each other's lives. I wanted what she had – a wonderful husband and a beautiful, incredibly witty and charming daughter, the whole bit. And Cheryl tolerated and defended my free-spirited nature because she could always live vicariously through me. But not this time. This time was different. This time it wasn't just silly Helena stuck in some jam for big sister to bail me out of."

"So, Cheyenne gave you the money, then?" Penny presumed prematurely. "And that's why her and the Accidental Plagiarist have *carte blanche* around here?"

"Not exactly," I said, and turned away from Penny to get myself a drink. I was going to need one.

Thankfully, I was interrupted by a phone call from Cheyenne, asking me if I could come and pick up Chet – he'd gotten into another fight at the strip club when one of the patrons got a little bit too friendly with Cheyenne – and the manager had threatened to fire her if Chet ever showed his face in there again.

So it wasn't until later that I finally had to tell Penny about my brief and regrettable stint as an exotic dancer.

accidental portrait of my friend bethany

$\mathcal{F}$irst of all – WATCH THIS SPACE. Helena told me to say that, 'cause she was called away on business, and wasn't able to finish telling the story of Cheyenne Wyoming and the Accidental Plagiarist, but she promises to finish when she gets back (which will be soon I hope, because they are driving me fifty shades[1] of bat shit). Anyhow, I escaped the confines of our suddenly overcrowded abode and grabbed a coffee with my friend Bethany (never Beth, always Bethany), and I took this picture of her on the sly, and once I comic-posted[2] the crap out of it, Bethany allowed that yes, she is almost pretty, at which point I smacked her and told her she is gorgeous! Isn't she just beautiful? Anyhow, gotta go... Chet's asking me to hear his new song, which kinda sounds like something by Iggy Pop, but I gotta go humour him. Laterz.

Penny - MWAH!

---

[1] A reference to that smutty nonsense *Fifty Shades of Grey* that supposedly intelligent women ate up like it was steak instead of the horrid tripe it was.

[2] You can't just take pictures anymore, darlings, you have to run them through cheap filters on your phone!

cheyenne wyoming and the accidental plagiarist - part three

When I finally told the Countess what happened to me, and how I ended up getting home after being effectively stranded in Cheyenne, Wyoming a few years ago, she had already done some digging of her own, and was full of angry questions and accusations and hurt.

I had been called away to do some work as an extra for a film being shot in Hamilton, and it was going to be long days, so I'd stayed with a friend there for the weekend rather than travel back and forth at ungodly hours of the morning and night. I am not a morning person, so there was no way I was getting up at five o'clock to be on set by seven-thirty.

When I arrived at home again, home again, jiggety jig, I found my house guest Cheyenne strapped to a kitchen chair, a look of confusion and mild terror on her face, as the Countess Penelope of Arcadia (which is apparently somewhere in the neighbourhood of Nuremberg) stood over her with a waterpik and a flashlight, repeating "Izeet safe? Izeet safe?" with a faux-German accent that have made Laurence Olivier blush in embarrassment. Chet/Chester/Chuck/The Accidental Plagiarist sat playing a melody on his guitar that could only be the Theme from Marathon

Man[1], though later he would protest that he had never heard it before.

Cheyenne looked up at me like a puppy happy to see its owner, stood up from the chair, that she was apparently not really strapped to at all, that was just your favourite unreliable narrator taking artistic license (again!), and gave me a big hug, and then breezed past me saying she had to get to work, dragging Chewie behind her.

I looked at Penny and then at Cheyenne, and then back at Penny, who wouldn't look me in the eyes, and then back at Cheyenne, who quickly disappeared out the door before I could ask her anything, and then back at Penny, who was fidgeting with her hands, and I knew then that Cheyenne had said something that I'd rather wish she hadn't.

"So what'd she tell you?" I asked delicately, my head already pounding with a headache, and really being in no mood to talk about this.

"Oh, not much," Penny began, "just some stuff about finding you passed out drunk after some sleazy one night stand, something about finding your rental car totalled, and then a delightful tale about how you thought that the best way to get yourself out of that mess was to take off all your clothes in front of strangers!"

"Penny, darling, I know you're upset, but..."

"I'm not upset, Helena," Penelope said, "I'm just... I dunno... disappointed. I can't picture you... doing *that*."

I sat down and put my arm around her and gave her a kiss on the top of her head. I would have never thought that it was something I was capable of, either, but when I found myself desperate, and the opportunity presented itself – well, at the time, I didn't see as I had many options available to me. It's not like I could have found any respectable work in Cheyenne. I was afraid and I was vulnerable and I allowed myself to be helpless. It was the

---

[1] *Marathon Man* is a 1976 spy-thriller starring Dustin Hoffman as a man who, due to a case of mistaken identity, ends up being interrogated by Laurence Olivier who tortures him with dentists tools, repeatedly asking him "Is it safe?" Poor Dustin doesn't know whether 'Yes' or 'No' is the correct answer.

lowest point of my life, not some adventure that I just added to my C.V. as a professional dilettante, but sometimes you have to hit bottom in order to learn how to never find yourself there again.

"Did she tell you she saved my life?" I asked, burying my face into Penny's hair.

Penny pushed me away and looked up at me in disbelief. "Her?"

I nodded. "She may be obnoxious, overbearing, and, well, let's face it, not the sharpest cheese at the deli..."

"Very nice," Penny said.

"Thank you, my dear," I replied. "But when the chips were down, she protected me like I was family, even though she didn't owe me a thing."

(Cue Mister Peabody and the WABAC machine!)[2]

On what would prove to be the very last night of my short-lived career as an exotic dancer...

Um, stripper, Penny interjected with not even a trace of open-mindedness or understanding. I replied that I simply cannot bring myself to refer to myself as a stripper, even though there was nothing exotic about shaking your ta-tas for a bunch of off-duty grease monkeys, wannabe cowboys and of course, all the zipper-suited sun gods[3] from the Air Force base. I mean, it's not like I was doing the dance of the seven veils, or Russian folk dancing or something. I'd understand it if they called it erotic dancing, but I guess that's just too 'on the nose', so exotic dancer it is.

While I am generally an exhibitionist by nature, I confess, I had never dreamed that I would find myself on stage in such a

---

[2]Mr. Peabody is a talking cartoon dog from the Rocky & Bullwinkle Show, (late fifties, early sixties, so, yeah, before my time, too, darlings – but I grew up with the re-runs) who, along with his boy Sherman (yeah, it was a dog and his boy story, instead of the other way around) travelled through time to tell comedic versions of historical tales. The WABAC was his time machine.

[3]I didn't make this term up, but it refers to military pilots, who tend to think very highly of themselves and wear jackets and G-suits that are covered in lots of zippers. Don't say I didn't teach you anything useful.

vulnerable state. I've been on stage before, sometimes as a singer, or the occasional foray into theatre, but nothing so (I hesitate to sully the word, but) intimate. Other than a one-night-only gig as a go-go dancer in a cabaret nightclub (and that only as a favour to a friend who was in the band that was playing that night – what can I say? I have a soft spot for guitarists), I had never really danced before, and certainly never in pasties and a G-string (at least not professionally, darlings). But Cheyenne had assured me the proficiency of my dancing would not be under such strict scrutiny as much as my ability to attract absolute attention and extract the maximum amount of money from my many admirers while withstanding any actual unwanted advances, of which, she attested with a warning, there would be many. Well, perhaps she put it a pinch less loquaciously.[4]

"Just keep 'em thirsty," Cheyenne told me my very first night. "Keep 'em thirsty and wanting more. Just keep it in your head that you're the one who's got the power – they may want more, but they ain't gonna get it. The best dancers are the ones that make those poor schmucks believe that you want them as much as they want you – but we know different. Sometimes I feel sorry for them – once the blood starts runnin' to their peckers, there ain't nothin' they won't pay to get one more look at yer precious Vertical Stripe.[5] It's like taking candy from a baby."

Except it wasn't. Every time I had to step out on to that stage was harder than the last. I wasn't stupid or naive – I'd seen men many times before worshiping at the altar of flesh, drooling like dogs, but I'd always been outside of it. Being in the spotlight (or, in this case, rather, in neon and black light) was a different thing altogether, and I dreaded it each and every time. It was no wonder that many of the dancers there were high off their heads the whole night, and, while I admit I had a couple of drinks to take the edge off, I made sure that I never lost control – not after the disaster that I'd brought upon myself that landed me in this mess to begin with.

---

[4] "No one's gonna give a shit if you can even keep time to the music so long as they can see your tits" were, I believe, her exact words.
[5] Oh yeah – you learn all kinds of charming slang names for the vagina if you travel. In the Air Force, one vertical stripe outranks all horizontal ones.

No, I wanted to be in control – I wasn't going to let anything else bad happen to me. And I was doing all right, until that final night, when Cheyenne saved me from being raped – or worse.

"How about a drink?" I asked Penny. "I think that before I continue, I am going to need a nice stiff drink."

"I thought you were going somewhere else just now." Penny replied, picking her mind up from the gutter it had fallen into.

"Conjecture and innuendo, darling." I sighed.

Penny went to the fridge for the grapefruit juice, and I used her absence as an opportunity to retire, as I was exhausted from my long day.

The Countess of Arcadia was not amused, and yelled after me to come back and finish the story.

"Tomorrow night, perhaps," I responded, praying that she'd take the hint that not only was I physically exhausted, but that reliving that time was not particularly pleasant for my emotional state either.

"But you can't stop there! You're not finished! I want to hear the rest," Penny protested, shaking my glass so I could hear the clink of ice cubes. "Don't you even want your drink? I used pink grapefruit juice, just how you like it."

"Penny dear," I called to her affectionately, "if there's one thing that I've taken away from my experience, it's that there's nothing wrong with walking away leaving them wanting more – as Cheyenne says – you gotta keep 'em thirsty."

"I see what you did, there, Helena!" Penny yelled after me. "You're not going to get away with this, you hear me!"

I laughed maniacally; throwing my head back and MU-HAH-HAH-ing like a cartoon villain, and then crawled into bed and shed a few secret tears before falling asleep.

accidental portrait of the countess penelope of arcadia — the newsprint edition

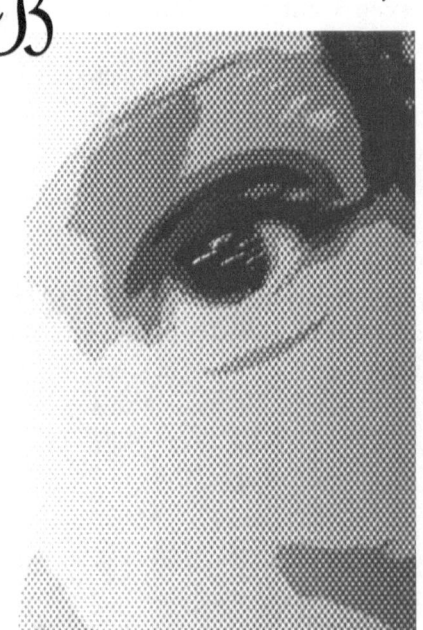

Before I had even had my coffee, before I had even begun to process, before I had even put on clothes, before I had even remembered that I had a male house guest, who was currently playing a passable rendition of *Foxy Lady*,[1] (which flattered me until he asked what I thought of his new song), the Countess Penelope of Arcadia, still miffed by my misdirection the night before, was in my face demanding to hear the rest of the saga of Cheyenne Wyoming and the Accidental Plagiarist.

Wrapping a terry housecoat

---

[1] Jimi Hendrix, in case you didn't already know.

around my pale, sun-starved body (note to self – go somewhere sunny soon), I put my hand in the pocket and found, to my surprise, my iPhone, which I pulled out and began snapping photos of my dear Penny, warding her off with it like some type of sacred talisman. This was the result of fiddling with Pudding Cam.[2]

[2]It might have been Paper Camera – I can't remember.

cheyenne wyoming and the accidental plagiarist - part four

"**S**o," the Countess began artlessly and impatiently, licking a bit of powdered sugar off a square of waffle she had skewered on her fork, "finish your story."

Telling the never-before-told tale of attempted rape and dramatic escape would be easier, I'd decided whimsically, with waffles. So, after I'd gotten dressed semi-presentably and consumed a (couldn't really call it copious[1]) amount of coffee, I packed Penny into the passenger seat and sped along in sweet introspective silence (which I'd made Penny promise to practice prior to departing) to the fair Waffle Bar[2], where we lay our scene.

"Okay," I said, defeated. I sympathized with the skewered bit of waffle that Penny had trapped on her fork. "But keep your voice down. So, did you ever see that Jodie Foster movie *The Accused*?"

"Are you saying that you got raped on a pinball machine?" Penny asked in as hushed tones as she could manage.

---

[1]This is a cheat, darlings, for the sake of alliteration, and I can't even let myself get away with it without saying something. Copious does not mean "excessive", but rather, abundant or plentiful. It is not really a qualifier, and I pray you forgive me just this once. But don't let me catch you using it improperly!

[2]281 Scarborough Road in Toronto – you simply must visit if you're in town.

"No," I said, "It was nothing like that. See, if you'll remember, in the movie, Jodie Foster wasn't doing anything wrong, other than being a little too flirty with the wrong boys and not being sober enough to get the hell out of there. With me, well, I'd just been pretty much shoving my hoo-ha in these boys' faces for the last couple of hours, and took an awful lot of money from them, so I suppose they figured they were entitled..."

"Woah, woah, back up there, Steubinville,"[3] Penny interjected, "rape is never the victim's fault, and no one is ever entitled to anything. What you were doing may have been overtly sexual and, I'm not going to deny it, absolutely intended to invoke a reaction, but there's an implicit social contract between the stripper..."

"Ah, I prefer the term exotic dancer," I mumbled.

"Fine," Penny relented graciously. "Between the exotic dancer and the audience member – because that's what they are, ultimately – the audience for a performance. Now, in that particular line of work, I'm sure the lines are blurred all the time, and..."

I snorted at that, and nearly choked on my waffle (which was delicious, by the way. If you want to have real Belgian waffles and can't make your way to Belgium, the Waffle Bar is simply to die for, darlings).

"That's one way to put it," I said after I recovered. "The lines are blurred so much that it's more like a dotted line. I mean, why do you think there's a cheap motel right beside every strip club?"

"Fair enough," Penny admitted, "but you can't hold yourself responsible for some redneck with more spunk than smarts. Or, that is, you can try, but I won't let you."

I smiled at the frowning and very serious-looking Countess Penelope until my heart felt it would burst with love, and reached out and gave her hand a squeeze.

---

[3] In early 2013, Steubinville, Ohio was all over the news, as the nation watched with furious attention the trial of two football players accused of raping a sixteen year old girl. The phrase *rape culture* became something of a thing, as people tried to examine why things like that are allowed to happen, and victims were re-victimized by people who wanted to say that they had it coming to them.

"But I do feel responsible, Penny. I'm not responsible for their actions, but I was responsible for being in that situation in the first place. I never would have been there at all if I'd been responsible to begin with."

(Alright, Doc, let's get the DeLorian up to EIGHTY-EIGHT MILES PER HOUR!)[4]

I remember it was a Tuesday, because Tuesday was ALL-NUDE night at The Den, as opposed to just being a topless joint the rest of the week. I say just as if that's a concession, but believe me, darlings, it's still a vulnerable position to be in, and you wouldn't believe how tired the ta-tas get after a few hours being bounced around like ice cubes in a cocktail shaker. I never thought I'd be so happy to strap my bra back on at the end of the night, but every night the blessed blissful relief was akin to Dorothy waking up back home in her bed in Kansas[5]– and there's no place like home.

Home. The place I was trying to get back to. My *raison d'être*[6]at the moment. And I had proven, perhaps to my detriment, that I was willing to do whatever it took to get back there. I'd finally paid off the garage after six weeks of the hardest work I've ever done, and figured that I only had to come up with enough scratch to get me home – so I was in good spirits, relatively speaking, that night when I went in to work. One or two more nights, and that was it. I'd wipe the sweat, grime and sleaze of Cheyenne, Wyoming (setting of three Phillip K. Dick novels[7]– who knew?) from my back, get in my good-as-new convertible rental car and drive home with the top down the whole way, and never look back.

---

[4]That would be Doc Brown, played by the amazing Christopher Lloyd in the *Back to the Future* movies, where the time machine was built out of a DeLorian and would only travel back in time once it hit 88 MPH. By the way, it makes me feel really old having to mention this, but it's possible that someone reading this might not know what I was referring to.
[5]Dorothy Gale from *The Wizard of Oz*, of course.
[6]Purpose – literally, reason for being.
[7]The most famous of which being *The Man in the High Castle*. You may have never read any Philip K. Dick, but you've seen something based on his stories – *Blade Runner, Total Recall, Minority Report, A Scanner Darkly, Screamers* – all based on his stories.

As I said, I was relatively happy that night when I went to work, so perhaps it was my smile that led those three men to believe that I'd like nothing better than to be thrown into the back of a pick-up truck at two-thirty in the morning, already sore and tired, and in no shape to fight off one horny redneck, let alone three.

At this point in the story, Penny was looking nervous, so I reminded her that there was a reason that we had house guests who had, for reasons about to be made clear, not quite run out of goodwill and overstayed their welcome.

I lay face down in the bed of the pick-up truck, its country back-road odour flooding my suddenly alert senses as I took deep, panicky lungfuls of dirt, oil, and old beer. I kicked and bucked the best I could, but one of them punched me in the side and knocked the wind out of me, and after that, all my energy, all my sense of being went into simply willing myself to breathe again. Breathe or die.

I felt the cold night air against my bottom as my jeans were forcibly removed, and heard the tell-tale jingle jangle of a belt buckle being undone, but far away, as if I was hearing it from underwater. Then I heard a loud bang from behind me – a sound that could only be a gunshot, followed by a stream of profanity and threats of permanent prophylaxis[8] from a voice that could have shattered glass. There was a brief pause where I feared everything might go very wrong, and then felt the weight lift off of my body, as the three drunken idiot would-be rapists scrambled to get out of the truck bed, climbed into the cab and sped off, sending my sorry naked ass sprawling in the dust of their wake. Cheyenne screamed curses after them, and fired another shot in their direction, but only succeeded in waking up everyone in earshot.

"Oh, honey," she sighed, looking down at me. I was weeping and shaking in anger and terror. For the second time, Cheyenne picked me up out of the dirt and put me to bed.

---

[8] "I'll blow your peckers clean off!" Is what she actually said. Later, I'd wish I'd been clever enough to come up with something like "I didn't know you were a sharp-shooter," but at the time my mind was otherwise occupied.

When I woke up, I was in the passenger seat of my car, with the sun coming up, as Cheyenne drove me away from town.

"Stop," I said weakly, still in shock, I suppose. "Where are you taking me?"

"Denver," Cheyenne said. "I looked it up on the internet – that's where you've got to go to get your passport and stuff."

"No," I said, trying to take charge of myself. I was done. I felt like I was waking from a bad dream, and I needed to take absolute charge of my situation. "Turn around. Fuck Denver. I just want to go home. Turn around and let me go home. I'll head north, and when I'm back in Canada I'll deal with all that official bullshit, but right now I just want to go home. Do you understand? Home."

Cheyenne slammed on the brakes, and may or may have not said "There's no place like home," and turned the car around back towards the city she stole her name from.

We stopped for breakfast at a tiny little diner/gas station outside of Cheyenne, where I thanked Cheyenne and promised her that someday, somehow, I would pay back her kindness – that I was in her debt, and that I could never ever be out of it, and in the end I was just babbling and blubbering, and she hugged me and held me as I cried into her hair while the other early morning patrons tried politely not to stare.

"Do you want me to come with you?"She offered. "Let me get you home."

"No," I said resolutely, blowing my nose on my only napkin and wiping my tears away. "No, I need to go the rest of the way on my own."

So I gave her my home number, said good-bye, and while I meant what I said at the time about how, if she was ever in Toronto, she was welcome to stay with me, it never even occurred to me that I would ever see her again. And yet here we were.

Penny was crying, and I might have been a little teary, too, because the guy behind the counter at the Waffle Hut came over with some extra napkins and asked if everything was okay.

Without missing a beat, Penny warbled through her tears: "These are just the best damn waffles I've ever had!"And broke into a sob, which sent the poor man away, obviously uncomfortable.

Which was our cue to exit, and so, of course, we did.

On the way back home, I told Penny the last few details, about crossing the border into Saskatchewan in the middle of nowhere after thirteen gruelling hours driving through the last great frontier of Wyoming and Montana, only to end up in Regina, which is not exactly a cosmopolitan paradise, but was, in that instant, one to me.

I summarized in sufficient detail my battle with the bastards at the rental car agency (which shall remain nameless – but it rhymes with Mavis), and how they'd wanted me to drive the car to Calgary, which was one of their depots that accepted cross-border drop offs, and how I'd described, in glorious, X-rated detail, exactly what they would have to do to themselves if they thought for one millisecond that I was going to acquiesce to their absurd request.

In the end, I broke down in tears (again!) and convinced the young, terrified looking man behind the counter that I was at the end of my tether, and after giving him a quick and heavily edited synopsis of how I came to arrive on his doorstep, so to speak, he agreed to accept the car, pending an inspection. And of course, there would be the matter of the balance owing, and a processing fee for transferring the car to Calgary, and I tuned him out around that point, remembering everything I had done over the past six weeks. I smiled weakly at him and nodded in, I hoped, all the right places, and handed over the keys to him while he went to process the car. And as soon as he was out of sight, I walked out the door, and calmly but quickly walked away.

I caught the first cab I saw and headed to the airport, where I blew the last of my remaining cash on a one-way ticket home.

Later that afternoon, when Penny saw Cheyenne, she didn't bristle as much as she had been. She made polite conversation, and restrained herself from making sarcastic remarks about her accent, or her profession. She was even nice to Chet when he came to us all excited, guitar in hand, and said:

"Hey, you guys want to hear the new song I've been working on?"

Chat/Chewie/Charles then proceeded to play *Fell In Love With A Girl* by The White Stripes.

Penny rolled her eyes at me, but, to her credit, said nothing. Of course it wasn't his fault. In his mind he was a genius and had just accidentally written the best punk pop love song since *Janie Jones* by The Clash.

"What do you think?"He asked with such naïve, innocent hope in his eyes. "Do I have a hit?"
"Oh definitely, squire," Penny deadpanned in her best cockney urchin accent.
"I love it," I agreed.

Penny had other plans, however.

"Oh is that all?" She said, smirking. "I believe you can do better than that, Helena."
"What?" I sputtered. "Oh no. Oh no, you're not going to make me say it."

The Countess Penelope of Arcadia, a suburb of Wonderland, just looked at me, arms crossed, a giant Cheshire cat grin on her face.

"I'm waiting," she said, tapping her foot.
"Fine," I sighed, and then recited, for Penny's benefit: "I don't know, there's just something about Jack White that makes me want to be a 19-year-old girl in a Go-Go cage again."[9]
Penny laughed triumphantly, and exited stage left.

---

[9]If you'll recall, Penny advertised that I would say this, and I vehemently denied it. However, with the White Stripes song being accidentally plagiarized by Chet, it only seemed appropriate. Sometimes, you just have to let the Countess win some.

vive les differences

I was deleting photos off my iPhone last night (we never used to waste this much film, I tell you) and came across this photo – another refugee from la belle province. Some urban artwork for a community centre called, appropriately, "Village".

This translates into the brilliant sentiment: *At Village, we believe that our differences (or diversity) can enrich us more than they can divide us.*

What impressed me most about Montreal was its true cultural diversity. It may be the only actual bilingual city I've ever visited in Canada – I heard as many people speaking English as I heard French, and was greeted or served in both languages equally. If I tried to speak French, they appreciated but didn't expect it. It was clear, as I'd approach the counter for a coffee that the person behind the counter was just as unsure as I was whether they should speak English or French. Montreal was just lovely, and I hope to see her again. *Vive les différences!*

the unholy power of nyquil

I feel awful, darlings.

Tossing and turning and coughing and snot-filled and most unladylike.

I can't sleep, and it's having disastrous effects, the first of which is the obvious, that I am writing in first person present tense, which is, as everyone knows, the laziest and most *Hunger Games*-iest of crimes against narrative.[1] (God were those books poorly written. Great idea – not very original, but great idea – but a big BLECH on the writing, darling).

I mean, we're led to believe that there are all these horrible things going on in the Districts, but we never actually get to see

---

[1]Everyone thinks first person is so easy to write in, but it's so frequently used for the wrong type of story. First person is for memoirs, darlings, as every good dilettante knows. Or for psychological thrillers where the reader is supposed to experience only what the narrator experiences. *Hunger Games* was completely ruined in my not-so-humble and definitely correct opinion by the choice to write in first person. It was a lazy choice that catered to teenage girls who just wanted to be Katniss. Again I say BLECH! If you have no idea what *Hunger Games* is, I can't help that you've been living under a rock, darling. Next you'll tell me you are completely unaware of the *Twilight* franchise.

what is going on, because it's written in first person subjective present tense, so it's all Katniss, Katniss, Katniss!

But I digress, and you'll just have to please forgive me if I'm a little bitchy, but nasal congestion evidently has detrimental designs on my demeanour.

That's when I turn to the unholy power of NyQuil (cue NyQuil theme music. Does NyQuil have theme music? Note to self: find out if NyQuil has theme music, because it's going to be driving me 50 shades of ape shit (and don't even get me started on those literary abortions – far too easy, darlings. And by the way, did I just open a parenthesis inside another parenthesis? Can I do that? Apparently I can). and also don't forget to close original parenthesis).[2]

Okay, where was I? Oh yes, the night-time, sniffling, sneezing, coughing, aching, stuffy head, fever so you can rest medicine.[3] Green gold. Like crack cocaine if you are, like me, suffering from cold or flu type symptoms. (And apparently, just as bad for you![4])

Yeah, you're not alone. I wish I'd never read anything bad about NyQuil either. I drink NyQuil straight from the bottle, and I drink alone. With nobody else. I drink NyQuil like George Thoroughgood drinks whiskey.[5]

---

[2]This was written at two o'clock in the morning after tossing and turning and being unable to sleep. After reading it the next day I decided not to edit myself so you could enjoy the full effect of my NyQuil induced mania.

[3]If you've not seen the commercials, you might not recognize that this is NyQuil's slogan.

[4]I couldn't sleep, and I did a Google seach for NyQuil (never a good idea) and found an article from *Wired* magazine (Issue 15.11) that revealed that taking NyQuil is tantamount to taking a bong hit, then washing down a bunch of PCP down with a shot of moonshine. When tripping the light fantastic on NyQuil, I can only assume that light has a greenish hue. Like dropping acid in OZ or something. The article can be found here: http://www.wired.com/science/discoveries/magazine/15-11/st_nyquil if you want to read more.

[5]Another glimpse into the stream that was my consciousness at 2 a.m. I got *I Drink Alone* by George Thoroughgood stuck in my head and looked it up on YouTube. For those of you who want the full effect, please feel free to watch the video now.

When I'm sick and drinking NyQuil alone, I prefer to be by myself. I don't want anyone around. You can stick around, though, dear reader. For you I'll make an exception. I'm glad we're on this trivial trip together.

Which reminds me of my favourite line from any show ever (though, admittedly, this might just be the NyQuil talking) – in Rudolph, the Red Nosed Reindeer, the elf that wanted to be a dentist, what's-his-name, Hermey, or Harvey or whatever, when Rudolf tells him that he's independent, his response is "Let's be independent together!"[6]

Wow, this stuff is pretty strong. Like "the power of Christ compels you" strong. I wonder if maybe Father Karras had given Linda Blair some NyQuil, all that nasty business could have been avoided.[7]

Alright. Second attempt at sleep forthcoming. Better stop whining to you all before I do more damage or wander too far into pop-culture obscurity.

G'night all. Thanks for listening to me gripe.

---

[6]There's only so much I can assume, darlings, but please tell me you're aware of the 1964 TV Movie *Rudolph, the Red-Nosed Reindeer.*

[7]Father Karras is the priest from *The Exorcist,* and Linda Blair is the actress who played the little girl who was possessed. At the time, I remembered her name but not the character's name. It was Regan, just in case you needed to know.

gratuitous pussy cat

"Get some fresh air, Helena, that'll make you feel better," Penny said with all good intentions, despite the fact that I'd just told her to do most unladylike things to herself and given her explicit directions on the best route to Hell (it's somewhere near Scarborough, by the way).

I'm really quite miserable to be around when I'm ill, and I don't recommend it to anyone. (Being around me, that is, although being ill is no box of chocolates, either).

Ooh, chocolate. That'd make me feel better.

But anyway, the suggestion became more of a decree, and Penny loaded me into the car and drove me to a park, where we got out and walked for a bit, taking in the first signs of Spring. After the bleak winter, whose only hues seem to be myriad shades of grey, it was refreshing to catch glimpses of orange on the breasts of robins out having their breakfast, or the pale yellow of the first daffodils poking their way out into the sunlight. And then there was this lady, lounging in a bed of blue-eyed grass.[1] She caught my eye and was kind enough to pose. The fresh air may not have cured me, but this little gal brightened my mood a little bit. I guess I better apologize to Penny. Oh dear.

---

[1]These pretty little flowers are called *Sisyrinchium*. Never say I didn't teach you anything, darlings.

valley girl version 2.0

ell, it certainly is a good thing that I never committed to write a poem a day for National Poetry Month, but since Amanda Palmer has dropped the gauntlet and single-handedly re-popularized poetry[1] (you know I love her, darlings, but she can be a little, well, full of herself, sometimes), I figured that, with it being the very last day of April, I'd share a little something I wrote after meeting Penny on campus one day. Penny was finishing up her last exams, and so I thought I'd drop by for a celebratory latte or whatnot, and had to bite my tongue (as I so often do) when I overheard snippets and snatches of conversation. I remarked to the Countess Penelope that Moon Unit Zappa[2] sounds positively

---

[1]This was right around the time of the bombing at the Boston Marathon in April 2013. Amanda Palmer (she of the fancy eyebrows and famous writer husband, among other things) wrote a poem called *A Poem for Dzhokhar* (one of the bombers) that provoked a crazy amount of response, much of it negative, because people felt she was being sympathetic to a terrorist. She received a gamut of responses ranging from threats of violence against her to outpouring of support and love. The next day, she wrote another blog post about the whole experience and reposted people's responses (many people actually wrote poems in response) and she remarked how amazing it was that a thousand people were arguing about poetry. Just a cautionary tale about how perhaps you shouldn't post for public consumption every little thing that pops into your head, whether you be a creator of art or a commenter.

[2]Daughter of musician Frank Zappa, and vocalist on his satirical song *Valley Girl*, which gave us such choice phrases as "like, totally" and "gag me with a spoon".

eloquent in comparison to some of these girls, and then of course, I had to explain to her who Moon Unit Zappa is.

Le sigh...

But I'm over-selling it, darlings. Here's my offering:

Valley Girl Version 2.0

the sweaty perfume of bus-trapped youth
among the huddled masses longing to be free,
but if you want to know the truth,
   these refugees from university

are more adept at swearing,
and smell of too much stale coffee;
theomygoddidyouseewhatshewaswearing?
   liketotally

of high school lingers,
and coffee is my drug of choice, so i don't mind.
it's her perfectly manicured fingers
   i just can't get behind –

adult indulgences on a child's hands.
like, you know, omygod totally,
and somehow, her audience understands.
   and then, a text message: ROTFL OMG

and her friend, sitting right next to her, replies:
   (and something inside of me dies)

   LOL
and i LMAO; what the hell.[3]

---

[3]ROTFL = Rolling On The Floor Laughing. OMG = Oh My God. LOL = Laughing Out Loud. LMAO = Laughing My Ass Off. Just in case you didn't know, or like me, loathe LOL-speak.

just another blizzard casualty -a tragedy told in twenty minutes

So, some of you have been asking: *Helena, how can you possibly be single? You're smart, witty, interesting — you've got the looks, the moves, and you don't let any of it go to your head.*

Why, thank you, darlings. Good to know some people still have taste.

But just the other day, Penny delicately reminded me that I'm not getting any younger, and, like, whatever happened with Steve, anyway?

"I liked Steve," she said. "I didn't like some of the other men you dated, but I liked Steve."

"You sound like your grandmother," I sighed with a bit of a laugh. "And I'll tell you what I told her – if you like him so much, you marry him. Besides, I lived with Steve for nearly two years and that entire time, he had no ambition. He couldn't commit to anything that wasn't that fucking video game.[1] It was always *Just*

---

[1] That fucking video game is, of course, Blizzard Entertainment's *World of Warcraft*, though you shouldn't think that I'm singling them out for my ire. It just happened that WOW was the game he played, though I've heard similar stories from other people involving other online games or activities.

another twenty minutes. Well, sometimes, all it takes is twenty minutes to show you just how little you mean to another person."

Everybody has a sad break up story, and I don't know how sad or tragic mine is, but it's mine, I own it, and while it was never a great love story, maybe it will serve as a cautionary tale of sorts.

I remember the day I left. Painful at the time, but when I think at what kind of life I could have ended up with, I'm glad I had the good sense to walk away when I did.

———

"Just another twenty minutes, I promise," Steve said, eyes glued to the monitor, where a purple-skinned creature was dancing what appeared to be the Macarena.[2] "I just have to kill this boss."

"You said twenty minutes forty-five minutes ago," I sighed crossly.

"Just twenty minutes, babe. I wanna hit seventy."

"Fine, whatever," I spat, and stormed sulkily out of the room. I'd had enough – enough of cleaning up after him, enough of always coming second to that fucking video game. What did I care that it had 11.5 million monthly subscribers worldwide – all that proved is that there were 11.5 million other idiots out there that were in serious need of a twelve-step program.[3]

Look at him, I thought with disgust. His desk was covered in empty candy wrappers, half-empty bottles of pop, sticky with age, and potato chip crumbs of several varieties. There were plates with partially eaten food on them, three coffee mugs with God only knows how old coffee in them, and notes containing codes and messages that meant nothing to anyone but the man sitting in the soft glow of the 27 inch screen; the man I lived with, the man that I was apparently wasting what might be the best years of my life with.

———

[2] A One Hit Wonder in the mid '90s, the dance took the world by the throat and refused to let go. In the Massively Multiplayer Online Role Playing Game *World of Warcraft*, characters can be made to do the dance.

[3] If there isn't already a Clinic for Video Game Addiction, there bloody well should be, darlings. Just recently, a friend of mine called me to complain that her husband cancelled their anniversary dinner plans because he wanted to go on a raid.

A man who was, in many ways, still a boy. Case in point: he once called in sick to work because an expansion pack had come out at midnight the night before, and he had to stand in line to get it right away, and then stayed up until two in the morning installing it and then spent the next day playing for fourteen hours straight.

Fourteen hours straight!

"Woo hoo!" He yelled. "Helena, come here! Come see! I got fat loot!"

I was expected to care that he'd scored some gear or whatever in an on-line role-playing game – a glorified version of *Dungeons and Dragons*. You know, the same thing that only complete losers played in high school. The kind of kids that never see a woman naked outside of a magazine and end up living in their parents' basement until they're forty. But now – now it's a cultural phenomenon, and it's got B-list celebrity endorsements and corporate sponsorship.[4] So now I'm supposed to cheer and get all excited because he managed to push enough buttons and spend enough time in front of the goddamn computer in order to get 'fat loot'. Well, whoopty-fucking-doo!

"Helena, look!" He called again. "I got me some fat loot. Aren't you excited?"
"Ecstatic," I murmured, shaking my head at him.
"Awesome," he said, never taking his eyes from the screen.
"So are you done, now?" I asked, doubting that I'd get the answer I desired.
"Not yet… almost… I'm gonna ding[5] soon."
"Right," I said. "Well, I'm going out then."

---

[4]This is, in a way, a true revenge of the nerds. People who are considered 'cool' are now playing and endorsing a game that they would have laughed at back in high school, and bullied those who played it. Now, those same 'nerds' developed a highly addictive version of what they loved back in high school, and are making themselves rich off the bullies they despised. Circle of life, indeed.
[5]If you've never played one of these games (and one can only dream, darlings) you may not know that when a character reaches the next level, an alert (or 'ding') sounds, and players have taken that onomatopoetic 'ding' and turned it into a verb. To ding. Shall I conjugate it? No, I'll spare you, darlings. You get the picture.

He didn't say anything. He never listened anymore. If I called him on the phone, I could tell he was playing his game because he answered without thinking; without comprehending. All I'd get were simple uh huhs or mm hmms or nothing at all. It was beyond rude, and I'd told him so, but it didn't change anything. He'd sit at his computer and play all day long and into the night, and when I was around, he'd order me around. Oh, nothing cruel or bossy – I'm nobody's bitch, darlings. He'd just ask me to get him this, or get him that, or ask me to go to the store for munchies. Which I didn't mind, because I didn't have anything better to do. Which was kind of the point – I didn't have anything better to do – and how sad was that?

"Did you hear me?" I asked. "I said I'm going out."

"Mmm hmm," he said. "Bring us back some munchies, will ya?"

"Why don't you get off your fat ass and get your own goddamn munchies?" I said under my breath as I turned away. I was past the point of caring enough to be confrontational.

"Cool Ranch[6], please," he called after me, oblivious. "And a 7-Up."

I'd had enough. I was stronger than this, better than this and I wasn't going to do this anymore.

"You need help, you know," I said, not without compassion. "You seriously do."

"Uh huh," he replied, and clicked the mouse repeatedly.

"I mean, have you looked in the mirror lately? Or smelled yourself? You haven't showered in days, haven't shaved in weeks. You look like a bloody homeless person!"

"Just twenty minutes, honey… I'm just about ready to ding… FUCK! I just got totally pwned![7] Shit!"

"And you completely ignore me. I'm lonely. You're always right here and I'm lonely. Hell, I masturbated right beside you the

---

[6] A flavour of Doritos, in case you've never consumed these products before.

[7] A made up word that actually has its origins in *World of Warcraft*. It's a neologism based on a typo – apparently someone meant to type 'owned' as in *you got owned* (ie. beaten, dominated) but typed pwned instead, and somehow, this took. Yes, seriously.

other day and you didn't even notice! I mean, do I have to dress up like one of those elves or dwarves or hobbits or whatever the hell they are to get you to pay attention to me?"

"Hmm? Yeah, that's hot."

"Fuck you, Steve! I'm outta here."

"Mmm hmm. Don't forget the chips."

Eyes glued to the computer screen, Steve didn't notice as I packed a suitcase; didn't notice as I took my favourite picture down off the wall; didn't notice as I took all the cash out of his wallet. He didn't notice any of this, just like he hadn't noticed that I'd lost weight; like he hadn't noticed that I often slept out on the couch; like he hadn't noticed how much I'd been crying. He certainly didn't notice that I was crying then, as I picked up the suitcase and took a last glance around the apartment I'd called home with him for two not-always-horrible years.

"Goodbye, Steve," I said plainly, as I walked out the door. "I'm leaving you."

"Goodbye, honey," he replied absently, eyes never leaving the screen, "I love you, too."

So now you know my silly little tragedy. I picture Zack Galifianakis[8] as Steve in the movie adaption, but who could be glamorous enough to play yours truly?

---

[8]You've seen him in *The Hangover*. Yes, yes you have.

suddenly seeking ssris, or, how i learned to stop worrying and love the pills**

*Q*s in, anti-depressants, darlings...

Or maybe just a little Lorazepam[1] to lull me into complacent contentment.

Nobody's favourite dilettante is having trouble coming to terms with the fact that she's simply not cut out for life in a world where LOL-cats and Justin Bieber are of more interest than, well, whatever it is that she has to offer. She just can't for the life of her recall what that is again...[2]

Single white female seeks magic pill to make everything a little rosier, to blur the edges a bit, because I keep cutting myself on the sharp corners and rough edges (figuratively, darlings – it's a metaphor – no need to alert the authorities). Must make all desire for anything more than just existence disappear – See also: Apathy.

I'd drink myself into oblivion, but that's frowned upon by polite society, whereas pharmaceutical lobotomization is not only

---

[1]A common anti-anxiety medication.
[2]I was feeling very sorry for myself, darlings – it happens. I'd recently come off of anti-depressants and was feeling very conflicted.

acceptable, why, it's downright trendy! In fact, I expect that soon, they'll just be putting Prozac in our water like they do Fluoride.[3]

The hardest thing to come to terms with is not that nobody cares (because that's just maudlin and melodramatic and morose and a bunch of other 'm' words, I'm sure, but I'm just too tired to try thinking right now), but rather the disappointment in yourself – I mean, at one point, you thought highly of yourself – or at least, you thought enough of yourself to put yourself out there, to share a bit of yourself. But now, well, now you realize that not only were you wrong, but that you are so laughably uninteresting that not even you are laughing, and that you're not even worth the time or tears it took to write this sentence. So, rather than make excuses, or just claim that you don't know how to play the game, or some other petty, sour-grapes loser bullshit, why not just own up to the fact that you're just bloody awful?[4]

There's liberation in accepting one's mediocrity. I'm not going to lie, though, it is a lot easier with medication, darlings. Oh, I could write horrible love poetry odes to anti-depressants, and their apathy-inducing ways. It's not euphoria, per se, but when one is mired deep in the depths of disinterested apathy, you simply do not care. And the ability not to care means not thinking about how you desperately despise your job, or your situation. Not caring means that rejection or disinterest doesn't hurt a bit, because you are numb right down to the little empty spot deep inside you where your soul used to be, but of course, you sold it for a bottle of sweet apathy. Those precious little pills turn you into the uninterested, uninteresting, dead inside, talk-show TV watching, cog-in-the machine, talent-less consumer who contributes nothing at all to the world around them or the world at large that you always feared you would become, but you know what? You don't care! You're not happy, per se, you're more – how do I put it – you're sleepwalking through life.[5]

---

[3]Studies (don't ask me to cite them, I'm just saying) show that 1 in 10 Americans (and I imagine the Canadian trend is similar) are on anti-depressants.

[4]I had considered leaving this chapter out altogether, but thought that seeing me at my bleakest and most discouraged might serve some purpose.

[5]If you recognize yourself or someone you know in this, you have my sympathy.

People talk condescendingly about those who abuse drugs or alcohol as escaping from their problems – as if that is a bad thing. Well, dear reader, I am here to testify that apathy is the only way I know how to stop myself from becoming a statistic. It's a hell of a choice, really – either wake up every day disappointed in myself, faced with the realization that it doesn't get any better than this, loathing what I've become and lugging all my failings and shortfalls behind me (even I don't have a purse big enough), or else medicate myself to the point of dead-numbness, so that I don't care about any of that, so that I don't have even a hint of a desire to strive for something more; something better, so that I can function as some sort of automaton cog in the machine.

It's either that or draw up the curtain and join the choir invisible, like that Norwegian Blue with the beautiful plumage. (Thought you could use a laugh right about now. And I knew nothing I could say was going to work in that regard).[6]

So what can I do? I don't want to feel this way about myself, but all evidence points to me being pretty much a waste of time hiding behind pathetic attempts at self-deprecatory humour as some sort of post-modern ironic statement.

Like the world needs more of that, right?

So I'm faced with the age old "To be or not to be," and we all know how that turned out.[7]

Oh, do read a book now and again for God's sake!

But I've been in the other place, and it's not exactly the blissful abandon I may have suggested it is. In reality, it's like being trapped inside your own body, looking out through a window filmed over with soap scum, with the volume turned down on everything, and while outwardly you give the appearance of apathy (and the world loves you – you are complacent and dull and boring and you do what you're told), inside you are rotting and crying and, well, dying.

---

[6]Monty Python – the dead parrot sketch – you remember that one, darlings.
[7]*Hamlet* – William Shakespeare.

There's no right answer here. Only choices. Things I have to live with. There is no studio audience I can poll, I can't take a 50/50 or phone a friend, and there's no brand new car or trip to Tahiti hiding behind door number three.

There is no door number three —or, rather, there is, but I don't even want to discuss that. It's not an option. I peeked behind door number three once or twice in my time, and have since decided that it is off the table. I will admit that it is sometimes difficult to maintain my resolve on that matter. It would be easier than choosing either doors one or two. And just like that Danish prince (I'm not going to annotate this one – if you have no idea what I'm referring to, then I have nothing but contempt for you and your little mind), my inaction is, in itself, a decision of sorts.

Oh, I know what you're thinking, darlings. *Don't look for affirmation from others. Your self-worth is not dependent on what others say (or don't say) about you, etc, etc…* and I'm glad that's working out for you, but let's be pragmatic for a moment. Let's cut the touchy-feely and be honest – what we do requires an audience. An audience to either affirm or reject, and therefore encourage or discourage us. Without that audience, we are merely masturbating.

What I'm saying is that I don't want to care anymore. I don't want to be an attention-seeking baby looking for a pat on the back. I want to be rid of this useless desire to create something, whether it is a character or a story or just a series of thoughts put into some sort of art form. I want to be rid of it, because it is evidently not good enough, not interesting enough, not catchy enough. And if I can't be rid of it, then I need to find a way to turn it off. And that's where the pills come in.

Sigh. Now my headache is back. Being a self-pitying melodramatic narcissist is hard work.

** With all respect to Stanley Kubrick[8]

---

[8]The title of this chapter is a riff on *Dr. Strangelove, or: How I Learned to Stop Worrying and Love the Bomb*, a satirical film written and directed by Stanley Kubrick.

does everyone stare? (why i so rarely take public transportation)

irst of all, in my defence, the guy was rather large, darlings. Ape-like.

But, like a shaved ape that's been kept out of the sun for too long, with fingers like a carnival clown's balloons.

"Are we going soon?"He asked no one in particular.

When he spoke, his voice was a low raspy growl, dry and harsh, like he'd been eating kitty litter.

Maybe he had.

"I have an appointment downtown."

And then a snide murmur from the back of the bus:

"You are downtown, you fucking freak."

I froze, close enough behind him to smell his body odour – for some reason a coppery odour, like blood, or old pennies – and I feared his reaction, feared that I might be in the line of fire of the metal cane he gripped tightly by his side, but thankfully, the heckler's comment was too low for him to notice.

"I don't know my way around so much. I've been gone for thirty years."

He was quiet then, as if considering the time that had passed, or where he was, or his appointment, or maybe he was remembering what chocolate tasted like.

Where had he been for thirty years?

"I'd walk," he told the bus driver loud enough for all the passengers to hear, "but I took a pretty bad beating from the cops yesterday."

I saw the bus driver smile politely in the rear-view mirror and say something monosyllabic and non-committal.

Nervously, she picked up her radio. With her eyes darting from the road to the mirror and back again, she spoke quietly into the black handset that connected to the dashboard with a long dangling curled cord.

All the better to strangle you with, my dear, I thought, trying in vain not to visualize the poor bus driver's purple bloated face and bulging eyes, with the big man's monstrous balloon hands pulling the curled cord tight around her neck until... POP!

Shuddering back to present reality, my own eyes shuffled suspiciously from the rear-view mirror to the back of the man's head, twitching involuntarily. He seemed tense and nervous and unable to relax.[1]

"They're gonna lose their jobs," the guy continued in his unconscious impression of Tom Waits[2] after a half bottle of Jack.

---

[1] A very deliberate nod to *Psycho Killer* by Talking Heads, 1977.

[2] Tom Waits has made a career of his trademark growl, and while he's not everyone's cup of tea, he is one of the greatest songwriters of all time – also one of the great drinkers of all time, but that's another matter. Even if you've never heard his original renditions, you've heard covers to be sure. In fact, Scarlett Johansson did an album called Anywhere I Lay My Head of all Tom Waits covers that even featured a duet with David Bowie.

"The doctors're gonna sue. Unnecessary abuse of a patient. I have to be downtown at two."

Thirty years, I thought again.

What would thirty years locked away do to someone?

Thirty years of shock treatments, and ice water baths, screaming protests, doctors dragging sticky fingers through the dusty corners of his mind, and then smearing the results on a piece of paper and asking him to tell them what he sees, what it all means.

Days that blurred into one another thanks to the magic of Haloperidol and Clozapine – days of drooling and blubbering, of counting tiles on the floor.

The interchangeable ammonia smells of urine and Lysol the only perfume he smelled *–thirty years!* The darkness, the fear, the rates and the cold stone – I pictured all this and more – I pictured him eating cockroaches because Jesus told him to, but not that Jesus – Jesús, a little Mexican hairless dog that only he could see, and who promised him that if he could only rid the world of cockroaches, then he would be a good boy, a clean boy, and no longer A DIRTY LITTLE SHITHEAD NO GOOD MOTHERFUCKER which is what his mother's boyfriend always called him... and speaking of his mother, where was she for the last thirty years?

Coming to see him faithfully every week, tears in her eyes, makeup smeared, hair a mess, crying to the doctors that he was always such a sweet little boy, that he wasn't a bad boy, that he was just ill, and to prove it, she show them pictures of him dressed up for Hallowe'en, or in his Little League uniform, or in the 8th grade production of *Bye Bye Birdie*.[3]

Then one day she just stopped coming, and he was left alone again, with only Jesús to cry to in the dark.

I could nearly taste the tears of confusion and frustration on my own cheeks as I imagined the clinical hospital staff explaining to him that his mother had passed away, asking him, as they would a child, if he understood what that meant; what DEATH is, and the cold consoling words they would utter out of obligation, and for an

---

[3] A 1960 Broadway musical inspired by the story of Elvis Presley being drafted into the Army in 1957. I remember my grade eight class performing it rather poorly.

instant, I looked at him with pity, despite his intimidating appearance, overwhelmed by the thought of thirty years being stolen from this poor man.

And then I pictured the newspaper headlines:

ESCAPED MENTAL PATIENT KILLS EIGHT ON CITY BUS

And I rang the bell and got the hell off at the next stop.

get me away from here,
i'm dying

$\mathscr{G}$ caught the Accidental Plagiarist playing something that sounded like *Waiting for the Man* by the Velvet Underground this morning, and I realized that I'd hit the wall. I am losing my taste for being a polite hostess. It's getting crowded in the apartment and the couch smells like ass and sex and dirty socks. I need to get away from my life for a bit, but it doesn't look like it's in the cards.

Oh, get me away from here, I'm dying...[1]

I just want to get in the car and drive until I'm out of gas, then fill up and drive back home again, with the sun on my face and the wind in my hair.

I want to close my eyes and dream it all up again, re-invent myself as someone I could stand to look at in the mirror in the morning.

I need to find Cheyenne an apartment of her own, and air out my apartment.

I need to figure out where it is I'd like to see myself in a year.

I need to have realistic expectations of myself and others.

---

[1]*Get Me Away From Here I'm Dying* is a song by Belle & Sebastian off of their seminal 1996 album *If You're Feeling Sinister*, which everyone should own and enjoy.

I need to talk to the Countess Penelope of Arcadia about the note she left me this morning: *Dearest Helena, I am going to be gone this weekend, see you when I get back. Love, Penny*

I need to know where she's going to be, if only for my peace of mind.

I need to pick up grapefruit juice.

I need to go somewhere interesting soon or else I'm going to lose my mind.[2]

I need to dye my hair black, powder my face white, apply heavy eyeliner and start wearing an ankh and sit around feeding pigeons,[3] or else I need to put on something much happier than Belle & Sebastian and dance around in my underwear. Perhaps I'll take Andra Watkins'[4] lead and throw on some Talking Heads. You can't really be sad or mopey when you're burning down the house.

Dear readers, I do hope this all gets sorted, soon. I am absolutely losing my *joie de vivre*.[5]

---

[2]Stream of consciousness writing when you're barely capable of consciousness. Sometimes it's good to take a grocery list of priorities big and small. It seems perfectly natural for me to have a list that includes both "re-invent myself as someone I could stand to look at in the mirror…" and "pick up grapefruit juice." If you don't put some easy tasks on there, darlings, you'll feel as if you've accomplished nothing.

[3]This is a reference to the character Death in Neil Gaiman's brilliant comic *Sandman*. The first time we meet her, she is sitting on a park bench feeding pigeons. She is drawn as pale skinned with black hair, and is actually the least scary of her siblings. She is usually pictured wearing an Ankh, the Egyptian key of life.

[4]Andra Watkins writes a blog called The Accidental Cootchie Mama – a constant source of amusement for me. This day, when I was feeling worn out and discouraged, she'd written a funny story about her and her husband's disagreements on the genius of Radiohead. Andra prefers Talking Heads, the band whose song Radiohead took their name from, but her husband continues to subject her to Thom Yorke et al. Her reminder that people do crazy things for love made me smile that day right when I needed it. She tends to do that a lot. Look her up at www.andrawatkins.com

[5]That's pronounced JWAH DUH VEEVRUH, darlings, and it simply means joy, or, more specifically, my joy of living.

los angeles, i'm yours[1] - the california years part one

𝔗 he story of how I ended up in California goes something like this: the wind was blowing that way.

I'd been dating a musician, and while his band was doing just fine here, they'd done some recording with a guy in L.A. who'd been trying to convince them to move to the west coast, where of course, he would make them famous. Now, not to get ahead of myself, darlings, but suffice it to say that my ex-lover is a bit famous, but just not as famous as he'd like to be, and I guess that's how fame works. Apparently, it's a monster.[2]

No matter how much you get, it's not enough, you just want more. Well, that's what happened to Robert (that's not his real name, of course). He got a little taste of fame and became a L.A. cliché– a completely plastic humanoid victim of his own success. Which is crazy, because, if I told you who he is, I imagine maybe 60% of you would know who I was talking about, but not in an *ohmygod Helena! You dated Robert!* way, because he's not really that big

---

[1] *Los Angeles, I'm Yours* is the title of a song by The Decemberists.
[2] At least according to Lady Gaga, who has made a career out of being weird and famous. This was a specific reference to her album *The Fame* and its follow up, *The Fame Monster*.

a deal, ergo, I'll call him Robert so that I can fantasize that he was Robert Smith[3] and not, well, who he really is, but let that be.

When he broke the news to me that he was moving to L.A., I figured he was breaking up with me, and to be honest, it had come out of nowhere. Our relationship worked, I recall, partially because we were never together all that much, what with him touring and travelling, and of course, I had my own stuff going on. So he hadn't told me that he'd been thinking of moving for some time. I recall reacting rather wretchedly in response to his revelation. He'd told me in the car one night after a gig, and it was about two o'clock in the morning, and in retrospect, we were a long way from his apartment when I pulled over, kicked him out of the car, and sped off. Don't ask me why I did it, dear readers, I just didn't want him to see me cry. He was still a decent human being at that point, and I loved him and his dreams, which at the time didn't involve snorting cocaine off the thighs of porn actresses. That came later.

So when he called me up the next day, I was expecting it to be one of those 'come by and pick up your stuff' (or vice versa) type conversations where you argue over who bought whom which Smashing Pumpkins CD or Chuck Palahniuk first edition[4], but instead, he was calling up to ask me if I would come with him. As nothing was working for me where I was, and being that I was restless as a butterfly and in dire need of a change of scenery, I said yes.

I didn't give much thought to what I would do, or, what I was leaving behind. I felt the wind blowing, and figured that if I followed it long enough, I would eventually end up where I belonged, and anyway, there were so many interesting things to be seen between where I was, where I was going, and wherever I would eventually end up.

I wish I could forget the young Countess's tears when I said my farewells. She was only ten or so at the time, and I had to show her on a map where I was going. I assured her that I would come

---

[3]Lead singer of The Cure and daydream of every gloomy goth girl that ever was, even if she has grown out of that phase.

[4]One of my prized possessions is a first edition of Fight Club. I honestly don't remember if I bought it or if Robert bought it for me. But possession is 9/10ths of the law.

and visit, or that, once I got settled in, she could come and visit me. I showed her a picture of Santa Monica pier and promised her a ride on the Ferris Wheel.[5] Which was all well and good at the time, and the guilt her tears elicited lifted slightly when I saw her eyes light up at the thought of seeing the ocean, but the fact remains that I was, and always have been selfish and whimsical in my wanderings, and it's not until recently that I've begun to consider what I've missed. When I left for California, Penelope was a young, bright, ten-year-old whose taste in clothing still involved pink (and not ironically), and whose favourite music was generally that which was featured in animated films like Shrek[6] or Lilo & Stitch. When I returned almost four years later, her Hello Kitty t-shirt had been replaced by Emily the Strange[7], the colour black had begun to permeate her wardrobe, and she was torturing my sister/her mother by professing a profound and undying love for Marilyn Manson.[8]

But that's the drawback of blowing where the wind blows – when you lack the personal volition required to plot your own course through life, sometimes you find yourself like that proverbial rolling stone that the poet laureate (or is Bob a patron saint now?) of Hibbing, Minnesota sang about.[9] Sometimes you get lost without really meaning to, and when you're lost, you end up missing out on what went on while you were gone. I met a lot of people like that in my time in LA. People like me, I should say. Lost angels. Selfish seekers. Dabblers and dilettantes, all. Not all running from something, but all rootless, homeless wanderers. If you were to take a poll of people in L.A. in general and Hollywood specifically, you could make a strong anthropological argument that L.A. has no indigenous population. No one is actually from L.A., and most people never stay long enough to become part of the scenery. The

---

[5] In case you're wondering if you've seen Santa Monica pier, you have. It is featured in pretty much every movie that takes place in Los Angeles ever.

[6] I have *Shrek* to thank for the Countess recognizing the wonderful song *Hallelujah* by Leonard Cohen. John Cale performed it in the movie, but I'll always be partial to the Jeff Buckley version.

[7] Emily the Strange is actually an interesting phenomenon. She was created by Nathan Carrico as a logo for a professional skater's skateboard in 1991 and has since evolved into a character with her own clothing line, comic book, video game, and Gibson guitars has even made an Emily the Strange edition of one of their guitars.

[8] Goth/shock rocker who terrifies today's conservatives (and mothers everywhere) the way Alice Cooper did in the '70s and '80s.

[9] That would be Bob Dylan, of course, and the song *Like A Rolling Stone*.

word transient isn't exactly the right word I'm looking for to describe the population, but it's the one that keeps getting stuck in my head.

A transient-at-heart myself, I left without much thought of when I'd be back, and within six months of moving to the city of lost angels, I found myself on my own again, with no direction home, sun-soaked and head over heels in love with the seaside. I'd hated L.A. and the whole Hollywood scene, where everyone's either an actor, a model, a writer, a musician, or else they're a Scientologist, (and most likely, both) and either way, they're all trying to sell you something, recruit you into something, or get you hooked on something.

I'd bailed before I got sucked in, but Robert ate it all up like a tourist, somehow ignoring the stench of Hollywood Boulevard and donning a pair of obligatory wayfarers (the official sunglasses of wannabe douche bags everywhere) and posing like Tom Cruise in *Risky Business*[10] for the screaming teenage girls who flocked to his shows. Our relationship was a casualty of celebrity, but by the time I left L.A., I was so sick of who he'd become that I wasn't really all that broken up about it. The kind of success he'd contracted was like a foul and communicable disease, and I wanted no part of it.

A lot of people describe the climb to success in terms of sleeping your way to the top. Well, if all a person had to do was sleep with a few people in order to climb that ladder that might be forgivable. I think that a more apt metaphor might be voluntarily allowing yourself to become host to the most disgusting and violently hungry parasites imaginable, who then proceed to eat your insides out until you are hollow, and then take a great big shit in your mouth until they fill up the void they themselves created. And then, once that's done, those same shit-eating parasites start the whole process all over again, repeating ad nauseum. Believe me when I tell you that Hollywood is only glamorous on TV – look a

---

[10]You know which movie I'm talking about. Bob Seger's *Old Time Rock N' Roll* playing while a young Tom Cruise slides across the floor in a collared shirt and his boxers. These are pop culture icons, darlings, do try to keep up.

little closer, and it's dirty and gritty, populated almost entirely with fake and plastic parasites and their prey.

Only two good things came out of my short time in Los Angeles. First, I got to meet David Byrne[11] backstage when Robert's band opened for him – and he was every bit as strange and wonderful as I'd imagined. Second, as a way of apologizing for dragging me all the way out to California and then tripping and falling dick-first into some small-time actress (whose career, as karma would have it, is doing better than his these days), Robert bought me a cute little convertible Nissan Z.[12] I can honestly say that the only thing I miss now about my time in L.A. is that car.

I hopped in my guilty parting gift on a beautiful sunny morning in Venice Beach[13], pointed my nose north and hit the accelerator, destination unknown, never looking back.

---

[11]David Byrne was the lead singer of Talking Heads, and continues to be a musical tour-de-force. I especially enjoy his recent-esque collaboration with Brian Eno (their second, in fact – the first being 1981's *My Life in the Bush of Ghosts*) called *Everything That Happens Will Happen Today*. (Okay, it's not *that* recent – 2008) Interesting fact – he's also an avid bicyclist. Who knew?

[12]It was metallic orange and drove like a dream, darlings.

[13]If you're ever in L.A., Venice Beach is where I'd recommend going – lots of crazy street musicians and artists, and beach volleyball, and surfers, and everything you think Southern California *should* be. Also, there are all kinds of great clothing stores, but *caveat emptor* – your credit cards will get maxed out.

zen poetry and the
macaroni art maneuver

*P*enny and I were at our favourite coffee shop last night, me
secretly celebrating her safe return, she simply succumbing
to her insatiable caffeine addiction, when the Countess,
without warning, launched a contemptible campaign of secret
challenges.

Ridiculous assignments, inspired, she insisted, on something
she learned from a Zen poetry class. Write a poem inside a china
cup, and then smash that cup, and then write a poem about that.
Penny had risen to the occasion by writing a dirty limerick inside
my favourite china cup – a souvenir from (yes, actually) China –
and then composed a poem about how vexed I was with her upon
discovery of this vainglorious act of vile vandalism:

What hurtful heartbreak?
What rage could make her wits as
Fragile as a cup?

My assignment was to put up or shut up – to contribute rather
than criticize – to create, compose, construct, concoct, contrive or
conceive something inspiring rather than just moan, mewl and
malign like some maladjusted misanthropic malcontent. I probably

should have been offended at the implication, but I was just so impressed by her alliteration that I let it pass.

Also, I suppose I did have it coming, as I had just finished shooting my mouth off about the tacky artwork (and I use the term loosely) that they have in trendy hipster cafes in general, and this one in particular.

"They'll hang anything on the wall," I said, sipping my deliciously overpriced triple-foam half-caff vanilla hazelnut cappuccino, "so long as it's intentionally ironic and/or unintentionally horrid. Andy Warhol[1] is spinning in his grave, Penny. Spinning!"

"I see," said the Countess Penelope of Arcadia, recently returned from Paris, and so therefore affecting a Parisian accent, even though the Paris she'd returned from was Paris, Ontario. "And, what izz, oh, how you silly Americans say, le art, in your 'umble opinion."

I continued sipping my cappuccino. I wasn't going to let her bait me.

"Nossing? Not even a, oh, what iz ze *mot juste*?[2] A retort? Ooh la la, how rude! 'Ere you are, uh, complaining about ze quality of ze art in ze galleria, and yet tu n'as pas un suggestion! Qu'elle fromage, 'Elene."[3]

Hot hazelnut and vanilla shot out my nose and my eyes teared up from pain and laughter. Penny continued.

"Sacre bleu cheese! What iz this?" She pointed to an empty space on the wall. "Why look 'Elene—zey 'ave an opening. Per'aps

---

[1] Andy Warhol was a pop artist/filmmaker/eccentric who popularized a form of art that celebrated the mundane and challenged what could be considered art. His fame is only trumped by his infamy, really – to some he's a genius, to others, his work is garish and disrespectful. He made art out of celebrities, Coke bottles and Campbell's Soup cans.

[2] The right word.

[3] The expression the Countess was looking for was *Qu'elle dommage*, which means That's too bad, or What a shame. Instead, she said What cheese.

what zis– what was it you called it? Pretentious little 'ipster 'aven–needs is an 'Elena 'Ann-Basquiat original, *n'est-ce pas?"*

I was positively choking with laughter, which had progressed to the point where I wasn't making laughing noises so much as I was red in the face, trying to catch my breath, wheezing like an asthmatic kitten and probably did look like I was choking. It was a good thing we were tucked away in a corner where we had some privacy, because that allowed me to clout the Countess Penelope across the head, which drew a sharp and angry yelp from her, and also, as a secondary benefit, made her quit talking like the Inspector from the Pink Panther movies, which is, I now realize, where she likely picked up the accent in the first place. My sincerest apologies to all French speakers out there – I do know that not everyone in France speaks like Inspector Clouseau, nor are you all bumbling idiots. Although I'm sure that you have your fair share of bumbling idiots. Er, that is not to say that the French have a higher ratio of bumbling idiots than any other nationality, like, say, Belgians. And it need not be said that I am speaking unfavourably of Belgians, because we all know what an enormous fan of their waffles I am. Oh, I'm really not making things any better, am I?

Anyway, where was I? Oh yes, clouting Penny across the head for making hot coffee shoot out my nose – let's see that again.

"Ow!" Penny said, sulking. "What'd you do that for? I didn't bite him."

Well, okay, maybe I embellished that last part (it's what I do, darlings) but I'm telling this story, and when I remember it, the Countess Penelope of Arcadia (which is, I insist, a regional district of the merry old land of Oz) cowered like the Cowardly Lion upon being slapped by Judy Garland, pre-prescription medication and alcohol abuse.

Really, Helena? Aren't you about thirty years too late to be taking pot-shots at Judy Garland? What's next, another Mickey Rooney/Breakfast at Tiffany's reference?

Quiet, you. If you want topical humour, just Google[4] Katy Perry. Hey, everyone else is.

Well, not Russell Brand.[5]

Fair enough. May I continue? Thank you.

Back to the tale at hand –after recovering from the clout to the head (isn't clout a great word? Why don't more people use the word clout anymore?) Penny dropped the gauntlet and challenged me to bring in some of my macaroni art to see if it is ironic and post-modern enough to be worthy of the wall of a coffee shop.

Dear readers, I am not proud to say this, but I let her goad me, and this morning I went back to the coffee shop, macaroni art in hand, not because I wanted to sell it, or even because I think it is art that is worthy of hanging on a wall somewhere, but rather, out of spite. I'd love to say that I was doing it to challenge myself, to broaden my horizons, or to add something to my *Curriculum Vitae*. I'd love to tell you that I am bigger and less petty than this, darlings, but the truth is, I just wanted to be right. They will hang anything on the wall just to be ironic.

But Helena, you say, *isn't that what Andy Warhol was all about?*

I'm not even going to dignify that with a response. Just know that I am right about this, and that is why I brought in a framed piece of macaroni art to hang in the café's gallery – not to prove that I am an artistic visionary whose genius will likely only be recognized posthumously, but rather, just to be right. So I can wipe that smug aristocratic smile off of the Countess' face. She tasks me. She tasks me, and I shall have her! I'll flog my macaroni art in coffee shops on the Moons of Nibia, and round the Antares

---

[4]The funniest thing about the fact that Google has become a verb (as in "to search for using the Google search engine") is that it doubles as a dirty euphemism.
[5]Funny man Russell Brand and flash in the pan sexpot singer Katy Perry divorced in the summer of 2013 after only fourteen months of marriage. There were allegations of infidelities from both sides. Who cares, right? Moving right along, darlings.

Maelstrom (isn't that that Star Trek themed cafe that just opened over on Spadina?) and round Perdition's flames before I give up![6]

As it turned out, I gave up long before Perdition's flames. At the end of the day, there was a much easier way to get my macaroni on the wall.

Later that evening I took Penny out to show her the latest addition to the gallery at Cafe Lindo, a Helena Hann-Basquiat original, just as she had suggested, and hanging over our usual spot, to boot. It was a single macaroni on a black background about 4"x4", with the caption *And my soul from out that shadow that lies floating on the floor shall be lifted - Italpasta.* I'd considered my macaroni representation of a lemon tree, entitled *When life gives you lemons, make Italpasta,* but in the end, went with pretentious pseudo-gothic over product placement humour. If this goes well, I have an entire series depicting cellular mitosis set on a back drop of a picture of James Dean, entitled *You're Tearing Me Apart!*[7] that would look just fantastic on the wall.

"Well, congratulations, Helena," the Countess said, sipping her coffee, suspiciously graceful about the whole thing. "I didn't think you had it in you to ask them to put it up."

"Well," I said mock-sheepishly. (Is there such a thing? Can one be mock-sheepish? I know you can have a mock turtleneck, but... anyhow...) "I think now you know better than to issue ridiculous challenges to your unflappable Aunt Helena."

"Hmm," Penny agreed amicably, affecting the Clouseau-eque accent once again, "Zere iz just one sing, zough. I think, zat does not, 'ow you say, make ze sense. Zat iz, if zis piece of macaroni *merde*[8] iz for sale, zen where iz ze price tag?"

"I, uh, good question," I said, trying for indignation for only achieving a mild desperation.

---

[6]The very clever (or very geeky) among you might recognize this diatribe as a paraphrase of a speech given by the late Ricardo Montalban as Khan in *Star Trek II: The Wrath of Khan.*
[7]This is a reference to the angst-ridden scene from *Rebel Without A Cause,* (1955) when James Dean yells this line.
[8]Shit (shortest footnote annotation ever).

"Oh *garçon! Garçon!*" The Countess Arcade called. "'Ow much for zis masterpiece in macaroni?"

"Shh!" I shushed her, not wanting my ruse to be uncovered by anyone but me. "Keep it down, will ya? I put it up there myself! There, are you happy? You win. But I'll have you know, it's not like I asked and was turned down - I didn't have the nerve to ask, so I just put it up quietly and without being seen, and it will gain legitimacy in time, you'll see."

"So, you're squatting, then?" Penny laughed, dropping the foppish faux-French façade.

"Yeah," I chuckled back, "I guess I am."

"Aren't you worried someone will take it down?" Penny asked.

"Are you kidding?" I asked, having learned nothing from this experience, nothing at all. "Have you seen some of the shit they have hanging here?"

Penny just rolled her eyes and smirked.

accidental still life - calla lilies (the mother's day early edition)

*P*enny made me cry a little bit when she came home with these flowers, presenting to them to me as a gift to her mother by proxy.

We don't talk very often about my sister, and I'm not sure why, or whose choice that is.

"Happy Motherless Day," the Countess Penelope said, trying to smile ironically, but failing miserably.

What could I do?

I just gave her a hug, and held her until she stopped crying.

la vie boheme - the california years part two

$\mathcal{I}$t was never my intention to stay in California, darlings, but by the time I reached Big Sur[1], I'd fallen in love with the ocean, and believed with all my heart that if I could just drive that cliffside highway up and down the coast forever, well, that would be heaven for me.

Unfortunately, one can only wander without wanting when one is wildly wealthy, and well, that has never been an apt description of yours truly, darlings. I suppose I could have just gone home, but people do funny things when they're in love.

Oh, there was never anyone special like that. There were a couple of nice men who tried their best to keep me around, but the truth is, I was never really there – not in any tangible way – I was like smoke being blown by the breeze, and any time someone tried to wrap their warm arms around me, they came away with nothing but cold air.

No, I was in love with the sun, and the sea, and the wild sense of abandonment I felt while driving up and down the coast, walking

---

[1]Big Sur is an area of the coastline between Los Angeles and San Francisco, but just south of Carmel and Monterey. Driving along California One is a transcendent experience, and I highly recommend doing it with a friend – if you are driving, you'll likely drive yourself into the ocean staring at the beautiful cliffs and the crashing waves.

along the little beaches, or visiting little seaside towns with charming names like Half Moon Bay, or discovering San Luis Obispo, where I could spend all day walking the Avila Beach Pier, laughing with the wide-eyed wonder of the girl I once was at the sea lions basking on the rocks or at the surfers crashing on the waves.

Further north I finally stayed somewhere for longer than a day or two, when I discovered Monterey, with its rich history, both literary and musical, and spent two weeks drinking in pubs that had been frequented by the likes of John Steinbeck[2], Jack London[3] and Robert Louis Stevenson[4]. There were still old timers around that would, if I plied them with alcohol or smiled nicely enough, regale me with stories of that magical summer of '67, the summer of love that began with the world's first rock festival. Back when everyone was California dreamin', and no one could have known that it would soon all turn sour. But at the Monterey Pop Festival, Janis Joplin was still alive, and so was Mama Cass, Brian Jones, Keith Moon, and a young guitar player named Jimi Hendrix, who made his US debut in that gorgeous seaside town, and commemorated the event by setting fire to his Fender Stratocaster at the end of an outrageously noisy and brilliant cover of *Wild Thing*.[5]

I had all kinds of misconceptions about geography and history completely turned upside down as I discovered the rolling countryside of Salinas and the forests outside of Carmel. I'd read *Of Mice and Men*, and I never once pictured George and Lenny[6] traversing rolling hills, but I guess I must have read that wrong.

---

[2] Pulitzer Prize winning author of *Grapes of Wrath*, *Of Mice and Men*, and *East of Eden*.

[3] Author of *Call of the Wild*, *White Fang*, *The Sea Wolf*, he grew up in the San Francisco Bay area before he went to join the Klondike Gold Rush in 1897.

[4] Yes, the Scottish writer of *Treasure Island* and *The Strange Case of Dr Jekyll and Mr Hyde*. He stayed in Monterey for a few months in the fall of 1879, and the story goes that he based some of the setting for Treasure Island on his walks taking in the sights of the Monterey Peninsula.

[5] Although the version everyone knows is The Troggs' 1966 version, it was actually written by a guy named Chip Taylor for his band The Wild Ones in 1965.

[6] George and Lenny. Guys like us. They are the main characters in Steinbeck's *Of Mice and Men*. They are migrant workers during the Great Depression, and you've seen them spoofed in Bugs Bunny cartoons and elsewhere. Lenny is the big dopey ox who is a bit simpleminded, and doesn't know his own strength. George looks after Lenny and tries to keep him out of trouble, with varying degrees of success. George is always telling Lenny a story about how someday, they're going to have a place of their own,

It's said that no one is ever poor in love, but by the time I pulled into Santa Cruz with less than a quarter of a tank of gas and two hundred dollars left to my name, the threat of poverty had begun to rear its ugly face, and the reality of my situation led me to seek some sort of employment. It was summertime, and the boardwalk in Santa Cruz was hopping with tourists and locals alike. There was music every day and every night, alongside the magical sound of the surf's ambient backdrop to the Midway's carnival cacophony. I rode the roller coaster and played Skee-Ball and went searching for vampires on the carousel. (I didn't find any, but did see a Kiefer Sutherland lookalike and managed to give myself a tiny case of the heebie-jeebies).[7] It was a little bit of sea-scented heaven, and if a young, attractive woman could flirt and serve beer and mussels, she could make enough to live in such a place.

Santa Cruz was the first place that I might have called home, were it not for my insatiable wanderlust. It was in Santa Cruz that I learned to love Spanish architecture, and sangria, and the smell of lime and fresh cilantro and avocados – those smells will forever remind me of El Chino, a little family style Mexican bar where I met the first well-intentioned but ultimately temporary man who tried to make me stay. Manuel was the first, and the one who tried the hardest and who nearly succeeded, and probably why I never got so close again.

Manuel was everything I loved about California – he was a surfer, he played guitar, he spoke Spanish and had a mother who barely spoke English and who just adored me, and whom I loved in return. He taught me how to make mole[8], and awakened my taste buds to taste the agave in tequila rather than just the burn. (In retrospect, I'm not sure I'm thankful about that bit). We shared a love of the open road, and he started me on what will surely be a lifelong love affair with the music of Conor Oberst, and specifically

---

and they can even have a little hutch where they can keep rabbits. Lenny will often ask 'Tell me again about the rabbits, George.'

[7] Santa Cruz is where they filmed *The Lost Boys*, a 1987 vampire movie starring Kiefer Sutherland and the Coreys; Haim and Feldman. The boardwalk and carousel feature prominently in the movie.

[8] Far too complicated to explain without showing you, darlings, mole (pronounced MO-LAY) is a sauce that starts with poblano chile peppers, has about 20 other ingredients including chocolate (who knew?) and it simply amazing.

his band Bright Eyes, which I would play at full volume as we drove down the coastal California One, where, one particularly beautiful day about a year or so after I first arrived in Santa Cruz, Manual pulled over and proposed to me.

I didn't want to break his heart, so I said yes.

I left Santa Cruz the next morning before sunrise.

I never even said goodbye, and I have never been back.

the good, the bad, and the hipster

S itting in our second favourite coffee shop (second, because it's my choice, darlings, and I so rarely get my own way when the Countess Penelope of Arcadia is in attendance), the Countess and I rolled our eyes as we were subjected to yet another Mumford, Lumineers and Sons song, which seems to be a requisite accompaniment to coffee these days.

"Helena," Penny began, faking actual interest. It was a game we'd played before. "Which Mumford and Sons[1] song is this?"

"All of them," I replied deadpan.

"Doesn't it make you want to smash a banjo over some random hipster's head?" The Countess Penelope asked, channelling the homicidal spirit of Lizzie Borden[2] with vicious glee.

---

[1]Mumford and Sons is an English folk band that took the world by storm in 2010 by capitalizing on shifting paradigms and cycles of musical trends. It's not that I think they're a shit band; it's just that their fans seem to think these guys invented folk music. The Lumineers are just another band cashing in on the sound. Also, all their songs sound the same – whether that's lazy song writing or poor production, I don't know, but they do.

[2]Lizzie Borden was the O.J. Simpson of her day – she was tried for the brutal axe-murders of her father and stepmother, acquitted (something to do with the glove found at the scene of the murder not fitting her – or maybe I'm confused) and set free, but then nobody else was ever arrested for the murder. In a ballsy move, she continued to live in the town where it happened until she died many years later.

"No," I said, but if I admit the truth, then yes. Yes, it does. "But if you like, we can mess about a bit. Do you want to have some snobbish fun?"

Penny was always up for a bit of the old aristo snobbery, particularly if it was musical, and at the expense of hipster poseurs, or the like. Teenage girls who've just 'discovered' a new musical trend that has its roots firmly planted decades before were an obvious but irresistible target.

Now, I should note that, by the strictest of definitions, I myself could be considered a hipster. But ah, I recall a time before Al Gore's insipid invention (we call it the Internet, darlings) when people had less access to information and knowledge, and yet, somehow had a sense of what came before, unlike the current generation of hipsters who, despite having the world quite literally at their fingertips, have the memory of goldfish, as evidenced by their lapping up of music or film or literature that is quite obviously (at least it's obvious to me, darlings) derivative and regurgitated.

And so to ease my indignation by immaturely poking fun at those who know less than I (and really, darlings, the list is enormous) I approached the barista on the sly and asked him very sweetly if he wouldn't mind playing a couple of songs from my iPod. After an unenthusiastic attempt at refusing my request, he relented and winked at me conspiratorially as he took my iPod from me and plugged in into the PA behind the bar.

I re-joined the Countess Penelope back at our table, where she'd positioned herself for maximum viewing and waited for the farce to begin.

I felt like a film director, or a puppeteer pulling strings on her creation, shaping them to her will. The scene played out like it was rehearsed, darlings, and I could scarcely contain my giddy amusement.

The first song on my Spirit of the West[3] playlist came on, and as *And If Venice Is Sinking* reached the first chorus, two girls dressed

---

[3] A Canadian folk-rock/alt-rock band that began in the '80s and is still (sort of) going today, but who had their peak around 1988-1995, with the *hits Political, Home For A Rest*, and *And If Venice Is Sinking*.

in nothing but environmentally friendly earth tones approached the bar in that awkward, self-conscious way that only hipster girls are capable of, and asked if it was the new Mumford and Sons. One of the girls brushed her Deschanel-esque[4] bangs off of her forehead, where they were resting on her lens-less glasses,[5] and stared expectantly up into the face of the barista, awaiting his answer.

"Lumineers, actually," the barista said slightly snarkily, scolding them. "Honestly, can't you tell the difference?"

Penny nearly jumped out of her seat to correct the barista, but as I looked up and caught his eye and saw the trace of a smirk on his lips, I knew we'd found a kindred spirit (of the west, perhaps, but that was yet to be seen) in this quick-thinking coffee *colporteur,*[6] and so I tugged Penny's arm and bade her sit back down and told her to keep watching.

"Oh, right, of course," said the other girl, who was wearing a toque despite the fact that it was 23°C (that's 73°F, American darlings – warm for Toronto). "There's like, totally a different vibe going on with the Lumineers than with Mumford."

"Oh, totally," agreed Hipster One. Hipster Two perused the CDs for sale on the bar, searching for the new Lumineers album. Finding it, she searched for the song that was ending, to be followed by a little number called *Home For A Rest.*

"Is it on here?" The toque-wearing hipster asked my new best friend, the Barista With No Name, who even looked (because I'm

---

[4]That would be Zooey Deschanel, actress, singer, patron saint of hipsters, and ex-wife of hipster icon Ben Gibbard of the official hipster band Death Cab For Cutie. No one's hipster cred is better than hers. She re-popularized the hairstyle of brushing your bangs down on your forehead.

[5]This is an actual thing – girls wearing, essentially, horn-rimmed glasses with no lenses in them. To *intentionally* look geeky. I guess this is what bothers me most about hipsters, is that they intentionally go out of their way to be 'uncool' ironically. But when I was growing up, that would have gotten you your ass handed to you. I listened to unpopular music and was mocked for it. Now, I would be a hipster goddess.

[6]French for peddler – someone who sells something. I just love how it sound like Cole Porter, and as I referred to him as a *colporteur,* I confess I had romantic notions on my mind, as well as the Cole Porter penned *Night and Day* and *I've Got You Under My Skin.*

writing this and you can choose to believe it or not, darlings) a bit like a young Clint Eastwood.[7]

The B.W.N.N. squinted at Hipster One and Hipster Two, judging just how wet behind the ears they were, then proceeded to tell them that the song they were listening to was not on the actual album, but was only available on 45.

I held my hand over my treacherous mouth to stifle my approaching peals of laughter. I saw the twinkle in the ice-blue eyes of the B.W.N.N. and knew that I had made a connection.

Hipster One looked at Hipster Two and a moment of awkward silence passed between them before the uselessly bespectacled hipster finally spoke.

"What's a 45?"[8]

I think I'm in love, darlings.

---

[7]Clint Eastwood is famous for playing The Man With No Name in the so-called Spaghetti Westerns of Sergio Leone (so called because they were made by Italians — the term came from a much less politically correct age). *A Fistful of Dollars, For a Few Dollars More*, and *The Good, the Bad and the Ugly* are considered some of the greatest westerns ever made, and Eastwood's character in them has become a cultural icon.

[8]The 7 inch 45 rpm record was what singles used to come on before the cassette tape and compact disc. Whereas a full size (12") record (or LP) would play at 33 1/3 rpm (revolutions per minute), singles would have to be played at 45 rpm, or else they'd sound really slow and creepy. Apparently, these are making a real comeback as hipsters everywhere are declaring that vinyl is so uncool that it's cool again. Break out your spider and those old 45s and party like it's 1989. Next up: Reel-to-reel. I hope you kept your old machine!

calgon, take me away[1]

$\mathcal{I}$f there's anything worse than a migraine on a beautiful sunny day, I don't know what it is.

Oh, well, I mean, I'm sure it'd be awful to be a quadruple amputee, or to be suffering from third degree burns, but the egocentric narcissist in me thinks that a migraine on a beautiful sunny day is right up there with getting a bikini wax from a drunk with a bad case of DTs, the ending of LOST, or Elephantitis of the nipples.

I've tried lying in a dark room, and I've tried good old lonelyTylenol[2], lots of water, some Gatorade (for re-hydration and restoration of electrolytes, darlings) and my head still feels like it's

---

[1]Calgon Bath Soap had this infectious catch phrase as their slogan, and their commercials always featured a very busy woman complaining about the stresses of her day, and then slipping into a bath full of Calgon bubbles, and then having all her stresses melt away. I love a good bubble bath, darlings, but the kind of pleasure the woman in the commercial is enjoying does not come from soapy suds alone. If you've never seen the commercial, check it out. Here's the link, darlings: http://www.youtube.com/watch?v=WVf1lClfBng

[2]I just love making a palindrome out of this. You'll just have to put up with me, darlings.

being squished in a vice while Gilbert Gottfried[3] recites the lyrics to a Ke$ha[4] song through a megaphone.

Perhaps I need a bubble bath, like the woman in this commercial, who has quite obviously dropped a couple of tabs of Ecstasy before stepping into the tub, where some talented pool boy with astounding lung capacity is clearly performing some pretty capital underwater cunnilingus, darlings. I mean, just look at her face at about the 0:16 mark, and tell me she's not getting her happy on.

Fear not, dear reader, I will get through this, and when I do, I will have a tale for you. Oh yes.

---

[3]You know him as the voice of Iago the parrot in Disney's *Aladdin*.

[4]My greatest wish would be that this annotation is completely necessary and that you have never been subjected to Ke$ha's 'music'. When your trademark is excessive use of auto-tuning, calling yourself a singer is kind of an insult to those who can sing. Her lyrics are generally odes to debauchery, and not in a melancholic, self-reflecting, romantic poet type of way. Of course, when she drinks herself to death, the music community will call her a misunderstood genius.

... and that's how the countess killed bambi's mother part one

ll I wanted was a nice, quiet, relaxing Victoria Day[1] long weekend.

What I got instead was a phone call on Friday night asking me to come to the hospital, a migraine on Saturday, a screaming exodus on Sunday, a positively surreal Monday, and then accidental venison this morning.

Settle in, darlings, and put on a bib or something, because this one might get long and messy.

Friday was supposed to be a good day for me – because I had finally convinced Cheyenne and her boyfriend, the Accidental Plagiarist, that they needed to be elsewhere. They had to decide if they were going to stay in Toronto, or move on. I was more than willing to help them out whichever route they decided to take, but whatever debt I owed Cheyenne had surely been at least honoured, (I knew that I could never fully re-pay) and besides, my debt to her did not extend to Chester, or Chuck or Cheeto, or whoever, whose behaviour of late had become increasingly bizarre. At first, we just thought him eccentric, but since he'd been staying with the

---

[1] In Canada, the last Monday in May before the 25th is Victoria Day, in honour of Queen Victoria's birthday. Victoria was the Queen in 1867 when Canada became a country.

Countess and myself, that diagnosis kept getting upgraded (or downgraded, depending on your point of view) as his behaviour kept getting stranger, and to be honest, at times, downright disturbing.

I think it may have all started when he suddenly stopped sleeping. And if Chupacabra or Chili Fries or Chop Suey (or any of the other pet names Cheyenne used instead of his real name, which I still insist she doesn't actually know) wasn't sleeping, then nobody was.

He would come home with Cheyenne at 3 a.m. or so, which is the life of a str... exotic dancer, so that was just something we – that is, the Countess Penelope of Arcadia, which is in the province of Snores Like A Moose And Can Sleep Through Just About Anything, and I, who cannot, had gotten used to. But there came a morning when I was awoken to the sound of glass breaking, and so I climbed out of bed (where I have, of late, taken to sleeping fully clothed, despite the humidity) to investigate, and found the Accidental Plagiarist picking up shards of glass barehanded.

My initial response was varied – the caregiver in me was concerned for his safety, but the owner of the broken tumbler (a souvenir from Reno, Nevada) was annoyed (but not really angry, I mean, whatever –*Que Sera Sera*)[2], while the woman of the house in me – that is, the Helena that has been putting up with his freeloading ass for the past (oh dear God, I've lost track now – how many weeks has it been?) however long, well, she just wanted to know what the hell was going on.

But first, caregiver Helena.

"Hey," I whispered, trying not to wake anyone else, "Let me get a broom – you don't want to cut yourself."

He looked up at me like he'd just noticed I was there, even though I'd made enough noise coming down the stairs. In fact, he looked right through me, like I wasn't even there, like his eyes weren't even registering my presence.

---

[2]Whatever will be, will be. Of course, this is also a song made popular by Doris Day in the Alfred Hitchcock film *The Man Who Knew Too Much*.

And then he snapped out of his dull stupor, and smiled at me, a big, eyes-popping-out-of-his-head, toothy smile – like a comic book drawing of the Joker, complete with anatomically impossibly long and numerous teeth – or like one of Giger's Aliens.[3] It was, not to put too fine a point on it – unsettling. It was the kind of smile you picture on a man who drives a windowless van and smells of NyQuil and candy, but kind of also the smile you picture on a Disney Prince, right before some doe-eyed damsel rides off into the sunset with him, after having just met him five minutes before. Stupid damsels in distress. I say they get whatever's coming to them.

Hmm... maybe there's a crossover there. Disney Princes who drive windowless vans, singing songs about true love's kiss to attract their victims, who willingly get in the van with visions of happily ever after on their brain, only to end up decomposing in a basement bathtub full of acid after having to perform all kinds of unspeakable acts while dressed up as Snow White while seven cannibal dwarfs bid for her sweetmeats while enjoying a nice bottle of Chianti and some fava beans.[4]

But I digress, darlings, as I tend to do when I'm nervously recounting an uncomfortable scene. And did I mention that the Countess Penelope killed Bambi's mother? Oh yes, do remind me to get to that at some point, because that is just the icing on this shitcake, darlings.

"Helena," Chico(?) said, suddenly aware that I was there, "Oh hey, sorry, did I wake you? I was just trying to figure out how to play slide guitar, but I didn't have a slide, and did you know that

---

[3]H.R. Giger is a Swiss painter, sculpture, and designer whose style blends organic and industrial elements. He is famous, among other things, for creating the Aliens for the franchise starring Sigourney Weaver.
[4]The Chianti and fava beans is, of course, a reference to Hannibal Lector from *Silence of the Lambs*. He claims to have eaten a census takers liver with these accompaniments. After I wrote this, I took part in a 100 word fiction challenge, where the photo prompt was a phone booth with a broken receiver. With this in mind, I wrote a story that re-imagines Prince Charming as something more sinister. For your pleasure, I've included the story in the bonus materials found at the back of the book.

you can use a glass to play slide but I think that it's better if you have something smaller that you can fit over your fingers because I tried playing with the glass and it fell and it broke and now you're here so you can see that it broke and did I wake you up, I'm sorry, I didn't mean to wake you up, but I couldn't sleep and I was playing guitar and I was trying to play slide but I broke the glass and I didn't mean to and now I think I woke you up, did I wake you up, I was playing guitar and I dropped the glass but I didn't mean to wake you up."

He stammered that out at about 100 kilometers per hour (about 60 mph, American darlings) and all in one breath, and then he stopped talking just as abruptly, and wrapped himself around me and started bawling into my shoulder.

That was night one of the weirdness, but I shook it off, figuring that everyone is entitled to one inappropriately emotional outburst, especially at four in the morning.

But during the next day, and the days that followed, both Penny and I noticed a change in the A.P.s demeanour – he seemed agitated all the time, or excited. He'd talk in rapid, disjointed half-sentences, never finishing a thought before he'd start a new one, and he'd seemed to have developed a sort of facial tic – several, if I am to try to describe it properly. It was like he couldn't relax, couldn't be still, even for a moment. He was constantly moving, constantly fidgeting, constantly twitching, blinking, wobbling his head, bopping it like there was a tune in his head that only he could hear, and smiling, grinning that child molester/Disney Prince/H.R. Giger's Alien grin.

After about a week of this, (and yes, I am a saint, darlings – just call me Saint Helena, patron saint of both putting up with shit and/or looking the other way toward that fantastic river in Egypt – you decide) I took Cheyenne aside and none too gently asked her what his problem was. Was he on drugs? Was he schizophrenic?

"He smokes pot, that's all I know," was Cheyenne's only reply. Anything else was news to her, and she didn't even seem to know what I was talking about. If you were to ask her, Chuck was just a little different, that's all, but he was a sweetie, and besides, it's not like she could just cut him loose, I mean, shucks (yes, she said shucks) what's he gonna do with himself?

I wasn't buying it. I'd been around enough pot smokers, and I'd never seen behaviour like this from smoking pot. So I used his behaviour as a scapegoat. I put up with it for another week or so, but then I told Cheyenne that they needed to start find another place to stay. I prefaced it by saying that I'd help her however else I could, and that if she needed anything, just to ask, but that they couldn't stay with us anymore. I told her I felt uncomfortable, and that I didn't want to be worried about Penny.

I'd love to tell you that she was calm and understanding and appreciative, darlings. I'd really love to tell you that, and have it be the truth. I'd love to tell you that she didn't break down crying and tell me that they were broke, and that they had nowhere to go, and that if I turned them out that they'd be living on the street within a week. I'd also really love to tell you that I hadn't been snooping for drugs in my former spare room, and that I hadn't found close to $10,000 in cash bundled up, but that would also be less than truthful. And so I'd very much like to tell you that I didn't call Cheyenne a lying cunt, because that would be most unladylike of me, and that I certainly never accused her of taking advantage of our friendship, or told her that she had to be out by the end of the week or else I would turn Chester or Chihuahua or Cheerio, or whatever the hell his name is over to the police, and that they could sort out just what his story was. I'd really love to tell you that nice little lie, darlings, but the truth is, I did do and say all of those things.

Am I the villain here? I mean, I'm not that naive, am I? Do I have the words *Gullible Twat* tattooed across my forehead? I knew she was dancing at least four nights a week, did she really expect me to believe that she was broke?

So Friday morning, I helped pack up Cheyenne Wyoming and the Accidental Plagiarist, and I dropped them off at a much nicer hotel than the one Cheyenne and I lived in during our stay in the town she took her name from, went home and washed that crazy man and his fool of a girlfriend right out of my hair.[5]

---

[5]This is a reference to the song from the Rogers & Hammerstein musical South Pacific *I'm Gonna Wash That Man Right Outta My Hair*, which was adapted by Clairol for a

It was absolutely beautiful, and there was finally peace and quiet in the house. After I'd had the argument with Cheyenne, at the very height of the weirdness a few days earlier, I'd sent Penny down to stay with friends in Niagara, just in case things got, well, uncomfortable. She hadn't wanted to leave, but I convinced her that I'd be okay, and besides, if I needed a big strong man to protect me (I really don't, darlings, this is just a frequent joke between the Countess and myself) then maybe it would be an opportunity to make the better acquaintance of a certain Barista With No Name who is the virtual doppelganger of young Clint Eastwood – perhaps a clone grown in a serape-wrapped bottle somewhere in Carmel[6] by a doctor with the unlikely name of Leone, who would blow the pungent smoke from hand rolled cheroots into the future coffee-slinger's glass womb, while Ennio Morricone[7] played the theme from *The Good, the Bad, and the Ugly* on one of those colourful Fisher Price xylophones.

Or maybe I'm just fabricating the entire resemblance, darlings. I've been accused of much worse in my days as a delightfully entertaining, yet unreliable narrator, the least of which is a pathetically poor penchant for digression, which I am proudly partaking in presently.

Penny graciously allowed that I could take care of myself, and that she was grateful for the excuse to excuse herself from the situation. So it was that I found myself having the apartment all to myself on Friday, with nothing to do and nowhere to go.

---

hair dye commercial and has kind of become part of pop culture. But if you were wondering where it came from, well, now you know.

[6] Clint Eastwood was mayor of Carmel, California for a couple of years in the late 1980s.

[7] Composer of the famous theme from *The Good, the Bad and the Ugly*. You've probably heard people whistle it and then follow that up with WAH WAHWAH, even if they've never even seen the movie. It's like a race memory or something, like how everyone knows *Twinkle, Twinkle, Little Star*.

After a fantastically frivolous yet thoroughly thrilling discussion with a friend online[8] as to what type of gauntlet a vampire would wear (were one to drop the dreaded vampire gauntlet) and coming up with a few different ideas (ie. frilly àla French Revolution aristocracy and/or Madonna circa 1985, or perhaps leather with studs a la a steampunk vampire or a member of Judas Priest), I decided to open the place up, crank some Ryan Adams, and give it a good cleaning (the apartment, not Ryan Adams, as I don't know him well enough, or not at all).

Yes, things were just going wonderfully, as far as my empty apartment could go. I mean, I felt a little guilty, but that would pass, and a good dose of Kermit the Frog singing *New York I Love You, But You're Bringing Me Down*[9] went a long way to making me feel like everything was going to be right with the world again.

But that was before the Friday night phone call, the Saturday migraine, a screaming match on Sunday that made me feel like the worst human being since Al Gore (inventor of both global warming and the Internet), and then all of that unwanted knowledge on Monday – a day that will be forever remembered as the day that I just couldn't make up anything stranger than the actual facts.

Oh, and then somewhere along the way, Penny killed Bambi's mother.

Make sure you remind me to tell you about that.

---

[8]This would actually mark the start of what has become an irreplaceable friendship with my editor, Hannah Sears, herself a writer of no small talent. Do check out her work here: http://secondstaronther.wordpress.com/
[9]One of Penny's favourites by LCD Soundsystem, she found a video on line where someone uses a Kermit the Frog puppet to create an entire video of the song.

...and that's how the countess killed bambi's mother part two

I arrived at the hospital to find Cheyenne weeping and furious, as they refused to let her see Chet. (It turns out his real name is Chester Atkins – which, considering his status as the world's greatest accidental plagiarist is just surreal and hilarious, and if you don't know why, darlings, then just do a Google search for Chet Atkins).[1]

The first thing that you need to know is that the Canadian healthcare system is wonderful, darlings, and I'll not brook any complaining about it[2]– but the fact of the matter is, Chet was brought in (by the police, no less, but more on that later) in a total state of confusion, unable to provide the nurses or doctors with any semblance of a sensible explanation of his situation, and had, in

---

[1]Chet Atkins was a famous American country guitarist who helped create the Nashville sound of modern country music. He played a large bodied Gretsch guitar nicknamed the Country Gentleman, and Gretsch made a Chet Atkins line of guitars for many years. There, now you don't need to do a Google search, I've done it for you. You're welcome.

[2]Without getting into a political debate, and with the understanding of the strengths and weaknesses of both the American and the Canadian system, I stand firmly behind the philosophy that all Canadians have medical coverage and access to medical services according to their need and irrespective of their ability to pay. It's considered a basic human right in Canada, and I think that's a good thing.

fact, needed to be restrained. It was only by examining his effects that, by dumb luck, they had found my phone number as the last number dialled on his cell phone. The fact that he had a cell phone at all was only due to my suggestion that it might be a good idea only a couple of weeks before, so it would seem that the Fates were smiling on poor Chet. The hospital called me, and I called Cheyenne, who was already there when I arrived, and who had been begging the hospital staff to let her see Chet, and had been refused. Nothing personal, it's just that he had been restrained, and they had no records for him, and so the doctors and nurses, in order to protect his best interests, weren't allowing anybody in to see him. They were happy to talk to us, to get any background information, and give us the bare minimum of information regarding his condition, but other than that, we would have to wait until the doctor decided to talk to us or not.

And now we're back to where we came in, with Cheyenne crying and shaking with frustrated and terrified rage. It would be a long night of waiting with no news, a headache for me that lasted until Saturday night, and another two and a half days before Penny killed Bambi's mother.

Cheyenne never left the hospital, but I needed to go home and sleep off the migraine that was pounding in my head like a pulsing bass-drum played by a sadistic DJ, and as they weren't telling us anything, I didn't see the point of either of us being there. I tried to get Cheyenne to come home with me, but she insisted on staying. I think she was a bit angry with me still, and that maybe she blamed me for Chet ending up in the hospital. I had this confirmed when she showed up on my door on Sunday morning and screamed at me like a scene from Jerry Springer[3] about how I'd abandoned her when she needed me most, and how I was an ungrateful, horrible person to kick them out, especially when something was so obviously wrong with Chet, and now she didn't know how she was

---

[3]Jerry Springer has a daytime tabloid talk show that hosts the most dysfunctional people America has to offer and serves up their horrid antics as entertainment. The jury is still out on whether the people that appear on the show or those that watch it are lower on the sub-human scale.

possibly going to get him the help he needed, and on and on and on.

She was scared, and she was angry, and so I took it. I said nothing as she blamed me for Chet's problems, (which she still wouldn't come to terms with, and in all fairness, by this point, the doctors and nurses hadn't disclosed anything) and she blamed me for them being stuck in Toronto now, and she said she'd wished she'd never met me, and that she should have just walked away and let me learn my lesson back in Wyoming, and I took it.

Hell, she could have blamed me for breaking up The Beatles, creating the Internet, or for wasting six years of millions of viewers' lives with the criminally bad ending of LOST, and I would have just nodded and taken it. But when she brought Penny into it, well, there's only so much Saint Helena can take, darlings.

"And don't think I haven't seen the way that little tramp acts around my Chester..." Cheyenne began, and I recoiled as if I'd been slapped. Everything up until that point was washing over me, and I had numbed myself to it. But this statement made me wake up in a hurry.

I screamed back at Cheyenne like a possessed woman, straining my throat and all the muscles in my face until I feared my skin would split and the demon that she had conjured by daring to attack the Countess would burst forth and devour her whole. I threw aside all decorum and tact and social obligations and asked her exactly what she thought that she was doing with her life, and just how well she knew Chet, and how dare she bring someone so obviously volatile into my home, and blah blah blah until it was just white hot rage and I just don't even remember (or want to remember) everything that was said.

Still crying and exhausted, Cheyenne walked out my door, back to the hospital, where they finally allowed her in to see Chet, who had calmed down considerably since the police brought him in naked, babbling a bunch of nonsense about sheep and goats, and how Jesus promised to take him to the zoo, bleeding from his anus and covered head to toe in Gold Bond Medicated Powder.[4]

---

[4]For external use only, Gold Bond Medicated Powder is meant to be used as an anti-itch power, for temporary relief of pain and itch associated with minor cuts, sunburn, insect bites, scrapes, and is certainly not intended to be snorted or rubbed all over

I didn't find out about the circumstances of Chet's encounter with the police until the next day, when I got a call from a clearly shaken and shocked Cheyenne, who called to ask me to come and meet her at the hospital, not a word spoken about our vicious exchange the day prior. Nor were apologies required, darlings – I simply couldn't imagine what Cheyenne was going through, and was ready to forgive some anger that truly only came from a place of panic and fear. After all, both Cheyenne and Chet were a long way from home, if such a place existed for either of them, and this was not the kind of thing that one planned for.

Someone had called the police upon seeing Chet running naked from a known crack house, a cloud of white powder blowing off of his body like smoke, a bundle of clothes in his arms, screaming about going to the zoo. Apparently he was found about twelve blocks from there, trying to ride a fire hydrant like it was a mechanical bull, and that (thankfully? is that the right word here?) is why he was bleeding from his anus, and not from any sexual assault. I'm not sure that really makes it any better, but I find that avoiding being sexually assaulted is always a plus.

An old high school friend of mine always used to say that sooner or later, everyone goes to the zoo. She meant that everyone loses it sometimes – and that under the right circumstances – like, say, accidentally destroying your father's favourite Ferrari– anyone and everyone can break. I just had no idea how prescient those words were to become.

Sooner or later, everyone goes to the zoo.[5]

This, however, was an entirely new level of going to the zoo. This was going to the zoo, stripping off your clothes and trying to snort an entire container of Gold Bond Medicated Powder and then trying to have sex with a fire hydrant, and for that, well, they may have to invent a whole new classification of crazy.

---

your skin to make you invisible from whatever paranoid delusion you are currently experiencing.

[5] Sloane Peterson, ladies and gentlemen. Her boyfriend, Ferris Bueller, once convinced their friend Cameron to let them borrow his father's Ferrari, and after a day off skipping school that would never be forgotten by any of them. The Ferrari didn't fare as well.

I don't know what Cheyenne's going to do, and I've decided that it's not my responsibility. I don't even really want to know any more than I already do, though I'm sure that my part in this twisted play is not entirely finished. They've transferred Chet into the Psych ward, where he's awaiting a second assessment, and I'm sure they'll do what's in his best interest, and worry about the fact that he's an American with no Canadian health coverage later. Cheyenne, to her credit, is staying in Toronto, and continuing to work as much as ever.

Penny was furious when I called her Monday night to tell her everything that had happened. She had wanted to come home right then, but I convinced her to stay one more night in St. Catharines and then, if she wanted to drive up in the morning, I'd be simply overjoyed to have her back home.

So when I got the phone call yesterday morning from Penny telling me that she had killed Bambi's[6] mother, it didn't really faze me. I think maybe I'd gone into a bit of shock myself, but the Countess Penelope of Arcadia was sobbing and hyperventilating and clearly in shock as I calmly told her not to worry, that everything was going to be all right, and that sooner or later, everyone goes to the zoo (a sentiment that was, I fear, lost on poor Penelope, darlings). But after everything that I'd been through the previous seventy-two hours, Penny hitting and killing a deer, and in the process, destroying her practically brand new VW bug (I'm not even going to go into the details of how much blood they cleaned out of the back seat) seemed like business as usual for Saint Helena. So I was strong for Penny, reassuring her that it was not the end of the world, all the while being silently, deeply relieved that it was just a deer that died – that my sweet Penelope – the daughter I'd never have but was so grateful to be stuck with – was safe and relatively unharmed. I had lost my sister and her husband (Penny's parents) to a car accident really not that long ago, and the trauma, I now realized, was still pretty fresh.

It seems that the saying is true, though. Sooner or later, everyone does go to the zoo, and I guess that includes me, because when I hung up the phone with Penny yesterday morning, I pretty

---

[6]Bambi, of course, being the little deer from that tearjerker Disney movie and not some dancer colleague of Cheyenne's in case you were worried that Penny became a murderer.

much shut down. I sat in the bathtub and turned the shower on, and let the shower's spray camouflage my tears. I cried until the water turned cold, and then I got out, wrapped myself in a towel, sat in my favourite chair, and I watched *Casablanca*[7] with the sound turned down. I didn't need the volume, anyway, and I didn't want to hear any voices, nothing at all.

I'd promised Penny I'd come and pick her up, so when I'd stopped crying enough that I could see straight, I put on some clothes, got in the car, and drove down to meet her, to hold her, to tell her I love her.

Really, what more was there to say?

---

[7] Humphrey Bogart and Ingrid Bergman classic. I don't need the audio; I know the whole thing by memory.

seven days with no helena makes one weak title - day one

'K ayso Helena had the week from hell I think we can all agree, so she called up her agency, and as luck would have it, they had some work for her out of town. Thing is, it's way out of town, so she's off on location all week,[1] which leaves me holding down the fort. She asked me to apologize to anyone who had wanted to hear the rest of the California story, but also told me to remind you all that Stephen King took a seven year hiatus between Book Three and Book Four of the Dark Tower series, with Book Three ending in a literal cliff-hanger,[2] so she politely (ha! yeah right!) asked that you bear with her. Don't worry – she says there are more stories to tell. She'll be checking her email as time permits, but that's about it.

And so you're stuck with me. Aunt Helena said that I could fill you in on my solo adventures – kind of like how Robin got his own

---

[1]But that I am forbid (by contractual obligation) to tell the secrets of my work on set, I could a tale unfold whose lightest word would harrow up thy soul, freeze thy young blood, and make you wonder about the randomness of me speaking in the words of Hamlet's father's ghost.

[2]Well, it was more like six years, really. For those of you who picked up on that series after Mr. King had his near-death experience and decided to get a move on and finish the story, you missed out on the joy of screaming *What the FUCK?!*when the third book (*The Waste Lands*) ended with the protagonists on a train speeding them to their deaths.

book in the early '90s[3]– so long as I didn't go too crazy and post photoshopped pictures of me and Jeremy Renner[4] getting hitched at a wedding chapel in Vegas or something (as if Jeremy and I would get married in Vegas! Now, a beach in Maui, maybe).

Anyhow, I thought I'd tell you about the Children's Literature class I'm taking over the summer, and maybe you'll see where Aunt Helena's been plundering her fairy tale material from. I thought it would be a bird course – I mean, the reading would have to be light, right? Monday Matchstick Girl[5], Tuesday Tortoise and Hare, Wednesday Wonderland, Thursday Thumbelina, and Friday fuck your hat, 'cause it wasn't like that at all, I regret to say.

No, we're reading all kinds of books by people with PhDs in Literature, which makes them about as useful to society as... well... I'm at a loss for a simile, which is why I'm taking a literature class in the first place. Don't judge me! We're analyzing the simplest of tales and turning them into things that, in some cases, would have made Caligula[6] blush. (Sorry, I've wanted to use that ever since I heard *Heaven Knows I'm Miserable Now* by The Smiths.[7] I hope I didn't force the phrase. Helena says I sometimes try too hard, so I hope you liked it!)

For instance, would you ever, in a gazillion years, have imagined that The Princess and the Frog was an object lesson – if

---

[3]That would be Tim Drake, the first Robin to really get his own story and personality, and who actually got trained properly before becoming another piece of evidence stacked up against Bruce Wayne in that child endangerment suit against him.

[4]You know him as Hawkeye in *The Avengers* movie, and that's all you really need to know, darlings.

[5]It's actually The Little Match Girl, and it's a horrifying tale of a little street urchin who freezes to death because no one will buy her matches, and she's afraid to go home without selling any because her father will beat her. But then she freezes to death and gets carried up to heaven where she'll never be cold or hungry again. And the lesson – God doesn't give a flying rat's ass about your life here. Life here is cruel and painful, but if you can just endure, there's hot lunch in heaven. Good-night, wee darlings!

[6]Caligula was Roman Emperor from 37 to 41 AD, and will always be remembered for his cruelty, his perversity, and outright decadence. I'll always remember him as Malcolm McDowell in the X-Rated film (which also starred Peter O'Toole and Helen Mirren) dipping his fist into a bowl of fat in preparation for what I can only assume was a quite painful and potentially injurious anal penetration. Are you blushing? Caligula wasn't.

[7]The lyric is: "What she asked of me at the end of the day Caligula would have blushed." Johnny Marr, Morrissey, 1984

not an instructional manual – about fellatio. Yup. According to my feminazi professor, at whom even outspoken feminist folk singer Ani Difranco would roll her eyes and laugh, the hidden agenda there is that if you just kiss that frog, your man will be a prince.[8]

I know, right? I mean, I get some of the obvious ones – the Grimm Brothers stuff is pretty gruesome but transparent – it's all cannibalism and child abuse and rape and lechery. But what about Sleeping Beauty, climbing the phallic tower to her spinning needle, where one prick causes her to bleed and fall into a deep sleep? Yeah, you can probably figure that one out for yourselves.

And then there's another one – I can't remember if it's Bluebeard (oh, God I'm gonna flunk this course!) but if it's not, then it's a variation of it, anyway, where Bluebeard (let's just say it's Bluebeard, okay – crazy serial killer who locks his dead wives behind closed doors – what do all these women see in him???) has this magic key, and he leaves his wife behind and tells him not to go into any of the rooms, and when he comes back, he sticks the magic key in each door, and if it comes out clean, then all's good – she didn't go in – but if it comes out bloody, then she's guilty. Or maybe it's the other way around – yeah – blood = good, no blood = bad. It's supposed to symbolize virginity or something – which I can totally see once it's pointed out – but honestly.[9]

On one hand, it's fascinating; on the other hand, it's kind of scary how much time people have on their hands, and what they come up with after dropping the freaky acid and going on a Disney movie marathon.

Next they're going to tell me that Jack's beanstalk was a phallic representation of Jack's latent homosexuality.[10]

SHEESH!

---

[8]Peter Gabriel addresses this as well in his song *Kiss That Frog*.

[9]What this story is really about is how men view women – honestly – it's about how women just won't do what they're told and how their curiosity will always be their undoing – see also: Eve, Lot's wife, Pandora, Christine Daaé, Psyche.

[10]Actually, the Countess is joking here, but the word phallic comes up an awful lot during any literary examination of Jack and the Beanstalk. Penny's take is quite tame compared to some of the stuff out there.

Tune in tomorrow when you'll hear me say: "Pineapples would not really make suitable underwater dwellings, as they would just rot and get all mushy!"[11]

I may or may not say that. I make no promises.

MWAH!

---

[11]Bad news, one supposes, for one SpongeBob SquarePants.

seven days with no helena makes one weak title - day two

This one's for Helena, in case she's monitoring her blog to make sure I'm not posting pictures of animal husbandry or Care Bears in compromising positions – not that I find those things amusing – okay, I lie, the Care Bears thing would be a little funny – but I think Helena's paranoid I'm going to do something crazy just to shock you, her adoring public.

Well, you can relax, Auntie H – in fact, I've gone ahead and listened to all that Ryan Adams you told me to, and I gotta admit – the boy does have a soulful voice and some pretty deep cuts.[1]

See, Aunt Helena's secretly (and now not-so-secretly) in love with Ryan Adams, and she wants his body and wants to have his babies and everything.[2]

Helena and Ryan, up in a tree, kay eye essess eye en geeeeeeee.

---

[1]Penny was kind enough to post a Ryan Adams video on my blog that day – Oh My God, Whatever, Etc. which is one of my favourite songs of his, so that was much nicer than Care Bears in compromising positions.

[2]If Ryan Adams can dedicate his album Gold to Winona Ryder and add, "Damn, girl", then I can profess my love for Ryan Adams in black and white as well.

But she was right about his music. Me, well, maybe I'd just sit with him in the dark, sipping whiskey and listening to his voice. But the lights would definitely have to be low. Sorry, Ryan, but.... yeah.

Anyhow, I had a forshit night last night at work. Forshit, as in, nobody tipped forshit. (People use the word, but I believe I am the first to put it in print. That's me – I'm a goddamn trailblazer, couche-tards!)

So I came home and put on some Ryan Adams and listened in the dark until I fell asleep, but not before I heard this song, *Oh My God, Whatever, Etc*...which contained this very appropriate bit of lyric: "And everyone tips but not enough to knock me over."

I looked up this video of it, and he completely fucks up right near the beginning and berates himself for it in the funniest possible way.[3]

Anyhow, tune in tomorrow when I will definitely NOT be posting nude photos of myself, but may just do that Care Bear thing... I dunno.... gotta see if I can actually find some Care Bears, first.

MWAH!

Penny.

---

[3] The recording is live in the studio, and when he messes up, he is heard to declare: "Fucking stab me in the eye with the fucking Empire State Building."

seven days with no helena makes one weak title - day three

'Kayso once in a while – not all the time, but every so often – I will encounter someone so terribly ignorant and rude that they actually say some of the stupid things that their stupid little minds are thinking, and I will be forced to defend myself without losing my composure.

For example: "Why yes, I do like the way I dress. No I don't think it makes me look like a crazy person", or "I speak like this because I read big books with no pictures, I have an active imagination, an insatiable *joie de vivre*, and an expansive vocabulary, you illiterate fuck." (My superpower is the ability to use the word 'fuck' in the sweetest possible way so that the listener isn't offended. See, it's already working on you – SHAZAAM!)

I mean, sneer at me all you want, snicker behind my back, and I can ignore it. Call me names, laugh at me with your shallow little friends, and I'll let it slide. Because I have found that the appropriate response to ignorance is just to ignore it. But tonight, when some drunken idiot decided that he wasn't content with the answer I gave him when he crossed the line between inappropriate curiosity and obnoxious behaviour, I felt that dumping his Sausage Penne Pomodoro on his head was the appropriate response.

My boss disagreed.

Oh, Helena is going to be so pissed.

Until, that is, I tell her what happened.

'Kayso, recently, I decided that I'd look stunning with bright pink hair.

And wouldn't you know it? I totally do.

These assholes at the restaurant, though, they of the pretty, plain, perfect girlfriends and wardrobes from The Gap, they just couldn't stop bugging me about it, and I suppose they thought they were being terribly cute when they asked me, so charmingly, if the carpet matched the drapes.

I had briefly considered flashing them, but my Supergirl underoos had that ketchup stain on them that just wouldn't come out (lesson learned: don't eat french fries in your underwear while watching *Phineas and Ferb*,[1] which is, like, totally the new SpongeBob –omygod it's so hilarious. I totally want a pet platypus)[2], and it would kinda look like I was on my rag, and I didn't want to traumatize the poor idiots – at least not at that point, anyway. In retrospect, that might have been the way to go.

Instead, I laughed with them like I thought it was the funniest thing I'd ever heard – but, you know, totally over-doing it, so that they knew I wasn't impressed, and as I walked away, I heard a few choices words muttered as the time-delay caught up with their brains and they realized I was mocking them.

So then a few minutes later, I came out with my big serving platter, full of bowls of hot pasta and salads for the girls (the air was thick with clichés tonight, let me tell you), and my hands were obviously full, otherwise I would have been able to brush off the

---

[1]How this show has been around since 2007 without me noticing until recently I have no idea – oh wait, I don't really watch TV and if and when I do, it's not exactly cartoons that I first turn to. More fool me, because this show is hilarious, even if it is a Disney creation. It is so cleverly written.

[2]Named Perry, of course. Perry the Platypus is a character on the showthat has a secret life as a fedora-wearing secret agent for the OWCA (Organization Without a Cool Acronym).

foolish, foolish boy who decided to cross the line between idiot and asshole by lifting up my skirt to take a peek underneath.

And that's when I dumped the pasta on his head.

Tune in tomorrow when you're fairly likely to hear me say: "Do you want fries with that?"

MWAH-tever.

Penny

seven days with no helena makes one weak title - day four

All work and no play make Penny a dull girl.

All work and no play make Penny a dull girl.

All work and no play make Penny a dull girl.

All work and no play make Penny a dull girl.

All work and no play make Penny a dull girl.[1]

All work –who I am kidding? It is to laugh (pronounced LARF).

---

[1] A reference to *The Shining* by Stephen King: All work and no play make Jack a dull boy, which was so cleverly parodied in The Simpsons Hallowe'en Special as No TV and no beer make Homer something something. "Go crazy?" asks Marge. "Don't mind if I do!" says Homer. Actually, now that I think about it, I think that was only in the Stanley Kubrick movie, not Stephen King's book.

Well, I must say, I certainly do feel sorry for those convertible-less individuals out there who cannot bask in the sun on a day like today.

Oh wait... I am now one of those poor unfortunate souls that is sans convertible, thanks to an altercation with a deer which we shall never speak of again. What shall I do? Walk?

Listen to me! *Oh, poor Penny, you have no more car, boo hoo, don't you realize there are people starving in the streets getting diseases from monkeys?*

Really? Yes, really.

I dunno, I was up late last night and a rerun of Flight of the Conchords was on, and they were doing their Marvin Gaye mock up.[2]

I think that's all I have for you today. I doubt anyone's reading what I have to say, anyhow – well, don't worry, Helena will be back soon.

Oh, hey – I'll leave you with a joke!

'Kayso, there's this nunnery/monastery out in Napa, and the Mother Superior gathers all the nuns together, and says she has an announcement to make. It seems, she says gravely, that there is a case of Gonorrhoea in the convent. There are some gasps and stuff, but then one nun in the back row turns to her sister and says, 'Oh, thank God! I was getting so tired of Chardonnay!'

A WAKA WAKAWAKA.[3]

MWAH!

Penny

---

[2]That would be *Think About It*, and it's a parody of *What's Goin' On*.
[3]Perhaps in another universe, Fozzy Bear of Muppet Show fame might tell jokes of a more adult nature like this one. One never knows.

seven days with no helena
makes one weak title - day five

Twenty-nine degrees doesn't sound all that hot (especially if you're thinking in Fahrenheit, stubborn Yankees! Everyone else in the world is on the metric system, but never mind... think about eighty-five degrees) unless that's the temperature of your apartment, because the air conditioner has died.

Hi ho, Penny the Frog here – except that I'm not a beloved Muppet with a taste for bacon and a hand up his butt, but rather, I'm that fabled frog from the biology experiment where they keep turning up the heat and the frog slowly boils to death. Ick.

So I'm walking around the house in my skivvies, careful to avoid open windows for fear of the watching eyes of peeping pervs (that's why Al Gore invented the internet, you fucking freaks!) when I spotted movement out of the corner of my eye. It's not anywhere near Christmas, so there's no way that the clatter that arose on the lawn could possibly be St. Nick,[1] though even just the fantasy of snow at this point gave me a pleasant sympathetic shiver.

No, not a miniature sleigh and eight tiny reindeer, but a fleet of rental trucks and a film crew.

---

[1] A reference to the famous poem *A Visit from St. Nicholas* – or, as it's commonly known, *'Twas the Night Before Christmas* – Clement Clarke Moore, 1823.

'Kayso, the neighbourhood we live in (did you notice the 'u' in there, Yankees? The rest of the world spells it with a 'u'. I'm just fucking with you – I love y'all!) has a lot of big old houses in it – a remnant from a time when people had twenty-seven children, lived with their parents and their fifty-two brothers and sisters (do the math), and had servants to clean up the place. Oh, and only one bathroom. Now, most of these places have been converted into apartments, and they really are the nicest places. I'm not gonna lie, it kind of feels like living in a big old Victorian mansion, even though only part of it is ours.

But some people are still Lords of the Manor, so to speak, and the house right across the way from us is just one of those types – it's a gorgeous house – three-storey Victorian, complete with a turret on the corner. I find myself daydreaming about winning the lottery and buying it, even though I never actually play the lottery, which kind of pokes a big hole in my daydreaming.

Anywho, there's a film crew setting up all around it, as sometimes happens around here – they don't call us Hollywood North[2] for nothing – and so I don my cutest, sanest looking outfit, and go out to investigate.

As it turns out, leaving the house was the best possible thing, as I'm rewarded by a breeze that makes everything better, brushing the hair off of my forehead and the back of my neck, and blowing up my skirt to air out my unmentionables as well.

Now, in case you're thinking that I'm one of those girls that walks up to a guy and flirts to get what she wants, I'm not. None of that chest-thrusting, accidentally intentional physical contact, batting of eyes bullshit for me. Aunt Helena's cornered the market

---

[2]A lot of filming gets done in Toronto under the guise of other cities. Hell, Racoon City from the *Resident Evil* movies is pretty much all Hamilton and Toronto, and there's even a shot of the CN Tower in one of the films, which is just lazy film-making in my opinion. You don't put a recognizable landmark of a certain city in your film and then try to tell your audience that the story takes place in a different (even if it's fictional) city. You wouldn't shoot the Eiffel Tower in a scene and then try to convince your audience that it's actually Cleveland. (Never mind asking why anyone would shoot in Paris as opposed to Cleveland – now you're just being difficult, darlings.

on those moves,[3] but I find it much easier to just take the direct route and ask for what I want. I can't help it if I strike a stunning figure – I mean literally stunning – I approach men and they act like they've been hit over the head with a cartoon mallet. I swear sometimes I can almost see the cartoon stars spinning around their heads – in fact, this one time, someone gave me these mushrooms, and... Well, never mind about that.

So anyway, I walked straight up to the first guy who looked like he had nothing better to do and asked him what's what.

Turns out they're filming some ghost story type deal – one of those paranormal drama-documentaries – true life spooky stories. Which made me wonder – did that mean that our neighbour had a ghost or something? I mean, that would explain that visit from that little Munchkin-looking lady the other day, who just kept saying "Carol Ann, come into the light"[4] for some reason, but it also made me wonder why ghosts only seemed to haunt big old Victorian mansions. I mean, think about it – you never see a ghost story set in, like, I dunno, a one bedroom pre-fab flat in the suburbs. Or, a haunted trailer home. Which would be way more terrifying, if you ask me.

I mean, if you lived in a big old Victorian mansion, and discovered you had a ghost, don't you think you could maybe work out reasonable living conditions that were acceptable to both parties?

"Here here, Mr. Poltergeist – you just stay in the attic and leave us be, and we'll keep to ourselves down here. You may frequent the Kitchen, the Hall, and the Billiard Room between the hours of one and three a.m., but STAY OUT OF THE CONSERVATORY AND THE LOUNGE! That's my secret passage, dammit!"[5]

---

[3]So unfair. I tell her the horrible tale of getting stranded in Cheyenne, Wyoming and all that followed, and all she remembers is me flirting my way into an upgrade to a convertible. Maybe she should remember that it was my flirting that caused me to miss all that about the Damage Waiver?

[4]A reference to the film *Poltergeist*, Carol Ann was the little girl who got sucked into the TV, and the character of Tangina Barrons, whom Craig T. Nelson's character referred to as the Magic Munchkin.

[5]A reference to the board game Clue (or Cluedo if your last name happens to be Windsor and you enjoy a spot of tea now and again) by Parker Brothers. A murder

But if you lived in a bungalow in the 'burbs, why, where would you go? The phrase *This house isn't big enough for the both of us!* would be horribly apt, in that case. And a trailer home? Forget about it! No ghost with an ounce of self-respect would be caught dead in a trailer home (and yes, I see what I just did there, thanks for pointing it out).

I think someone should make a ghost story set in a single-family dwelling. Or, better yet, a spirit makes a long journey to try to return to her house, only to find that it's been torn down, and the whole neighbourhood (again with that 'u') has been converted to cheap pre-fab tract housing, and the ghost can't figure out which lot was originally hers, because all the houses look exactly the same. Call it *Scary Suburbia*– I figure this is the vehicle those ghastly Olson twins[6] have been waiting for to resurrect their careers (yes, I did it again, thanks for noticing – I'm not just a pretty face, you know – there are some people that say that I have a gift for turning a phrase. Then there was that creepy couche-tard down at the bus station who said he thought I'd have a gift for turning a trick, and I'm pretty sure he's still waiting for his testicles to descend, but that's a story for another day).

So, in conclusion (because I have to wrap this up), to quote the immortal Winston Zeddemore (who was, incidentally, supposed to be played by Eddie Murphy,[7] but that would have made a whole other movie): "When someone asks you if you are a god, you say YES!"

It's a Ghostbusters reference, people. C'mon, get with the program! Should I have been more obvious?

---

mystery set in a house where there are secret passages between certain rooms. This is useful for getting around the board if you happen to be stuck in one of the corner rooms and you keep rolling a two, which is completely useless, and of course, your niece cheats and always wins and you just wanted to play Monopoly, but no, the Countess doesn't like Monopoly... and I digress, darlings.

[6]Mary Kate and Ashley Olson, who have been on television since near birth as the Tanner baby on *Full House*, and who have since become... I don't even know – what do they do?

[7]True story.

Okay, conclusion take #2: So as I was walking back to my apartment, I overhead the pizza delivery guy say he had a pizza for Dana. Then I heard a low growl of a voice respond: "There is no Dana, only Zul."

Nothing?

Okay, conclusion take #3: Who you gonna call? (cue Ray Parker Jr. music video now).

Okay, people, that's a wrap.

seven days with no helena makes one weak title - day six

Hey Helena! Look who I found!
'Kayso, the A/C is still not fixed, so last night I caught the GO bus

down to Hamilton to visit a friend, and this morning we went down to grab a coffee at her favourite little coffee shop with the charming name of My Dog Joe, and lo and behold, there's a music festival on, and guess who was playing? The Bay City Rollers! I know, right – who knew they were still together? Ess Ay Tee You Are Dee

Ay Why... Night!

Nah, it was none other than Mr. Jacob Moon, he of the opening-for-Marillion fame. You know – Montreal, Couche-Tard, Jumping Asians.

Turns out he's from Hamilton, so, you know, home town boy makes good and all that jazz, blues, and electronica-bluegrass-disco-hip-hop fusion.

He was playing to mostly an empty parking lot, so I kinda felt bad for him, but it was only 10 O'Clock on a Saturday morning, so...

Anywho, I made sure to snap a picture so he knows we're stalking him (kidding, Jacob –omygod, what if he reads this? Then hit the delete button. Shut up, voices in my head, or I'll stab you with a Q-tip) and I made sure to hoot and holler so he knows we love him.

And then I made sure to filter it through effects so that everyone knows that I am an artiste and not just some schmuck with a camera. I am a schmuck with a camera phone and the basic ability to fool around with the Paper Camera app, thank you very much.

MWAH!

Penny

seven days with no helena makes one weak title - day seven

H ave you ever had anyone make a pop culture reference at you that you just didn't get?

Isn't that terribly awkward?

I admit I have put my foot in my mouth a number of times when I thought I was being terribly clever, only to want to have the ground swallow me up in embarrassment when I see the blank look of cluelessness staring back at me.

Like this morning, for example. I was on a roll, or so I thought. I mean, it was like the universe just kept setting me up, and who am I to deny the universe when it clearly wants me to spike that fucker? KA-POW IN YOUR FACE! (Doing victory dance, shaking my booty, fingers in the air white-girl style).[1]

First, I was at the supermarket to pick up some freshly baked pastries, and there was a boy in the parking lot rounding up the

---

[1]The Countess might have been an excellent addition to her high school volleyball team, but a dancer she is not.

stray grocery carts, and he was whistling the Elle Driver song from *Kill Bill.*[2]

So as I'm passing by him, I casually say "Elle, you're gonna have to abort the mission."

He looked at me, confused, and asked "What?"

So of course, I responded in kind, saying "We owe her better than that," at which point he smiled, pointed his finger at me, and laughed.

'Kayso then I'm in the store, and it's a Sunday morning, so it's like being in some post-apocalyptic zombie movie grocery store, and there's never anyone around to help you when you need it. Empty chip bags blow by like tumbleweeds, and no one's answering the repeated announcement that there's a need for clean-up in Aisle Three. I came upon a lady who was trying to get some olives or something at the self-serve Antipasto bar, but she couldn't find a spoon. She'd been trying to flag down someone from behind the deli counter, but to no avail.

Again, it was like the universe had just floated one up for me to smash like I was some bikini-clad bimbo in a game of two-on-two beach volleyball. I walked up to her and said, in my most zen-like voice, "Do not try to get customer service on a Sunday morning – that's impossible. Instead, only try to realize the truth."

"I'm sorry," the lady said, clearly uncomfortable that I was encroaching on her world – a world where nice girls didn't have pink hair or wear Ruby Gloom[3] t-shirts, and people clearly weren't randomly sociable with strangers, "what did you say?"

---

[2]Elle Driver, an assassin portrayed by Daryl Hannah, dresses up like a nurse and saunters down the halls of the hospital whistling a tune, and is interrupted by her boss Bill, who tells her to abort the mission just as she was about to issue a lethal injection to a comatose Uma Thurman.
[3]Ruby Gloom might just be the greatest cartoon ever made. If Robert Smith of The Cure made cartoons, they would look like Ruby Gloom. It's a Canadian animated series whose characters include a two-headed guitarist, a walking disaster named Misery, a cyclops named Iris, and a Raven named Poe. It's a cartoon for Goths, and it features

"I said, only try to realize the truth."

"What truth?" She asked, and there the ball floated, waiting for me to deliver the blow.

"There is no spoon," I replied, affecting my calmest voice and giving her a bow like a Buddhist monk.[4]

As I walked away, I couldn't help but smile to myself as I heard her repeat 'There is no spoon,' first seeming confused, but then eventually laughing and sighing. So I was feeling pretty good about myself as I stepped into the Ten Items or Less aisle, which should have been empty on a Sunday morning, but was actually occupied by a woman who'd decided to stock up on Tomato soup, because, hey, it was on sale, so why not, right?

Unfortunately, the cashier had decided to be the penultimate couche-tard, and was giving her a hard time about the fact that she obviously had more than ten items. There was, including myself, exactly three people in line, and he was the only cashier working, anyway, so I'm not sure what the woman with the surplus items was supposed to do, but he just kept pointing to the sign that read Ten Items or Less.

"The sign says ten items, and you have," he started counting, "thirty-five, thirty-six... thirty-seven!"

"Thirty-seven?" The woman asked, not amused. She might not have been amused, but I was suddenly overcome with amusement, and I was having trouble keeping it to myself.

---

incredibly clever writing with smart pop culture and musical references (Frank and Len, the two-headed guitarists write a rock opera called Quadrogloomia) and brilliant voice work. It's a much smarter version of the *Beetlejuice* cartoon, which was also directed by the same person – Robin Budd.

[4] A reference to the little Buddhist monk-esque child in the waiting room in the film *The Matrix*, who sits bending a spoon, apparently with his mind. When asked how he's accomplishing this, the boy responds in a very zen-like fashion that if one can realize the truth – that "there is no spoon" then anything is possible. Mind = blown.

"Thirty-seven," the dictatorial cashier confirmed. I could contain myself no longer.

"IN A ROW?!" I shouted with feigned disbelief.

Heads turned to stare at me and my outburst. I had a big smile on my face that faded as I realized that perhaps the films of Kevin Smith remained a mystery to my intended audience.

"Thirty-seven?" I tried again, weakly. "In a row? Nothing? Oh, never mind."

Oh well, I couldn't really complain. Two out of three ain't bad and all that. At least I had the good sense to not shout 'try not to suck any dick on the way through the parking lot!' as she left with her thirty-seven items.[5]

Thanks for bearing with me this week – I hope I maintained the high standard of quality that you're used to. (I delivered that with a straight face, hand-to-god).

Anywho, tune in next time, when you're quite certain to hear Helena ask "What the hell happened? Did the maid quit?"

She thinks she's SOOOO clever.

MWAH! 'til next time!

Penny

---

[5]Where do I begin explaining about the scene in the Kevin Smith movie *Clerks* where Dante's girlfriend confesses to him that while she has only had sex with a small number of men (by which she means intercourse), that she has performed fellatio on a grand total of thirty-seven different men, though not, as Dante asks, in a row. Dante is not very happy about the whole situation, and they have a fight about it, as she leaves the store, he shouts after her "try not to suck any dick on the way through the parking lot." I'm not saying that the Countess wouldn't ever say something like that, but I must say I'm glad that in this case, she did not.

d is for dilettante

I am a dilettante, darlings, no doubt about it. But don't you dare call me that as an insult. No, I'm taking the word back and re-branding it. I may not be a professional, but I am no wannabe, either.

See, dilettante is kind of the 'N' word for artistic types (the 'N' word being novice, of course – where did you think I was going with that? Did you think I was going to say neophyte?) as it is dismissive and insulting to those of us who delight in dabbling and experimentation, and brands us with a big scarlet letter that burns no less than the one dear Hester Prynne was forced to wear.[1] Only the letter that we dilettantes are forced to wear screams Dabbler. As

---

[1] Hester Prynne was the woman forced to wear the scarlet letter A (for Adultery) in Nathaniel Hawthorne's *The Scarlet Letter*. Of course, her lover, a prominent member of the community, was not forced to wear a corresponding letter. The D you see on this page would be scarlet but for the expense of printing in colour – so you'll just have to use your imaginations, darlings.

in, not good enough. Of poor quality. The work of an admirer, as opposed to an artist. As if we have no respect for the craft. As if we seek validation by putting ourselves in the same category as someone more talented – and there are degrees of talent, no question. As if we don't take what we're doing seriously – as if we are not artists unless we are on television.

I do have respect for more talented artists, and I do have respect for the craft, and I take whatever I do very seriously, and I refuse to be put into the same category as someone who does wonderful Paint By Numbers renditions of Dogs Playing Poker or twelve year old girls (or forty year old women) writing poorly constructed Twilight fan fiction, nor indeed with those computer savvy kids who cannot play an instrument, but can layer pre-recorded samples in GarageBand and call that songwriting.

I may not ever see my name in lights – but I am an actress.

I may never sit on a panel alongside Joss Whedon[2] and answer questions on how I brilliantly resurrected *Firefly*, but I'll keep writing nonetheless – I am a writer.

Macaroni art aside, I'll keep doodling, dabbling and someday learn to paint – I am an artist.

I am an occasional singer; I model intermittently, write poetry now and again, and who knows what else I may try my hand at.

But rest assured, darlings, that whatever I do, I will do my best – I will continue to hone my craft, and I will refine my raw materials down to the purest form, and sand off the rough edges, and shake off the dross and separate the wheat from the chaff, and only present the finished works when they are, indeed, finished – or, if not finished, then I will present them as a curiosity of sorts – portrait of a spectacular failure.

I am a dilettante, from the Italian *dilettare* (to delight), derived from the Latin *delectare* (to delight), and I will delight in my artistic dalliances, taking each new love like an adventure, and measure my success by the number of scars I acquire, and my failures only by

---

[2]Creator of, among other things, *Buffy the Vampire Slayer* and the tragically short-lived and posthumously much-loved cult classic *Firefly*. He is also responsible for making an entire generation of non-comic readers love The Avengers.

the number of things I never tried but always wished I had. And I will wear the word dilettante like a badge of honour, as one who is willing to try, as one will is willing to fail, as one who demands excellence from themselves, as one who is willing to get in the game instead of sitting in the stands waiting to be entertained.

So don't you dare call me dilettante – unless you mean it.

the persistence of magic - the california years part three

$\mathcal{I}$'d only been working at Amoeba Music[1] for about three weeks when Michael handed me a flyer for his band and asked me if I'd come out and hear them play for the first time.

I told him I'd think about it, see what I was doing. I tried to be polite and show interest in promoting his band, because hey, I was working in one of the coolest record stores in the world, and that's kind of what they do there, darlings – promote music, especially independent music.

I had arrived in San Francisco about a month before, after a meandering drive up from Santa Cruz, crying nearly the whole way and listening to Bright Eyes, which didn't really make it any better. I had driven away from a good man, a man I'd loved, and who had loved me but couldn't keep me, as I wouldn't allow myself to be kept, I guess. I'd driven away, never looking back, just trying to convince myself that I was doing the right thing. Some days, even

---

[1]Amoeba Music is the greatest and biggest independent music store in the world, with two locations in the San Francisco Bay area (one in the Haight District and one in Berkeley) and another in Hollywood. The store in the Haight really is an iconic part of the city, based in a converted bowling alley. They still have in store shows with both up-and-coming artists and seasoned veterans and legends of rock.

now, I have to convince myself all over again. But that was so long ago, darlings, and nostalgia is a dangerous drug.

So is cocaine, apparently, as Stevie Nicks[2] could attest to.

Speaking of Stevie Nicks...

Forced segues are a cheap trick, Helena.

Yeah, well, so's your mother.
Well, that's just rude and unpleasant.

Yeah, well, so's your mother.

Where was I? Oh yes, Fleetwood Mac.[3] As someone with a number of complicated relationships under my belt, I have always found the soap opera love stories behind the music of Fleetwood Mac fascinating,[4] and think that Rumours might just be the greatest pop album ever recorded (Michael Jackson's *Thriller* can go spike some kid's Pepsi with wine for all I care), so I made sure to stop in Sausalito on the way through to visit The Record Plant at 2200 Bridgeway.[5] I don't know why, but I just wanted to stand there and soak up the history or something.

Anyway, what is magical in our minds rarely measures up to what we might have imagined, and in this case, there really was no persistence of magic. Whatever magic there was there thirty years prior, well, they'd taken it with them when they went.

---

[2]Stevie Nicks, one of the singers the band Fleetwood Mac, had a notorious cocaine addiction that actually burned a hole in her nose, or so the story goes.

[3]You've heard Fleetwood Mac, and if you haven't you're also one of those rare people that claim they've never heard The Beatles, in which case, what are you doing with this book in your hand? Shouldn't you be playing Halo or World of Warcraft or something? Fleetwood Mac's 1977 album *Rumours* is so much a part of pop consciousness that it likely figures in your dreams (those in the know will realize that your favourite dilettante just made a clever joke, but it's bad form to have to annotate one's own annotations, so that one's just for those in the know) and you don't even realize it.

[4]Four of the band members were romantically involved with each other and then went through violently bitter splits – most of this was going on during the recording of *Rumours*.

[5]Famous record studio where *Rumours* was recorded.

Which is really too bad, because I surely could have used some of that magic to make me forget Manuel, or to help me figure out what I was going to do next. Instead, the only magic I found was the kind that got passed around the drum circle I found myself a part of shortly after I arrived in the Panhandle area of Golden Gate Park that afternoon.

I had gone looking for leftovers of the Summer of Love and so I went to Haight-Asbury, where I'd hoped to walk in the footsteps of Janis Joplin[6] and Grace Slick.[7] What I found, instead, were high-priced shoe stores, vintage clothing shops selling used jeans for $100, and psychedelia-themed souvenir shops cashing in on hippie culture. Jerry Garcia[8] would be spinning in his grave, darlings. (Well, he was kind of a big guy, so maybe spinning is a bit ambitious – suffice to say he would be resting uneasily).

I can't say that I saw Don Henley's fabled Dead Head sticker on a Cadillac,[9] but it wouldn't have surprised me. The magic had faded here, as well.

Disillusioned, I retreated back into Golden Gate Park, found some friendly faces, and got very high.

I stayed that way for nearly three days.

When my head cleared, and I decided that I didn't want to live in my car anymore, I rented the Peace Room at The Red Victorian[10] (because hey, when in Rome), took a long shower in the Starlight Bathroom and contemplated my next move.

---

[6]Singer of *Little Piece of My Heart* who died at twenty-seven of a heroin overdose.

[7]Singer of the band Jefferson Airplane, with the kick ass songs *White Rabbit* and *Somebody to Love*, and then later of Starship (kind of the same band – long story) with the less than kick ass song *We Built This City*. Which just goes to show that there really is no persistence of magic.

[8]Jerry Garcia was a guitarist, songwriter, singer and the unofficial leader of The Grateful Dead.

[9]A reference to the Don Henley song *The Boys of Summer*, which sports the lyric "Out on the road today I saw a Dead Head sticker on a Cadillac. A little voice inside my head said don't look back; you can never look back."

[10]Pretty much THE hippie hotel, darlings.

From what I'd already seen of San Francisco, it wasn't going to be like Santa Cruz. It was too expensive, for one, and too big. In Santa Cruz, I'd found a place to crash pretty easily until I found a room to rent, but I didn't dare try that in the big city. And I certainly couldn't stay in the hotel for very long. No, I figured I had enough money to maybe stay in San Francisco for about a week, and then maybe it'd be best if I moved on – perhaps I'd keep driving north until I arrived back in Canada – I'd never been to Vancouver, so it seemed as good a plan as any.

But you already know that I didn't do that.

That had been the plan, though, as I went for a walk through the Haight, playing tourist and even buying a box of Nag Champa incense and a Jerry Bear postcard[11], which I suppose I'd intended on sending to my sister Cheryl, though I don't know that I ever did.

I ended up walking into Amoeba Music for the first time that day, and discovered where all the magic had gone.

I wandered around, bewitched by the enormity of it – it's the size of a warehouse, the size of an aircraft hangar, the size of the music collection in my head. When God goes shopping for that hard to find, deleted, import only 7" Smiths single (*Still Ill* b/w *You've Got Everything Now*, perhaps), Amoeba Music is where she goes.

As I browsed, I couldn't help but notice what other people were shopping for, (I'm nosy like that) and when I saw what they'd picked up, I was often moved to start a conversation with them. I've never been shy with starting conversations with strangers in bookstores, music stores, or in line for concerts. It's just something I do, darlings.

Maroon 5 had just hit it big that summer with their debut *Songs About Jane*, and I when I heard two girls raving about it, I practically dragged them to the P section, where I was relieved to find that

---

[11]The Grateful Dead were almost as famous for the culture they created as for their music. A Jerry Bear was a marching bear designed by Bob Thomas for a compilation album called *The Grateful Dead, Volume One (Bear's Choice)*. They've become an iconic logo of Dead Head culture.

they had both of The Philosopher Kings'[12] studio albums, though not the live album, but insisted that they had to hear them, that it was, indeed, a crime that they hadn't already. Then there was the skinny boy in the skinny jeans, madras shirt and horn-rimmed glasses that had not yet become the official uniform requirement at that time, but would soon be seen everywhere. He was having a discussion with his androgynous, pixie-cut sporting girlfriend about this new band called The Decemberists, who I said I thought took a lot of cues from Jeff Mangum, which started a half hour discussion of the myriad of influences in their music ranging from old English folk music, sixties and seventies folk rock like Neil Young and Bob Dylan, through Morrissey, and into a world of their own. That conversation then ended with me gently pressing a copy of Neutral Milk Hotel's *In the Aeroplane Over the Sea*[13] into his hands, and saying "This will change your life."

Before I knew it, I'd spent all afternoon browsing and chatting with people, making recommendations (although when I recommend something, darlings, it's more of an insistence than a suggestion) and when I started to leave empty handed, my heart sunk a little. It was like having to leave Wonderland.

"Hey," a voice called after me as I walked past the checkout counter, "can you come back tomorrow at eleven?"

I turned, not quite sure I heard him correctly. I pointed at myself in the universally understood gesture that means "Who? Me?"

"Yeah," the guy in the Dead Kennedys shirt and dyed black hair said, looking up at me while flipping through some LPs a customer had dropped off to sell. "I figure you must have brought in a couple hundred dollars of business this afternoon, and you don't even really care about that, do you?"

I smirked. Was I being offered a job?

---

[12]The Philosopher Kings were a Canadian funk/blues/soul/pop band from the mid-to-late '90s that never got the recognition they so dearly deserved. When Maroon 5 was suddenly everywhere, I kind of felt bad for the Philosopher Kings, whose music was similar, but just didn't have the PR team that Maroon 5 did.

[13]Jeff Mangum's masterpiece and one of the best-selling and most beloved indie albums of all time. If you haven't heard it, you're missing out.

"I was just talking to people, darling," I said nonchalantly. "I just couldn't let someone who claims they love The Cure walk out of here without *Hyaena*."[14]

"Well, I would have gone with The Glove, but yeah, the Siouxsie Sioux album was a good choice, too," he said, almost daring me to disagree with him.

"I just wish Robert Smith had sung on those tracks instead of Budgie's girlfriend,"[15] I countered, and that seemed to clinch the deal. It was the coolest, most informal interview I've ever had.

"So I'll see you tomorrow, then?" He asked, without the usually upward inflection that would indicate that he was asking me a question. His confidence won me over, and I found myself agreeing.

"Yeah," I said, suddenly feeling very grateful – to whom or what, I'm not sure. God; the universe? Robert Smith, maybe? Perhaps it was the persistence of magic after all.

"Sure," I repeated. I could stay. Why not? "See you at eleven..."

"Steve," he offered.

"Helena," I replied in kind.

And that's how I ended up working at the coolest record store in the world. Sometimes, magic does happen, when you least expect it.

Three weeks later, Michael started showing up.

---

[14] *Hyaena* is an album by Siouxsie and the Banshees featuring Robert Smith from The Cure as part of the band. It features a stunning cover of The Beatles' *Dear Prudence*.
[15] The Glove was a side project that developed out of Robert Smith's involvement with The Banshees, featuring Steven Severin from The Banshees, and Jeanette Landray on vocals, due to a contractual prohibition preventing Robert Smith from singing with another band. In 2006, a Deluxe Edition of the album *Blue Sunshine* was released, which contained these much-coveted home demo recordings of Robert Smith singing these songs.

the return of the barista
with no name

"The Barista With No Name squinted into the sunlight to survey the line of patrons lined up for their daily espresso injection. A solitary bead of sweat trickled down one temple, but he dare not wipe it away. He kept his hands at waist level, rubbing forefingers and thumbs together, awaiting the order. When at last, the request came, his hands moved like lightening to the big sandalwood grips of the espresso tamper, its mother of pearl inlays glinting in the sun like the promise of gold in a prospector's pan."

"Then," The Countess Penelope of Arcadia interrupted, "suddenly and without warning..."

"Superfluous and redundant," I countered, annoyed that she'd interrupted.

"... The Barista With No Name tore away his smelly grey serape, to reveal a brightly-coloured cowboy costume of the Roy Rogers[1] variety, and then proceeded to sing *Rhinestone Cowboy*,[2] while the lovely Miss Helena blushed like a prairie blossom (whatever that is) and made googly eyes at him. Then, like something out of a

---

[1]Roy Rogers was a Hollywood cowboy in the 1940s and '50s, but Hollywood's idea of what was worn in the Old West differed greatly from reality.
[2]Written by Larry Weiss but made famous by Glen Campbell in 1975.

1980s movie starring Patrick Swayze[3], suddenly some other cowboy-themed song started playing, and Miss Helena got on the back of the BWNN's horse, a gentle nag with the lovely name of Cordelia, or Buttercup, and rode off into the sunset. Never mind that it's eight o'clock in the morning."

"I told you before, darling, I never make googly eyes," I insisted, though I'm pretty sure I was making googly eyes at the Barista With No Name, so named because he had the piercing blue eyes and steely glare of a young Clint Eastwood.

"You do and are," the Countess replied. "You also might want to wipe your chin. You're drooling."

"I am not dr- Oh, crap," I was drooling a bit.

"Way I reckon," said the Countess Penelope of Arcadia, which is apparently a small borough of Tumbleweed, Texas, in the County of Buttfuck, "all you gotta do is just mosey on up there and rope in that tall drink o' water with yer, whatchamacallit? Feminine wiles. Just go and say a friendly howdy-do. I reckon, well shucks, little trailhand, and so forth. Nothin' doin' and whatnot. Unless, that is, yer yella'. That's it, ain't it? Why, yer nothin' but a no good, darn tootin' yella-belly snake, ain'tcha?"

"Now listen here," I said to the Countess, trying to give her my I'm serious face, "I'm not just going to go talk to him – he's busy. And cut out the cowpoke."

"Why, yer just a lily-livered ol' chicken, ain'tcha? Why, I oughta hosswhup you right here and now, learn you some manners."

"Do you even know what you're saying?" I asked her incredulously.

"Everything except 'hosswhup'. Did I just threaten you with violence of some sort?" Penny asked in a more hushed tone than I would have thought her capable of.

"I believe so, yes," I replied.

"Well, good, varmint!" Penny the Kid retorted, slipping seamlessly back into Hayseed, in which her fluency was somewhat suspect. "Ah reckon that's more'n a cowardly cur like you rightly

---

[3]This never happened in Road House, but it could have. Or any 1980s movie, when musical montages and pastiches were very popular.

deserves! Why, yer nothin' but a lowdown, cactus-eatin' milquetoast."[4]

"Well, that's enough of that. I'll tolerate many things," I said, exaggeratedly exasperated, "but I'll not tolerate being called a milquetoast! Why, you just point me at that cowboy, and just watch and see what my feminine wiles can achieve."

But as I turned back toward the coffee bar to set my sights on the BWNN, he was gone – vanished as if into a puff of smoke. As the tumbleweeds tumbled, and the coyotes, uh, coyot-ed, somewhere, a mariachi band played *Save a Horse (Ride a Cowboy)*[5] with a distinctively Mexican flair, and The Countess Penny the Kid began narrating the moment in a voice like an old John Ford[6] film, like *How Green Was My Valley*, or *The Quiet Man*.

"He walked a hard path, and he walked it alone, blowing into town and back out again just as suddenly, leaving a trail of busted teeth and broken hearts in his wake..."

"Oh, Penny," I teased, "Do shut up."

---

[4] Milquetoast is a dysphemism for a weak, bland person, deriving from a comic strip character from the 1920s, Caspar Milquetoast. Perhaps one day, people will refer to villainous types as Gores. Penny made me say that.

[5] By the country duo Big & Rich, 2004. Innuendo absolutely intended – that's kind of all the song has going for it, really.

[6] Four time Academy Award winning director of *The Grapes of Wrath*, *Stagecoach*, and a whole shitload of other Westerns. He was famous for booming voice over narratives.

don't wake me - the california years - a sleepy intermission

When the Postal Service[1] re-issued their album *Give Up* earlier this year as a 10th anniversary edition, it made me painfully aware of the passage of time. This album came out while I was working at Amoeba Music – somehow I'd ended up there for nearly nine months, and that was just unsettling.

I lived a normal life there – I ended up renting a room in one of the beautiful houses they call the Painted Ladies, and I believe that is where my love of Victorian architecture began, and why I've sought them out to live in ever since.

I'd work at the record store all afternoon, and then I'd be out all night, drinking with my new friends, checking out bands in the bars in North Beach, and then, well, I actually got involved with Michael's band – but that's a tale for next time.

I'd get home at three, sleep 'til ten, roll out of bed and do it all over again.

Oh, to be young and insane again, darlings!

---

[1]An American electronic side project of Ben Gibbard from Death Cab for Cutie and Jimmy Tamborello. The songs on this album were heard everywhere, as they were used for TV commercials and movie soundtracks. The song *Such Great Heights* has been covered by everybody but Elvis, and I understand that they have necromancers working around the clock for the express purpose of correcting that grievous oversight.

Last night, one of the band members was in town, and called me up and asked if I'd like to get together. He has a new band that's doing reasonably well, and is currently on their first tour that includes dates outside the US. I'm terribly excited for them, and I'm afraid I got a little caught up in the nostalgia of it all, and I think I may have made quite a fool of myself when he asked me up on the stage to sing what had been my signature piece – a cover of *Sour Times* by Portishead.

I may or may not have then joined the after party (I am admitting to nothing that I can't remember with crystal clarity, which isn't much, darlings) and gotten more than slightly fershnickered as I reminisced about California days (and nights) with James, the only member of Quixotic Exotica (yes, there's a reason you've never heard of them) with whom I was still on speaking terms. The only one I hadn't slept with, alienated, or betrayed. The only one whose heart I hadn't broken.

Those times were sour, indeed.

Now leave me alone – I'm going back to bed. And don't wake me – I plan on sleeping in.[2] This staying out all night stuff is for the twentysomething crowd. Me, I need my beauty sleep.

---

[2] A reference to the song *Sleeping In* by The Postal Service

recipes from the hann-basquiat - sweet and spicy chicken pizza, helena style

I thought I'd throw you all a curve ball, darlings – a deliciously sweet and just spicy enough to make your lips tingle a bit – curve ball. I mean, what kind of dilettante would I be if I didn't dabble in a bit of cooking and sports metaphors?

When I'm recovering from a night of – well, debauchery is not an entirely accurate term – I mean my clothes remained on the entire evening, and there were no illicit substances involved – so let's say overindulgence. Yes. So let's back up, because that sentence was just terribly constructed, darlings, and the backspace key on my laptop is hooked up to a 500 volt (is that a lot? I don't know) battery and it gives me mildly painful shocks whenever I touch it, so let's just press on, shall we? Onward, ho! (Please, no overused who you callin' ho? routine, agreed? Good).

So, to continue – when I'm recovering from a night of overindulgence, I find that pizza soaks up the lingering libations splendidly. Unfortunately, no one makes my pizza. But now you'll be able to – I'll tell you how, darlings. You can thank me later.

What you'll need:

Some type of flatbread – if you really think that I make my own pizza dough, you've got to be kidding me - does the name beside my avatar say Betty Crocker?[1] No, it does not.

Some sort of Alfredo sauce (ooh, the first twist – no tomato sauce!) Again, go gaze into your navel until you unravel the secret of the universe if you think I make my own. I recommend something cheesy – Classico has a Four Cheese Alfredo that's actually my favourite, but you feel free to improvise.

Chicken breast - now, here I do actually recommend that you slaughter your own chicken, because it gives it that ever-so-fresh taste that you just don't get with store bought chicken. In fact, the chickens that I always use are hand-raised by the Countess and myself, and have only been fed the best grains and cornmeal, and they only drink single malt scotch. I call them my drunken chickens. I have a similar approach to raising geese for fois gras. My chickens enjoy an 18 year old Glenfiddich. I once enjoyed an 18-year-old named Glenn Finnegan, but that was a long time ago. Sorry darlings, again with the no backspacing. I tried and got burned so badly, I'm like Ringo Starr at the end of *Helter Skelter*, yelling 'I got blisters on me fingers!'[2]

But I digress. If you don't raise your own drunken chickens, store bought will suffice. I guess.

Frank's Red Hot Sauce. I've got nothing. Just pick up some Frank's Red Hot Sauce.

Also, some banana peppers – the pickled kind – they have a tanginess and the vinegar just adds something to the mix. Don't ask me – I didn't go to culinary school, I just know what I like.

---

[1] Betty Crocker is a cultural icon, but not, I repeat, not (underscore understood but not necessary) a real person, despite the fact that millions of people believed otherwise. In fact, in 1945, *Fortune* magazine named her the second most popular American woman. Not bad for someone who doesn't exist.

[2] I always assumed it was George Harrison screaming this ('cause that would make sense, right?) but after a little digging, I learned that it's actually Ringo. Who knew? Not me. But now I do, and so do you.

Pineapple chunks. Now, you can buy a pineapple, and peel it, core it and chop it up into chunks like a schmuck, or you can do what I do, and buy a can.

So, I guess you're going to need a can opener, too.

Clothes. You're going to require clothing to make this. Unless you're a nudist – and there's nothing wrong with that – I totally support alternative lifestyles. But if you are a nudist, and you're preparing this, and you invite me over, can you please give me a little warning, so I cannot eat anything you've touched. It's nothing personal; it's just, I don't want to have to keep watching my food for little curly hairs.

Seriously? How do you prepare your food? Do you rub your junk all over your food? What makes you think that a nudist would rub theirs on their food?

Don't be ridiculous! It's just that they might scratch, or something – I don't know –don't judge me!

I think that's really closed-minded, Helena, and I don't know if I want to read your memoirs anymore. I am getting hungry, though, so could you maybe get back on track here?

Oh, don't be like that. I'm sorry. Please don't go. Okay, I'll get back to the recipe.

On to the cheese. I shred a mix of Mozzarella and Mild Cheddar – about 2/3 Mozza and 1/3 Mild Chedda.

Now what?

Alright, the first thing I do is just grill up the chicken breast (boneless/skinless – did I mention that?). I find that if I just pan fry it, it's easiest. I cook it a bit on both sides to make it easier to cut, and then I take it out of the frying pan and cut it into strips (it's going to be raw in the middle, so be sure to be cutting on a clean cutting board, and wash your hands before and after handling the chicken. Penny and I use a hand soap that we make ourselves by rendering fat, scooping off the tallow, and then adding lye. We find that the best fat comes from liposuction clinics. OH wait, sorry, that's not us, that's Tyler Durden[3] from Fight Club).

Nevermind. Moving right along, after I've cut up the chicken, I put it back in the frying pan (did I mention you'll need a frying pan?) and then I coat it very liberally with Frank's Red Hot Sauce. Cook it until it's done.

Take your flatbread, spread a nice amount of the Alfredo sauce on, and then add your now spicy chicken, some banana peppers, and drained pineapple chunks.

Spread cheese over top – not too much, though – you don't want to bury the taste of the toppings. If you like a little more spice, you can put a few more drops of Frank's on top of the cheese, but it's not necessary.

So now, put it in the oven at, I dunno– 175 Celsius/350 Fahrenheit – for maybe 20 minutes or so, until the cheese is melted and a little browning – maybe put the broiler on for the last 2 minutes? What am I? Rachael Ray?[4]

Once the pizza's in the oven, put on some music –*The Tain* by The Decemberists is 18 minutes long, so that'd be a good choice, and not only for the track length. If you're, um, under the weather like I am today, you might want to go with something a little mellower. I'd suggest *Discreet Music* by Brian Eno, but then, that first track is 30 minutes long, and then you might end up with a burned pizza, and nobody likes burned pizza.

Might I suggest, then, if your head is being attacked by tiny invisible piranhas that are slowly nibbling your brain like mine is, that you just put *I Know It's Over* by The Smiths on repeat three times[5], or if you really want to mix it up, vary it by throwing in Jeff Buckley's cover version.

Enjoy your pizza, darlings.

---

[3]Tyler Durden is one of the main characters of the book and movie *Fight Club*. He makes money by making and selling soap that he makes using the fat he steals from liposuction clinics.
[4]Celebrity chef and Food Network personality.
[5]If you're shit at maths like I am, darlings, let me explain. The song is about six minutes long, and if you listen to it three times, then you've magically allowed about eighteen minutes to pass. And yes, I do realize that this was completely unnecessary.

special providence

"There's a special providence in the fall of a sparrow."
Shakespeare, Hamlet, Act 5, Scene 2

$\mathcal{I}$ was sitting outside enjoying a Soy Chai Latte and a maple pecan muffin the other day, and I suspect it was the latter that drew the attention of the sparrows. Having been utterly terrified by Hitchcock's adaption of the Daphne Du Maurier story *The Birds*,[1] I was at first apprehensive, but after a minute or two, when I remained pleasantly unpecked, I relaxed, and tried to enjoy their company, as they flitted and hopped about, picking and pecking at my muffin paper.

I was able to get a few snaps, and this one was my favourite.

It was one of those moments that made me forget about the rush hour traffic, or the bills I had to pay, and just enjoy what little communion with nature that my busy life affords me.

Shakespeare was referring to a bible verse about how God takes care of even the sparrows, and that not one sparrow falls without His knowledge (and presumably, consent).

And then, that we are more valuable than many sparrows, ergo... take that to the logical conclusion, and so forth and so on.

---

[1] 1963 film starring Rod Taylor and TippiHedren. Scared the shit out of me as a child, darlings, though I suspect it wouldn't hold up to today's standards of terror.

Essentially, Hamlet was telling his friend Horatio that whatever happens will happen; that it's in God's hands.

I don't know if I subscribe to that kind of logic or belief system - seems oversimplified to me, but the sentiment is nice – that we are valuable, that we are cared for. Unfortunately, when things go wrong (as they sometimes do), it is only natural to feel abandoned – like if God is supposed to be looking after us, what happened?[2]

I don't know, darlings – I temper any religious and/or spiritual inclinations I have with a healthy dose of scepticism. Like Fox Mulder of *X-Files* fame, I want to believe. I just don't know if I do most of the time. Anyway, I just remembered that verse from Hamlet and it got me thinking.

A dangerous pastime, I know.[3]

---

[2]This moment started me thinking about Halesowen – a story I hadn't really told before – not in any permanent way, anyhow. I hadn't known that I was going to write it here – it just kind of happened. Isn't that strange? If you have no idea what I'm talking about yet, just turn the page, and consider this a prologue.

[3]A reference to a song from Disney's *Beauty and the Beast,* when Gaston sings 'LeFou I'm afraid I've been thinking..." And now you'll be singing that to yourself for the next couple of hours. You're welcome. Earworms served daily.

son of a preacher man[1]
(a halesowen adventure)

I was seventeen and in love. Or, seventeen and crazy, as a character in a book I probably read for the first time at seventeen used to say.[2]

Seventeen and in love – or, at least, in love with love. In love with the idea of love, in love with falling in love, and all that it entailed. Irrational and romantic, grandiose and dramatic love, of the kind one is generally only capable of at seventeen.

I mean, had Romeo and Juliet had a few more years under their belts, they might have just knocked obligatory boots, and then eaten the customary breakfast of shame and then Romeo would promise to call Juliet, and Juliet would play along, having heard that particular brand of horseshit a dozen times before, and smile, knowing full well that she'd never hear from him again. The only trip to the apothecary necessary would be Juliet's for a morning-after pill.

But at seventeen, I fell in love on a weekly basis, and I confess I rode off into the sunset with a prince or two like some brainless Disney princess, convinced they were my true love before I even knew their last name.

---

[1] A reference, of course, to the classic Dusty Springfield song, 1968.
[2] Clarisse McClellan from Ray Bradbury's *Fahrenheit 451*.

My true love's name was Andrew, and our love was doomed from the start. For one, we were from different lands. I had been living in the wilds of the New World, whereas Andrew hailed from Albion[3] fair, and in his eyes I saw the beauty of centuries past – I was his Guinevere, his Isolde– if ours was to be a tragic opera, I would be Dido to his Aeneas, and I would sing arias describing in romantic detail the depths of my love for him.[4]

But alas, we were to be torn apart. Andrew was a missionary's son, and his father was returning to England, and taking my beautiful Andrew with him.

And so it was that I suddenly found Jesus, and wanted to dedicate my life to converting the heathens the world over, but more specifically, in Halesowen,[5] a town I'd never heard of until I met Andrew. But people do crazy things when they are seventeen and in love.

Perhaps I should have thought things through a little better.

This is what was circling around in my head two months later as I faked yet another headache and lay in my bunk, trapped by my own reckless abandon and impulsive nature. Self-imposed solitary confinement to avoid taking part in going door-to-door and trying to convince people that I, at seventeen, had discovered the meaning of life in Jesus, and that I wanted them to share in the beauty of that discovery, and find true peace, like I supposedly had. I may be a storyteller, an exaggerator, and a teller of tall tales, but even I couldn't pull that off.

The truth is, I knew nothing of peace, and certainly hadn't received any road to Damascus revelations that set me on the path

---

[3] An ancient name for Great Britain.
[4] *Dido and Aeneas* is a famous opera by English composer Henry Purcell. *Dido's Lament* is a famous aria from the opera, and has been performed by such unlikely people as Klaus Nomi and Jeff Buckley. Trust me, darlings, it's a classic, and you'd know it if you heard it (Oh yeah! *The Band of Brothers* song!)
[5] It's a small town in the West Midlands of England, just southwest of Birmingham. Robert Plant (singer of Led Zeppelin – really, do I have to explain everything?) actually grew up there, but obviously was long gone by the time I arrived.

of enlightenment.[6] I was seventeen and in love, not some whitewashed sepulchre out to make converts twice as fit for hell as I was myself (it didn't all go in one ear and out the other, darlings – and I was always quite fond of that little tongue lashing Jesus gave the Pharisees – he could be pretty badass from time to time).[7] I repeat for emphasis that I was but seventeen and in love, and actually by that point, it wasn't even Andrew I was in love with anymore, but that didn't change the fact that I found myself in a situation that required me to fake a certainty and energy that I simply did not possess. And I was beginning to wonder how much longer I could keep up the facade.

I was living in what amounted to a boarding school, sharing a room with five other girls in a sort of evangelist training centre, and it was like living the life of a goldfish. I was bombarded with well-meaning but naive admonishments and promises to pray for me. I was afflicted with nearly daily migraines, which they saw as demonic attacks (I couldn't make this shit up, darlings. Well, I could, but what would be the point?) that hindered my ability to serve the Lord. Their concern was both touching and creepy at the same time, and I wasn't doing myself any favours by being so anti-social. I know that now, but at the time I just wanted to die. If I'd known what I'd been signing up for, I would have found some other boy to be in love with. But, as the saying goes, hindsight is always greener in someone else's optometrist's office. Or something like that, anyway.

I couldn't keep sleeping the days away, I knew that much. The walls were closing in on me, and I'd begun to hear whispers about them sending me home. I just couldn't bear the thought of being sent back home, where I'd have to face the disappointed looks and *I told you so* stares of the *mater* and *pater familias*, not to mention the scorn of my older sister, who had been fairly transparent with her jealousy in the matter of me travelling abroad in the first place. And

---

[6]Paul, who wrote a lot of the New Testament of the Bible, supposedly had a divine enlightenment on a trip to Damascus, which changed him to a persecutor of the early Christians to their greatest proponent. The phrase *Road to Damascus* has become synonymous with dramatic revelations.
[7]In Matthew Chapter 23, Jesus gives the televangelists of the day a good dressing down.

so I decided to get better, and give them the answer to their prayers. Suddenly, Helena was a Do-Bee[8], and joined in their little games, praise God and hallelujah, it's a miracle. Not only were my headaches fewer, but I was suddenly enthusiastic to get outside, into the community! The truth is, it wasn't until I broke down and decided to play the game did I finally see the possibilities that awaited me outside of the compound walls.

So the next time that we went out, I wandered off on my own, and found other things to do with my time. After all, I was seventeen and carefree, surrounded by that accent that, to this day, makes me weak in the knees, and there was so much more to see, so much to do, and plenty of English boys to fall in love with. Pints wouldn't drink themselves, you know, and snogging was always better with a partner.

Andrew was but the first, but he wouldn't be the last. Not by a long shot.

---

[8]A reference to Romper Room, a children's television show from my childhood.

i'm with the band - the california years part four

T V Voice Over Guy: *When last we saw Helena, she was seventeen and swept up in sinful sedition and reaping the reward for her o'er-hasty commitment to an evangelical organization that she only joined because of some pretty boy. Though she didn't know it at the time (but she was beginning to suspect), pretty boys would be the cause of no end of turmoil in Helena's life.*

Meanwhile, ten years later (but not any wiser), somewhere in California...

"I'm with the band," I said, night after night, and they'd let me in without paying the cover. Michael had just kept coming in to the record store every day or so to chat, until finally, after a couple of weeks, I relented and agreed to come see his band play.

I was relieved and delighted to discover that they weren't awful. Their singer, however, really was. Horrible. And I found it very difficult to hide my distaste for her. Because of my, ahem, vocalizing of my disdain, I am willing to accept perhaps as much as thirty, maybe thirty-five percent of the blame for what was to follow, but the fact of the matter is, their singer really was truly awful. She was flat, she screeched the high notes, and she had zero charisma.

I guess I made the mistake of mentioning these things after Michael kept pestering me for an honest opinion, and after three hours, a pitcher of sangria, and I lost track of how many bong hits later, I finally blurted out that their singer, Charlotte, had the charisma of a Post-it note, and the grating voice of a dentist's drill in her good moments, and Foghorn Leghorn[1] in her not so good moments, of which there were many. Or, at least, I choose to recall being that articulate about it, and therefore, that is what happened.

I had sort of become an unofficial member of the band – groupie is too vulgar a term, darlings, because I wasn't sleeping with any of them – yet – so I guess I was just one of those rock and roll cliché hangers-on. A modern day Penny Lane, as portrayed by the fabulous Kate Hudson in *Almost Famous*.[2] Except I wasn't seventeen anymore, and perhaps I should have been doing something more, something better with my life, but instead I spent my days working in the coolest record store in one of the coolest places in San Francisco, which is one of the coolest cities in the world, and hanging out with some pretty cool people, listening to their music, drinking their booze, smoking their pot, and...

And you know what – it was – what's the word I'm looking for? Oh yeah – cool. I was having the time of my life, and I regret nothing, darlings. Not even blurting out how awful I thought Charlotte was, despite the fact that she was sitting not three feet from me at the time.

Oops. What can I say, darlings? I was pretty far gone at the time.

Of course, a grand debacle ensued, and some ugly things were said about my virtue, none of which were true, at that point, and then Charlotte blurted out that Michael was in love with me, which he denied so vehemently that it very nearly hurt my feelings, darlings, honestly! Not least of all because I knew full well that he was. He had never made any profession of love, had never even made any moves on me – which is kind of what made me

---

[1] The giant rooster from the Warner Brothers cartoons with the Deep South Texas accent: *Ah say, Ah say boy...*

[2] A fantastic movie that is a fictionalized account of director Cameron Crowe's life as a writer for *Rolling Stone* magazine, and in particular, with his experience with the Allman Brothers Band.

comfortable with him – but I knew all the same. We spent a lot of time together, just the two of us – he'd take me on little exploring trips around the city, or take me hiking in Muir Woods, where he'd invariably tell me he spotted an Ewok[3] (he thought he was cute, darlings). I was comfortable with him because I thought I was sure of how things stood between us – that we were friends. I knew he had feelings for me, but I thought that he knew that I didn't return those feelings, and that he respected that. Okay, sure, we'd never actually talked about it, or even said any of those things aloud, but he should know, right? Oh, why do men have to be so obtuse!

Charlotte picked up the bong and threw it against the wall, where it smashed into a thousand rainbow coloured pieces, flooding the room with the skunky stink of bong-water and jealousy. She started crying and spraying a stream of unintelligible curses at nobody in particular, but I do recall my name being paired with such flattering phrases as *interloping cunt, talent-less cock-gobbler,* and my personal favourite, *that Canadian bitch.* Sean, the other guitarist in the band, told her to calm the fuck down, and let's talk about this, and Charlotte advised him to participate in a physically demanding if not biologically impossible act of sexual congress with himself, and then stormed out, declaring that she was quitting the band, and if they loved me so much, why didn't they just make me the singer.

Patrick and James, the drummer and bassist respectively, were passed out together in the back bedroom of James' apartment, where we invaded most nights after a show, so they weren't really part of the whole decision – that was all Sean and Michael, but neither were they too shaken up the next morning when they woke and were informed that I was now the lead singer of Quixotic Exotica.

And so began my brief, intimate foray as a performer in the world of rock and roll, instead of just arm candy for a narcissist, or a as just another screaming fan.

---

[3]Muir Woods, as you already know because I told you, is where they filmed the Endor scenes of *Return of the Jedi.* Just thought I'd remind you, darlings.

Night after night, the bouncers would look me up and down as I strutted past them, head high, simply oozing charisma and charm as I flirtatiously cooed, "I'm with the band."

lover, you should've come over

After one too many Greyhounds (the nectar of the gods, darlings – a combination of Grey Goose and grapefruit juice), I declared to the unsuspecting Countess Penelope of Arcadia that "I miss Jeff Buckley."

I know that it was one too many, because the line between somewhat slightly dazed and morosely maudlin and melancholy is one Greyhound too many, and measures roughly four ounces of vodka long by maybe six ounces of grapefruit juice wide. But I can't really be absolutely specific about that, darlings, because really, who measures?

"So call him up," the Countess said glibly. "Invite him over. Who is he, anyway? Some old flame you've never told me about?"

"Can't," I said, finishing my... I dunno... my latest Greyhound. "He's dead. He drowned. He's gone."

All the warmth seemed to have suddenly been sucked out of the room, and the Countess turned pale (well... paler). She came and wrapped her arms around me.

"Oh, I'm sorry, Helena, I didn't know. When did he die?"

I thought about it for a moment, and did the math in my head, which is more difficult than you'd think after... um... several Greyhounds.

"It'd be fifteen years last month. I don't know how I missed it, how I forgot, I just..."

"Fifteen years?" Penny blurted, letting go of me and looking at me like I'd just thrown up all over her (which, if I stood up too quickly, was not outside of the realm of possibility). "Fifteen years ago, some guy I've never heard you speak about dies, and you're, what is it you're doing, exactly? Drinking to his memory? Who was this guy, anyway?"

How did I explain Jeff Buckley to Penny?

I could say:

"Jeff Buckley was one of the great loves of my life. I was introduced to him when I was about twenty years old. I only knew him for two years before he drowned – a terrible, stupid accident – but I've never stopped loving him. I have loved others since, but every so often, I'll listen to his voice, and hear him sing all the old love songs, and dream of what might have been."

But that wouldn't really do him justice, and while it sounded good in my head, it'd probably come off as speechy if I actually said it.

"So who was he?" Penny asked again.

What would Penny say if I told her that I only knew him through his music, and that I had never actually met him; never even saw him play? Penny is a sweetheart, even more so when she is drunk, but stone sober she might just pat my head like I was a senile old bird and tuck me into bed with a patronizing kiss on the forehead. No, that would not do. I would just have to show her; to introduce her to Jeff and his music. So I took Penny by the hand, poured her a drink, and we sat in the living room in the dark and listened to *Live at Sin-é*– all of it. We marvelled together at his genius as a guitarist and as a singer, and laughed at what a ridiculous person he was in his between-song banter. Penny, to her credit (another reason I love her to pieces) never even gave me any shit about crying over a dead musician. She's cool that way.

We sat for the whole two and a half hours and drank some more, laughed some more, and I cried some more. By the time *Hallelujah* ended and the concert was over, even Penny was a little choked up.

"Okay" she said, fighting back a tear, "I get it. He was a beautiful person. Now, let's get you to bed, you sappy drunk."

***Note from your favourite dilettante: My darlings, Jeff Buckley really was a beautiful human being, and I remember his death affecting me terribly – more than any of those drug-related, rock and roll excess burn-outs that while tragic, were essentially self-inflicted. Jeff died going for a night swim after a long day recording what would be his unfinished second album. All accounts say that he was happy, and in a great mood, and when they did the autopsy, there were no drugs or alcohol found in his system, and there were no mysterious circumstances surrounding his untimely demise. The world really did lose something special when we lost Jeff. If you have never heard his music, you really owe it to yourself to correct that grievous oversight. If you don't ever read another word I write, at least listen to the song *Lover, You Should've Come Over*. Oh, and if you like Edgar Allan Poe, do yourself a favour and track down the wonderfully moody and creepy reading Jeff does of *Ulalume*, which you can find on the Interweb without too much trouble, I'm sure.

the smurfette of
star wars

"I'm bored," Penny complained. She'd been reading *The Bell Jar*, after admitting the other night during our monthly back-to-back screening of *Fight Club* and *American Beauty* that while she understood the reference Edward Norton's character makes ('In the Tibetan philosophy, Sylvia Plath sense of the word, we're all dying.'), she had never actually read her work.

I suggested that that might just be the most horrible thing I've ever heard. More horrible than hearing that LCD Soundsystem broke up, more horrible than hearing that someone green-lighted a second Fantastic Four movie, even more horrible than when I heard that Akiva Goldsman might be writing the adaption of Stephen King's *The Dark Tower* for the screen.

"Oh no!" Penny exclaimed in an exaggerated deadpan. "Surely not that horrible, Helena! And could you be any more esoteric?"

"I mean, sure," I replied, ignoring her, "he wrote *A Beautiful Mind*, but he also wrote *The DaVinci Code*, *Lost in Space*, and both *Batman Forever* and *Batman and Robin*, which is arguably the worst movie ever made, never mind the worst Batman movie ever made. So, yeah, that was some pretty horrible news – but this – (and yes, I know I'm taking a long time to come back to it) this is more horrible yet!"

And so Penny is reading *The Bell Jar*, and while she may be bored, I am just glad that she is not clinically depressed. Now next month when we have our screening of *American Beauty* and *Fight Club*, she will have a richer understanding. (What can I say? Some people go to church. Penny and I have our own rituals, and this is one of them. There is so much to glean from those movies, both separately and together, but back to back, you can really see how they complement each other perfectly, *Fight Club* the dark Yin to *American Beauty*'s Yang).

"Speaking of Batman," Penny said, reeling the conversation in to a manageable size, "Doesn't that whole Batman Year Zero thing start this week?"

"Only one way to find out," I said.

"Well, no, actually," Penny said, spoiling my cliché. "We could just go on the Internet, and..."

"*Only. One. Way. To. Find. Out.*" I reiterated in all italics, punctuated by grammatically incorrect periods between each word. Grammatically incorrect or not, Penny managed to take my meaning, and we were off to the comic book store.

As always, we were greeted by the disembodied voice of Dave as we walked in the door, but we had also walked in on a discussion – an actual heated discussion on whether Timothy Zahn's Thrawn trilogy[1] was actually Star Wars canon or not – something to do with the clone processing planet from Episode II throwing a big monkey wrench in the cloning technology suggested by Zahn's books. Suddenly and ill-advisedly, my favourite clerk James, well-meaning but clearly clueless when it came to the etiquette of never bringing a woman into an argument between two geeks about Star Wars, turned to me and said "Helena, back me up – tell this guy that none of the books are canon – Lucas said so, right?"

---

[1]Back in 1991, Timothy Zahn wrote the first of three books that pretty much re-launched the Star Wars franchise, and expanded its universe. It's likely that we wouldn't have the Star Wars prequels without this renewed interest, so I'm not sure if we should be thanking Mr. Zahn or hunting him down, covering him with honey, and leaving him on an anthill.

"Lucas can't even keep his own continuity straight," I remarked, off-handedly, "But leave me out of this – I don't even like those movies."

"What do you mean you don't like Star Wars?"The bespectacled Star Wars geek asked – the one who had been insisting that the Zahn trilogy was canon.

"Did I stutter?" I asked, channelling my inner Emilio Estevez.[2]

Flustered, Star Wars Geek (or SWG for short – Star Wars geeks love their short forms –ie. SW ANH, or SW ESB or SW ROTJ)[3] laughed, and said, "Oh, you don't like the prequels. I get it – Jar Jar Binks, Trade Federation – yeah, kinda hokey– but *Revenge of the Sith* kind of rocked, no?"

"Nope," I said plainly. "I can't stand the whole franchise. It's the most sexist universe in the history of cinema. Frankly, I don't even know how the galaxy is populated, with only one woman under the age of sixty, and hundreds of planets populated seemingly only by men.Face it – Princess Leia is pretty much the Smurfette[4] of Star Wars – just one of the boys, only with tits."

SWG snickered at my use of the word *tits*, and I could tell he wasn't taking me seriously.

"Laugh it up, fuzzball," I said, hoping to get his attention by quoting the one movie in the trilogy that had actual redemptive qualities, except... "Except that even in *Empire*, Leia's not much more than a foil for Han Solo – and her entire character is just there to be alternately abused or ignored by a loveable scoundrel (oh, that's original), and yet – and yet, when he's being lowered into the Carbonite, she declares her love for him, to which he replies?"

---

[2]A reference to a scene from *The Breakfast Club* where Judd Nelson and Emilio Estevez are having a Whose Dick is Bigger contest in the form of a Whose Life is Worse contest.

[3]That would be short for *Star Wars: A New Hope*, *Empire Strikes Back*, and *Return of the Jedi* respectively.

[4]The female character – wait – do I seriously need to explain who Smurfette is? Suffice to say, she wasn't even a real Smurf – if you'll recall (or need me to recall for you) Gargamel created Smurfette as a trap for the male Smurfs – which makes no sense – the Smurfs couldn't be male, otherwise, how does their species procreate? Ergo they must be hermaphroditic, and therefore would not be attracted to a female. It'd be like a worm wanting to get it on with a female mantis. But I digress.

"I know," both SWG and James quoted in unison. I knew I could count on them.

"Right," I said. "Leia the doormat, Leia the sexist plaything – and I'm not even going to get into the gold lame bikini Leia of *Return of the Jedi.* I mean, all three movies, she's scowling the whole time, and yet she's got both the charming, loveable rogue and her annoying, whiney brother sniffing around her like a couple of dogs after a good bone. Yeah, that sounds about right. What do you think, Penny?"

The Countess Penelope of Arcadia took my inclusion of her as an invitation to bring out the Dickensian street urchin.

"Thass right, milords 'n ladyship. Iss loik, she don't really 'ave any real personality of 'er own, loik. Well, iss loik she's just one'a those, whatchecallits, archy-types, ennit? Just loik in that there Twi-loit book. Why, she's no different than that Bella Swan bird!"[5]

The SWG actually recoiled – physically recoiled in horror at that statement.

"You know, Countess, I think you may be on to something there," I said, goading her on. "Please, do continue. If Leia is Bella, then, pray tell – which one is Edward and which is Jacob?"[6]

"Out!" James said firmly. "Both of you, get out of the store right now! For your own good! Run! Run while you can!"

And run we did, darlings, as a crowd of grown men in T-shirts chased us out of the store with lightsabers raised (the Jedi version of torches and pitchforks) in righteous (I was going to say anger, but isn't anger the path to the Dark Side?) irritation.

I was going to buy the last couple of issues I'd missed of *The Unwritten,* by Mike Carey and Peter Gross (another great read,

---

[5]Penny is referring to *Twilight,* by Stephanie Meyer.
[6]In case you're not aware – Edward the vampire and Jacob the werewolf, in a love triangle with a girl with the personality of a used Kleenex in the *Twilight* series of books.

darlings, and I highly recommend it) but I guess I'll wait for the trade – I'm still welcome on Amazon.

schrodingers rabbit - the california years part five

I am a huge Neil Gaiman fan, darlings, and if you're not, well, what are you reading? Even his children's books (that is, his books written for children, not books written by his children for any of you English majors who caught that faux-pas and are currently clucking your tongues at me for how very long this parenthesis is getting) are wildly amusing, particularly if they are illustrated by his frequent collaborator, the incomparable Dave McKean. One of his books, *The Wolves in the Walls* has a repeated refrain of *When the Wolves come out of the walls, it's all over!*

Well, darlings, when the man who secretly (or perhaps not so secretly) loves you catches you in bed with some other man who really doesn't give a toss about you, but the two of you just happened to be drunk enough and horny enough and unclothed enough to end up in bed together, it's all over.

If the man in question in the previous equation (let's call him A) is the rhythm guitarist in the same band as the second man (called for the sake of argument B), and man B knew full well that man A was in love with you, had in fact spent many nights lamenting to man B that he was so heartsick over you, and yet, man B goes ahead and sleeps with you anyway – it's all over.

If man A leaves San Francisco bound for Sacramento on a train going 60 mph, and man B leaves the bar with woman C, ambling drunkenly at 1.4 mph, how long will it take until woman C is performing page 58 of the Kama Sutra with man B on the floor of man A's studio apartment because it was closer than man B's place, and besides, he was going to be gone all night at his sister's in Sacramento? Second part: from this position, how many moves will it take in order to successfully form the astrological symbol for Cancer? Solve for XXX.[1]

If you take into consideration that these two are at right angles to each other, and that I (represented by C) am the common denominator, then it is clear to see, by any logical person with a basic understanding of Pythagorean Theorem, that the square of the hypotenuse of any right triangle is equal to the sum of the squares of the other two sides. Or, expressed by this equation, $A^2 + B^2 = C^2$,[2] you can deduce that Helena is a completely heartless bitch with no regard for anyone's feelings but her own, and that she knew how Michael felt about her, and did she give any thought to how this was going to affect the band, and Sean'll fuck anything breathing, and…

And I pretty much tuned them out by that point, because I had other concerns that morning after Michael caught me in bed with Sean that were much bigger than breaking up the band, or breaking Michael's heart, but rather, they were about breaking a promise to myself.

It really all depended on whether Schrödinger's Rabbit was alive or dead.

Two weeks earlier, Michael had asked me if I'd ever been to Lake Tahoe, and I said that I hadn't, and, of course, he asked,

---

[1] I told you that I was shit at maths, darlings. I always loathed these types of problems, and so if I've confused you, don't worry – it was intentional. Incidentally, the astrological symbol for Cancer is 69. Does that make more sense now?

[2] Pythagorean Theorem is the only mathematical theorem that I really remember, and that only because it is what the Scarecrow recites right after he gets his brain to prove that he is smart. Go ahead – go watch *The Wizard of Oz* so you can have that 'a-ha!' moment.

would I like to go, and I said that yes I would love to go, and so we went.

There are two things that I can tell you about Lake Tahoe, darlings. The first is that Lake Tahoe is one of the most beautiful places I've ever seen. The mountain roads are amazing, and the glacier fed water is crystal clear, and sparkles in the sunlight, and the sunrise over the lake seen from a hotel balcony on the west side of the lake is like nothing you'll ever experience. The second thing I can tell you about Lake Tahoe is that I never want to go back there again.

Michael and I had been spending a lot of time together, as I may have previously mentioned, but, as I also said, I thought that we were clear on the nature of our friendship. Now, I say friendship specifically as opposed to relationship, because that always tends to imply romantic attachment.

It's not that Michael wasn't nice, or attractive, or kind – he was. Michael was very sweet. He's the kind of guy who will open doors for you, and get you your drinks, and give you a back rub at the end of a hard day, and every other thing that women say that they want in a man. Michael would have done anything for me, and if I feel badly about anything at all, it's that I didn't put an end to his puppy dog ways before things got out of hand. Because essentially, that's what Michael was – a puppy dog. I could have asked Michael to jump in front of a bus for me and he would have done it gladly – and that kind of loyalty is not attractive, it's just clingy and needy and you can never live up to it. As a good friend of mine once said, you can't respect somebody who kisses your ass. He also said that life moves pretty fast, and that if you don't stop and look around once in a while, you could miss it. He was right on both accounts, and his advice hasn't let me down yet.[3]

When Michael and I arrived at Lake Tahoe, it was early evening, and so we stopped at a tiny little taqueria in South Lake Tahoe for some dinner – they had the best pico de gallo I've ever eaten – and yes, darlings, I know that there's really nothing special about pico de gallo, but they must have just had the freshest, tastiest tomatoes, onions, and cilantro imaginable, because I still compare

---

[3]More gems of wisdom from the great Ferris Bueller.

any pico I've eaten since to that little hole-in-the-wall taco shack in South Lake.

Afterwards, I asked him if he wanted me to drive back to San Francisco – it was about a four hour drive and Michael had driven there, so I thought it only polite for me to return the favour – I am nothing if not polite, darlings. But it appeared that Michael had other plans, as he pulled into a rustic looking motel.

"I thought we could stay the night, and then go exploring tomorrow," he said nonchalantly. (Can someone say something chalantly? Is that even a thing?)

I looked at him dubiously. He smiled back like a cat that's just gotten laid, and then had an entire pitcher of cream.

"Maybe we could go check out Reno," he continued after I had said nothing, which he took as consent. This would be only the first such assumption he made that evening.

I had enjoyed Tahoe up until that point, and the thought of spending another entire day there sounded wonderful, and so I gave in.

"Okay, but no funny business," I teased him. In retrospect, I should have been firmer with him, but one does not simply find oneself suddenly in the midst of trouble. Trouble is always achieved in steps, or degrees. Whenever I look back at bad situations I've been in, I can usually trace back the steps to discover where I first stepped on the path to destruction. The tragedy is that I can also generally spot several points along the way where I could have stepped off and saved myself a lot of heartache, but you know what they say – hindsight shows objects closer than they actually appear – or something like that. I figure if you're always looking backwards, you're bound to bump into a lot of shit, and so I tend to keep moving forward.

Michael assured me that there would be no funny business, but the further along the evening went, the funnier the business got. I mean, it was downright fucking hilarious when we stepped into our hotel room, where it became bloody obvious to me that this whole affair had been meticulously planned. Champagne doesn't uncork itself, Brie and crackers don't magically appear, and unless there's a Jacuzzi fairy somewhere that no one told me about, that was arranged beforehand, too. All that was missing was some smooth jazz and a smoking jacket-wearing Hugh Hefner for it to be a scene from the Playboy mansion.

"I wanted this to be a surprise," Michael said, barely containing his excitement.

"Oh, I'm surprised," I said, heart pounding in my chest, a mixture of nerves and anger. Nerves because I knew what was expected of me, and I was incredibly conflicted about that, and anger that he put me in this situation; that he was making me feel this way.

I was angry with Michael for putting me in this position, and I was angry with myself for believing that he could respect me, and for allowing myself to be put in this situation. I was angry and I felt guilty for not loving him the way that he loved me. And so I fucked him. I fucked him, and it wasn't rape, because I said yes, and I let it happen, but it wasn't making love, either, and if you've ever fucked someone because you felt guilty or pressured or obligated, you'll know that it still feels like a violation. And in this case, I earned my self-loathing, because I let it happen.

Michael was delighted – he'd gotten what he'd wanted for months, and all he could talk about was how long he'd wanted me, how hard it was to be near me without touching me, holding me, kissing me, and all kinds of other obsessive bullshit. He was so wrapped up in himself that he was completely oblivious to how I felt.

Michael got in the Jacuzzi and invited me to join him. I said that I might take a bath later, but right now I just wanted to sleep. He made some crack about me being all worn out after what he referred to as the best sex of his life, and I sighed and purred like the porn star he wanted me to act like at that moment and told him that must be it.

When we left in the morning, my hatred for him had only just begun to grow. Two weeks later, after I'd been discovered in flagrant embrace with Sean, I'd tried to tell Michael that I never meant to hurt him, and that it was a stupid, drunken accident, but even as the words dripped out of my mouth, part of me knew that I was lying. Men aren't the only ones that can use sex as a weapon.

My fear that morning, as I sat alone in the bathroom, where such feminine rituals are oft performed, was that something else had begun to grow.

Was the rabbit dead or alive?[4] Until I looked, it was like Schrödinger's Cat[5]— either possibility was equally valid.

I sat thinking about the promise I had silently made to myself after a pregnancy scare a few years earlier. I promised myself that I would never have a baby with someone I didn't love. I promised myself that I would never become trapped by motherhood and be a miserable person and therefore a miserable mother. These are the promises I made to myself.

Then the two lines went blue, Schrödinger's Rabbit died, and all my promises went out the window. Because when Schrödinger's Rabbit dies, it's all over.

---

[4]In the early Twentieth Century, scientists used to inject the urine of a pregnant woman into a rabbit, and if the woman was indeed pregnant, it would cause haemorrhages on the rabbit's ovaries – of course, you'd have to kill the rabbit to find this out – so, if the rabbit dies, then the woman's pregnant. Actually, if you think about it, it's kind of a poor analogy – because you have to kill the rabbit either way to find out. But work with me here.

[5]Erwin Schrödinger devised a hypothetical thought experiment involving a cat locked in a box, which has become synonymous with any situation where two or more possible outcomes can only be determined when one 'opens the box'. In the specific example of Schrödinger's Cat, the cat can be alive or the cat can be dead, but until open the box, the cat is understood to be both. I'm actually reducing this to its most absurd understanding, but you get the point.

quentin tarantino & oliver stone present: natural born smurfers

"**I** don't think I like this Jessica[1] broad very much," the Countess Penelope of Arcadia said bluntly, tossing the half-unread draft of a horror story I've been writing at me.

"What?" I asked, perplexed beyond the pale. I was quite sure that Penny would love *The Best Medicine*.[2]

"Can't you just write something happy? You know, something where two people meet, fall in love, and die many years later of old age in their sleep, curled up together in their bed?"

"What's wrong with what I wrote?" I asked, honestly baffled by this point.

"She was only twelve years old, Helena! What'd she ever do to you that you would [spoilers] and then right in front of her mother, you let [more spoilers] and then that bloody handprint, why, that's just a slap in the face, and then, on top of that [sorry, you're just going to have to wait for it to be published!] —it's just wrong! People are going to think that you're miserable or depressed, or that I'm a horrible burden on you and that you hate me, and..."

---

[1]Jessica B. Bell is a pseudonym I use when writing fiction. Jessica tends to write dark and creepy stories where bad things happen to nice people.
[2]I've included this story in the bonus materials section at the back of the book

"And you're getting your period, aren't you?" I asked indelicately.

"OH!" Penny gasped. "That's just... that's just dismissive and... and..."

"And?" I asked.

"And yes I am, okay?" Penny burst into tears. "She was only twelve years old, Helena? How could you do that to a little girl?"

"Shh," I said, giving her a hug and rubbing her back like I've done for her since she was little and needed comforting. "You want some ice cream?"

"Uh huh," she nodded, looking very much like the little girl who'd once accidentally set her cat on fire and brought a very smelly, very frightened and very pissed off kitty to me and begged me to a) not tell her Mom, and b) make everything better. We had ice cream that day, which, in my experience, makes everything a little better.

"What kinds do we have?" She asked, sniffling.

"Let me see," I said, digging in the freezer and pulling out two containers. "We've got Death by Caffeine, or... For Unlawful Caramel Knowledge."

"Can I have a scoop of each?" The Countess Penelope of Arcadia asked sheepishly, batting her eyes at me. As she had been crying, and her mascara had run, it didn't have the effect on me that she had hoped. She kind of looked like Alice Cooper with something caught in his eye. I laughed at the image, and Penny pouted pathetically.

"Sure thing, darling. Anything for Alice."

She shot me a funny look and I brushed it off. I scooped her some ice cream, and some for myself, and then retired for the evening.

———

I'm not much of a Tweeter, but for some reason, the mood struck me (especially after the events prior to going to bed) and so I sent a message saying that Penny was angry with me about *The Best Medicine*. This got the response that perhaps I should write a nice story for Penny. And I thought, sure, why not? I can do that, no problem. But what to write? Ah well, I figured I'd sleep on it and something would come to me later.

Well, the next day, I got a suggestion from the very picture of pixie-osity herself with her tightly cropped coiffure[3] that perhaps pixie dust and Smurfette's breasts were the safest, most inoffensive topics that I could craft a tale around. Surely there was no way that I could twist something so sweet, pure and innocent into something sordid and sinful.

Not so, dear readers, not so. And so, in association with Quentin Tarantino & Oliver Stone (or at least, I'm sure they'd associate themselves with this if they knew anything about it), I present: Natural Born Smurfers,[4] starring Woody Harrelson as Dopey and Juliette Lewis as Smurfette. Special Appearance by Rodney Dangerfield as Smurfette's father.

Smurfette fell in with Dopey because he was wild, and brash, and impulsive – everything her father hated. And he always had the best shit – hence the name Dopey. Smurfette was raised in a strict religious home, where she was often subjected to punishments of a physical nature from her father, who seemed to enjoy spanking her for such offenses as wearing her shorts too short, or her shirt too tight, or for taking too long in the shower. Dopey rode into her life on a Harley Davidson flathead one day, a pack of Marlboros rolled up in the sleeve of his plain white T-shirt, his Wayfarers hiding his crazy eyes, and shot her father right between the eyes.

"Hop on, baby," Dopey drawled.

"Oh my smurfing God! You shot him!" Smurfette screamed, but was smiling. "You shot him right between his smurfing eyes!"

"You're smurfing right I did, baby," Dopey said. "Now are you getting on this smurfing bike or not?"

---

[3]This would be Jennie Saia, who is an excellent writer, critic, and all around nice lady. You can find her writing at http://jenniesaia.wordpress.com/
[4]This is, of course, a spoof of the movie *Natural Born Killers*.

"Smurf yeah!" Smurfette yelled in triumph, and got on the bike behind Dopey, wrapping her arms tightly around him as they sped off.

Back at Dopey's place, Smurfette lay on the couch smoking a big fat smurf, the world melting around her and her head expanding and spinning.

Dopey came back into the room with a small baggie of some kind of sparkly powder. Smurfette grinned greedily at him.

"Ooh," she said, purring smurfily. "What's that?"

"Pixie dust, baby," Dopey said. "Pure pixie dust. You ever smurf someone on pixie dust? You ain't never smurfed until you've smurfed on pixie dust. I'm telling you, my smurf's gonna be rock hard, and I'm gonna smurf you until you smurf, and then I'm gonna smurf you some more. You're going to smurfgasm like you've never dreamed possible."

Dopey cut open the baggie and poured a little on Smurfette's breast, then bent to snort the dust off it, giving her blue nipple a little lick as he did so. Smurfette moaned, and...

"Oh, you've got to be kidding me!" The Countess Penelope interjected. "You just couldn't do it, could you? Ooh, I will kill you! There will be death, and pain, and your stupid face on Missing Persons posters! You couldn't just write something nice, like, I don't know, *The Notebook*[5] or something?"

"You like *The Notebook*?" I asked, nearly laughing.

"No," she protested. "Yes, I like *The Notebook*, okay? Are you happy?"

"Yes," I laughed. "Yes I am."

"Well, you'd never know it by reading that miserable shit you write!" Penny accused.

---

[5]*The Notebook* is a book by Nicholas Sparks that was then turned into a movie, and it's a romantic tearjerker chock full of unapologetic sentimentality. Some things are just designed to make you cry. Hollywood is full of sadists, and movie-goers (particularly us women, it seems) are emotional masochists.

I ignored her, and reached out for another hug. She complied; crying into my favourite old concert T-shirt – a Ben Folds from 2003 with the inflammatory ROCK THIS BITCH slogan – and I asked her if there was something else bothering her, or if was really just the story and her raging hormones.

"I miss them," Penny finally admitted, and nothing else needed to be said.

I let her cry, holding her tight, and even shed a few tears myself.
"Can I have some more ice cream?" She asked eventually.

I laughed at her asking me for permission, and reached out with the tail of my T-shirt and wiped her racoon eyes.

"You're a grown-ass woman; you can do what you like." I said, and the spoken statement filled me with a strange fear of loss; the knowledge that someday (and really, it could happen at any time) Penny would leave. She'd meet some boy and move out, or she'd find some job and move away, or she'd simply just grow tired of my face and move out, and our dynamic duo would come to an end.[6]

Suddenly, I was also very sad.

"Can I have some, too?" I asked.

---

[6]Where did *that* come from? I don't know, darlings. This one was a rollercoaster, that's for sure.

losing my religion[1]
(a halesowen adventure)

*O*h, distinctly I remember, it was in the bleak November...[2]

I remember, because it was right around the time of Thanksgiving (for Americans, anyway)[3] and some ignorant American asked why they didn't celebrate Thanksgiving in England, and I just couldn't stop from laughing myself into a frothy-mouthed frenzy, which gained me looks of equal parts disappointment and concern.

Now, I need to back up a minute and stress that I used the qualifier ignorant *plus* American to indicate that it was an ignorant American, not that all Americans are ignorant. I feel that is an important distinction to make, as I have many American friends, and most of them are not ignorant. Again, I used the qualifier most because, well, most is not the same as all. It's just that for some reason, Americans abroad (especially if it's their first time abroad) are so prone to putting their feet in their mouths, and I can't help

---

[1] A reference to the song by R.E.M., 1991
[2] From *The Raven* by Edgar Allan Poe, 1845
[3] American Thanksgiving is in November, whereas Canadians celebrate Thanksgiving in October.

but find it hilarious. You'll excuse my laughter at your expense, darlings.

It just got funnier when the poor Yank didn't have the good sense to quit, and was getting quite upset at being laughed at. He just kept asking *No, I'm serious – why don't they celebrate Thanksgiving here? It's a Christian holiday. It's a time to thank God for all the blessings throughout the year.*

I'm not ashamed to say that I just kept laughing until tears were streaming down my face and I was hyperventilating and turning purple in the face.

When I finally calmed down, I said that I thought it was a bloody good idea, and that they *should* celebrate Thanksgiving in England.

A sweet but irritating girl named Claire chastised me for the use of the word 'bloody' and begged me not to use it again. I confess I intentionally used it around Claire because it was really the only way I could wind her up – but more on that later.

"Thanksgiving," I said, in a mock reverent tone. "A time to be thankful and remember that time where we kicked all the crazy religious nutters off the island!"

Considering that I was, at that time, surrounded by crazy religious nutters, my sentiment didn't go over very well.

Now, I've done some travelling, darlings, and I've come across various degrees of religious belief, some of it benign, and some of it bordering on psychotic, and I've always teetered back and forth between seeing the very religious as well-meaning if a bit obsessive and, on the other end of the spectrum, delusional and dangerous. And I'm not just talking about Evangelicals[4] here, though this tale I'm about to tell you if you've made it this far (welcome – pull up a chair, pour yourself some tea – I believe there may still be some Bourbon biscuits[5] left) is indeed about a damn near militant

---

[4]When I say Evangelicals, I refer to Protestant Christianity missionary types.
[5]Bourbon biscuits are cookies that I discovered while in England, and have loved ever since. Two dark chocolate cookies with chocolate fondant in the middle. Lovely.

evangelical organization which I shall, respectfully, leave nameless. But no, it's not just Evangelicals – why, one time I was accosted by a Muslim who told me in no uncertain terms that I was going to hell because I paid too much interest on my bank loans.[6] (And here, all the time, I thought it was because I drank too much and enjoy showing off my killer gams – but when you've got legs like mine, darlings, you don't keep them hidden behind ankle length dresses!)

And speaking of Muslims, it was a Thursday in November, and I remember this, because Thursdays were Muslim evangelism days. Monday was Hindu evangelism, Tuesday we converted the Pagans, Wednesday was Sikhs, Thursday Muslims, and Friday, we focused on all those nice folks who aligned themselves with the Church of England, because they weren't *really* Christians anyway.

So, Thursdays we sat in a seminar where some teacher would give us a history lesson on Islam, and what its teachings were, and why they were wrong, and how best to show any of the nice Muslim people that we met how and why they were wrong and why we were right, and it was all very patronizing and I really didn't want any part of it. Don't get me wrong, darlings, some of it was interesting – I found the history fascinating, and the timeline of events where certain doctrines or beliefs came into being, and how certain dogmas split churches, and the ways in which Islam was related to Judaism and Christianity.[7] From an intellectual standpoint, or even a philosophical one, it was engaging. But then it got into strategies and tactics complete with handouts and pamphlets on *How To Witness To A Muslim Man* (and its counterpart, *How To Witness To A Muslim Woman*). They'd talk about culture and etiquette, which was fine, but then they'd talk about overcoming objections, and when to listen for the ASK moment, and it all seemed very used car salesman-esque to me. A couple of years later,

---

[6]According to this man, the person who pays too much interest is the greater sinner than the one who charges it. Not sure about the validity of this claim, it's just what he told me. Seems in line with the patriarchal idea that the person getting fucked is the bigger whore than the one doing the fucking, though.

[7]When you realize that three of the world's biggest religions hate each other and can't agree on philosophy based on a 2000 year old game of Telephone gone awry, it makes you shake your head a little bit. One of the things I remember was something about a church that started a doctrine that described the Trinity as God the Father, Mary the Mother, and Jesus the Son, which apparently offended people so much that they killed a bunch of people over it. But I'm no religious scholar, darlings, I'm merely commenting on my observations and opinions.

I took a shit telemarketing job trying to sell magazine subscriptions or some nonsense, and they trained us using the same model.

I'm sorry (apologize for upsetting/challenging their beliefs) I understand how you feel (express empathy), I have felt the same way (make it personal) but what I found was...(make your sales pitch), and that's why I subscribe to Jesus Magazine.

So, apparently, God uses a basic sales/marketing strategy.

Our teacher was an American from some east coast state like Maryland, or maybe it was Virginia – I don't remember exactly, but he had a nasal Yankee drawl of an accent, was a big Jerry Falwell[8] fan, and was generally opposed to interracial marriages – but wasn't from a state that was so far south that he said y'all or spoke like Foghorn Leghorn. He smiled too much to be trusted, and was always telling me that I needed to dress more ladylike, especially on Thursdays, when we were doing Muslim evangelism, because (and I quote) "Those Muslim men have no respect for women, and they've got it in their minds that all white girls are whores."[9]

He was a literal bible-thumper, and liked to slap his hand down on his big black Bible to emphasize his point. He reminded me of a high school basketball coach giving a pep talk, or a general giving a rallying speech to his troops before a big battle. Well, really, he reminded me of movies I've seen of those things, because I was certainly never on the high school basketball team. As if.

Before we'd go out, he would lead us in a prayer – well, he would start, and other people would pipe in. This particular day I will never forget, because it was so surreal and comedic that nothing I could ever invent, exaggerate or embellish could ever come close to matching how terrifyingly depressing and hilarious this was. In fact, looking back, I think I can pinpoint this moment as the very one that forever killed any hope I may have ever held

---

[8]Southern Baptist televangelist infamous for co-founding the Moral Majority, and for attacks on homosexuals, whom he blamed for pretty much all of society's ills, up to and including the terrorist attacks of September 11,2001. He had a tendency to feel that he actually spoke for God, even when he was attacking such benign and banal things as Teletubbies.

[9]Is it only me that thinks that people have been saying this about whatever group is the subject of their ire forever? As in, substitute the word Muslim for whatever group you want, and it's really the same ignorant spiel?

for organized religion. Don't get me wrong – I still hold out a flicker of hope that there is a God, because there are some very long conversations I'd like to have with her, but this particular day was the final nail in organized religion's coffin for me.

"Dear Lord," he prayed, "thank you for the wisdom you've given us. Thank you for your Word, which is the Truth, and will surely win all victories. Thank you for showing us how to pierce the armour of the enemy, and overcome their brainwashing and their lies. Heavenly Father, help us to apply what we have learned here today, that we might win souls out of Satan's grasp..."

At this point, a small, warbling voice spoke up. I knew immediately that it was Claire, because just the sound of her voice made me want to beat her over the head with a shovel. She took exception to *everything*, and so you can only imagine that she and I got along like bees and honey. I mean, I'm sure her parents loved her and everything, but she took everything so bloody seriously that I wanted to smack her on a daily basis. But here's the rub – you couldn't be mean to Claire. No, nobody could say shit about Claire, because Claire was a miracle child. Claire had just gotten over cancer and had decided to dedicate the rest of her life to Evangelism. (Actually, I do believe that she had stopped medical treatment as she claimed that she had been healed of her cancer and – sorry to say this, and it doesn't really affect the story at all, but I thought you should know – Claire died about three months after I went home, so, proponents of faith healers, all offense intended, you can go to hell).

So Claire was our resident saint, and nobody was cruel enough to say *Boo* to Claire, not even much younger, much brasher, even, I dare say, much ruder me. So Claire was allowed to express her distaste for my clothes, or my music, or to question why I was there in the first place (implying that I didn't belong there, which, for some reason, I took offense to, though I'm not really sure why) and I just smiled and let it slide. Even Claire's prayer contributions could be considered argumentative and disagreeable. Case in point:

"Dear Lord," Claire warbled in her Channel Islands accent that to me will always be the voice of patronizing condescension. If you look up patronizing or condescension in the dictionary, as you open the book, Claire's voice will read out the definition for you. Don't ask me how that works, but try it sometime. If it doesn't work, take your dictionary back to the store for a full refund. Tell them Helena sent you – don't worry, they'll know who you mean. "Dear, dear Lord. As Your Word says, *Lean not on your own understanding, for I will direct your paths.* Father, let us humble ourselves, and not be so proud of this petty knowledge that we have gained here today – for does Your Word not also say: *Professing to be wise, they became as fools?* No, Lord, let us cast off all earthly knowledge, and instead be led by Your Spirit, and let you give us the words to say to convince the stony hearts of the Muslims. Amen."

Now, if you're thinking that this was a little more conversational than the prayer you've encountered, just keep reading, darlings, because while I was biting my lip at this point, it was about to get even more ridiculous.

"Oh Lord," the teacher replied – and I said replied, because at this point, it was pretty clear (to me, at least) that God was no longer the intended recipient of his prayer. "Let it be a combination of the two, Lord – let us both use what we have learned, but show true wisdom by allowing Your Spirit to guide our own hearts and give words to our tongues."

"Oh Lord!" I blurted, and every head popped up, every eye opened and looked my way. I was uncharacteristically quiet during these prayer sessions we had, and when I'd been previously pressed about it, I explained that I just would rather internalize my thoughts, and that I wasn't comfortable praying out loud. They seemed to buy it, so when I blurted this out I think that they thought I was about to burst into tongues, or start prophesying or something.[10] Instead, I just stood up, shook my head sadly, and

---

[10]Interesting side note: I don't know if you've ever been around people who 'speak in tongues' or if you are familiar with the phenomenon, but it fascinated me, and so I started asking various people about it in hope of understanding it. Maybe one day I'll tell that whole tale, but for now, try to wrap your head around the idea of someone trying to teach me how to do it. And here I thought it was a supernatural gift, not something you could learn by ordering a kit from Rosetta Stone (a language school, in case you didn't know).

stormed out of the room. I just couldn't grasp how incredibly fickle and stupid and petty it all was. How arrogant and presumptuous and even hateful at times. And this – this is what they were trying to sell?

Well, it was no wonder, then, that they had to use the same sales and marketing lies and trickery as those charlatans selling fake, plastic, and ultimately disposable shit on late night TV infomercials.

I wouldn't exactly say that I had faith, and that this was my long dark night of the soul, but I had wanted to believe – or at least, I think I wanted to believe. But after that day, I didn't even want that anymore.

I crawled into bed and pulled the covers over my head. I spent the rest of the day writing horrible poetry and trying to capture the moment by drawing a self-portrait. I'm pretty sure the portrait itself is long lost, but I remember the title:

Portrait of a Lost Girl - Disillusioned at Seventeen.

laid
(a halesowen adventure)

*B*rothers and sisters, I went to the mountaintop, and there I did pray. Oh Lord! Oh Lordy, Lordy, Lordy! How did I get myself into such consternation as this?

And the Lord did say unto his humble servant, Yea, verrily, thou art a fool in love...

Well, darlings, it was either God or Joe Jackson. (See, 'cause Joe Jackson has this great song called *Fools in Love*... oh, never mind).

I wasn't actually on the mountaintop, darlings, I was on the top bunk in the bedroom I shared with five other girls in the small town in the West Midlands of England, where I found myself marooned for four months during my seventeenth year. I was crying, as I seemed to do a little more each day while I was there. One of my favourite characters in all of literature introduces herself as 'seventeen and crazy'[1] and that was me, darlings. Most of the time it was just a youthful mania, mixed with an eccentric quirkiness that I am delighted to say that my lovely niece, the Countess Penelope of Arcadia, has inherited in spades. But as any manic maniac will tell

---

[1]Clarisse McLellan from *Fahrenheit 451*, in case you'd forgotten.

241

you, the crashes are intensely awful, and by about month three in the madhouse that was my home in Albion fair, I had days where I had honestly begun to doubt my own sanity. And at seventeen, with the imagination that I had, and the films that I'd watched, I had dark and terrible fantasies about being chained to some ECT table in some dungeon-like asylum where mad doctors performed unethical experiments on me. Shock treatments on Mondays, ice cold water immersion on Tuesdays, sleep deprivation experiments on Wednesdays, Rorschach interpretations on Thursdays, followed up by an experimental lobotomy on Friday. I figured by the weekend, I'd be locked away in a straitjacket drooling and incoherent, covered in my own filth and listening to the Joker cackle in the adjacent cell about how it was the Batman that was the crazy one, not him.[2]

Of course, it didn't help that I was constantly bombarded by people either honestly trying to comfort and help me through what was turning into an awful experience, or by people whose concern was more heavy-handed. These are the ones who were convinced that I had a demon in me, or at the very least was demonically oppressed. I had one girl try to teach me how to speak in tongues as a way to channel the Holy Spirit and cleanse me of my darkness.

But I had put myself there, darlings, and so I am the only one to blame. And how did I get there? Well, it is safe to say that there was a boy involved, and the fact that I desperately wanted to get away from my parents was a factor as well, but the specific geography of my exile in Halesowen was directly attributable to a boy that I followed home, as if I were some stray kitten. It was another boy, however, that had me crying in my bunk that day. And to think that the day had started out so well.

I had met James about a week before, after Andrew had told me that he wasn't allowed to spend time with me anymore –

---

[2]Grant Morrison and Dave McKean's *Arkham Asylum: A Serious House on Serious Earth* (1989) had come out a few years earlier and had made a huge impact on me – in fact, it's the first comic book I ever fell in love with, and is pretty much responsible for my love of the medium to this day. Not only did Grant Morrison change the game for storytelling and comics, but this book also introduced me to the work of Dave McKean, who challenged what was possible in the realm of graphic novels. It's brilliant and dark and twisted and if you haven't read it already I give you thirty days in which to procure a copy and send me a review or we are no longer friends, darlings.

something about a policy that the organization had that forbade dating – and I had needed a shoulder to cry on.

James had a broken arm, and not just a little wrist cast, either. It was one of those L-shaped deals with metal pins in the elbow for support. Someone had painted the Manchester United[3] red devil on it, and someone else had drawn in a cigarette in the devil's mouth. He'd been hit by a car, he said. I imagined that he'd been rescuing some little old lady who had a lorry bearing down on her, and James swooped in and pushed her out of the way, sacrificing his young, strong body to save an innocent life. In my mind, the first words out of his lips as the paramedics arrived would be to ask if the dear old woman was okay, and the papers would feature his picture on the front page with the words "LOCAL HERO WILL LIVE" with a by-line showing the smiling old lady with her cat, saying that when he gets out of the hospital, she'd simply love to have him 'round for tea.

Of course, that was all in my head, and I had been smitten with this boy from the first moment I heard his voice. His voice had all the dulcet tones of my beloved Morrissey. James didn't just support Manchester United, he was actually from the land of Stone Roses, Inspiral Carpets, Happy Mondays, and most importantly, Smiths. Now, if you don't realize that I am talking about bands, then I suggest you do yourself some musical archaeology and check these out. I was just amazed, as if it were the greatest thing in the world that he came from the same town as my musical heartthrob. James was somewhat less excited, but he liked to laugh at my excitement.

I was a ridiculous girl, and could listen to him talk for hours on end. And when he'd stop talking, I'd tell him to say something else.

"Like what?" He'd ask, smiling in exasperation.

And I'd say: "Um, say I'm the Last of the Famous International Playboys."[4] Or some other Morrissey related line.

---

[3]Manchester United is a football (that's soccer in North America) club, whose colours are red and gold and whose logo is a red devil/dragon carrying a trident.
[4]The title of a song my Morrissey, who was the lead singer of The Smiths, but then, you already knew that if you've gotten this far, darlings.

I'd sneak off to meet him on the pretence that I was helping his mother, who was in a wheelchair (I can't remember exactly whether it was Cerebral Palsy or Spina Bifida, but his mum was the sweetest lady I ever met, and she knew exactly what was going on – she kept warning me that if broke her little boy's heart that she was going to get out of her chair and kick my ass until I bled maple syrup. She thought my being Canadian was just the funniest thing in the whole world). When his mum wasn't in the room, we were physically inseparable, and, if I am truthful, it was James who really taught me how to kiss. Prior to that, I really had no technique, but James, well, he made my toes tingle, and I had to keep up or else risk being discovered as a rank amateur in the field of tongue-tangling.

Two days prior to the opening of this story (if you need a quick recap, it's quite simple, darlings – I was crying on my bed, listening to R.E.M.'s *Automatic for the People*, which was huge at that time, and rewinding *Everybody Hurts* and listening to it again and again on my Walkman. Yes, that's right – James is going to break my heart. Is that really a surprise? Should I have shouted SPOILERS?) James and I were walking to The Cornbow to go to the record store to pick up "The new album by James," he said, and the statement made no sense to me.

"C'mon," he said in his dreamy voice, "let's go get Laid by James."

I looked at him out of the corner of my eye and grinned. He turned an amusing shade of purple and then burst out laughing. He grabbed my hand and said he had to show me something.

"I'll bet," I said, and he just kept laughing.
"Nothing like that, you cheeky tart," he said teasingly, and as we turned a corner, I saw what he wanted to show me, and wondered how I possibly could have missed it before. It was lit up by the sun in a single spotlight ray, and I do believe I heard a choir of heavenly angels singing the falsetto refrain of the title track of the album being advertised on an enormous billboard.

It was 1993, and the album in question was called LAID, by a Manchester band that went by the simple name of JAMES.[5] Some clever marketing man got the idea to promote the album with the tagline *Get LAID... by JAMES*. From the moment I saw that billboard, which featured the entire band in tasteful drag I knew that I had to have it. And no, I didn't mean, *hey, let's go to the record shop and see if they have a poster!* I meant that I had to have *that billboard*; I coveted it, I wanted to steal it, I would kill to get it, and use the Lord's name in vain while doing it. I had sinning on my mind when turned to my James and told him that I would (and I believe I'm quoting here, though it was a long time ago) 'totally shag whoever got me that billboard'. I had just learned the word 'shag', darlings, and I was using it at every opportunity. Claire (you remember poor, dying Claire – she of the caustic personality and equally caustic accent) really didn't approve, and chastised me for being vulgar. I tried to find the proper context to be able to use the words bloody and shag in the same sentence, but the words seemed naturally at odds with each other.

Now (and this is merely an interlude, darlings, so that I can catch my breath) I can hear some of your brains grinding away doing the calculation, and some of you less clever folks have taken off your shoes and socks to perform such sophisticated mathematics in order to determine your favourite dilettante's age. My advice: never ask a lady about her age.

So, before that interlude, younger and brasher Helena had just made a bold statement – but, ultimately an empty promise, because that billboard was really big, and there's no way that anyone was going to...

Until the next day, when James called on me at the cult compound (I'm gracefully leaving them anonymous, darlings, but I never said that I would refrain from snark), and reminded my

---

[5]Interesting side note, and this all ties back in to Batman somehow – Tim Booth, lead singer for JAMES, played Victor Zsasz in *Batman Begins* – the bald, goateed defendant right near the beginning that Dr. Crane (played by Cillian Murphy) is testifying is clearly insane.

keepers that his mother needed my help with the laundry that afternoon.

When we were safely out of earshot, James informed me that his mother was actually away at her sisters' that afternoon, and that he had a surprise waiting for me.

I have been nervous, darlings, and I have been excited, but the way I remember feeling that day is very rare. I can likely count on one hand the number of times I've felt that way, and not all of them were good times. But in retrospect, the feeling wasn't about the result, it was about the anticipation. My stomach was twisted, my face was tight, and my mouth was completely dry. In fact, the first thing I did when we got to James' house was to request something to drink.

James thought I meant a *drink* drink, and got me a can of Strongbow[6], which I downed in one guzzling chug, and then wiped my mouth with the back of my hand. Having skipped a lunch of low protein gruel (the official food of brainwashing cults everywhere – nah, I'm just kidding – I think it was mushy peas and gravy or some other British starch-fest delicacy) the hard cider hit me nearly instantaneously, and I felt a bit lightheaded, but good. James stared at me, smiled, and offered me another, which I declined, having seen enough after-school specials to know better.

James led me to his room, where there, rolled out on his bed, was a strip of mostly orange poster paper that must have been about twenty feet long. Right near the top, I could make out the letters ME and below that, what I now know is a bit of Tim Booth's head.

"You didn't..." I started, knowing that he had. "That isn't..."

James beamed proudly, and then shrugged. "I couldn't get all of it – it's not one piece – I guess they put it up in strips, and..."

And then I jumped on him, knocking him down on top of the bit of poster he'd managed to steal for me, a feat even more amazing considering he had a badly broken arm in an extremely

---

[6]Hard apple cider which has the nasty after-effect of making your breath smell like vinegar. Delicious stuff, though.

awkward cast – a fact that clearly I'd forgotten about when I jumped on him, as he started yelping and caterwauling.

"I'm sorry! I'm sorry!" I apologized, and got up off of him.
"Don't stop," he said, laughing. "Just... be careful with me."

As I started to undress, all the nervousness seemed to well up, and I realized that I was trembling, though with fear or excitement I really couldn't say. I wondered for a moment if I should tell him that it was my first time, but decided to keep that secret to myself.

Another thing came back to me from the after school specials, though.

"Um, do you have any... you know..."

"Yeah," he said sheepishly, "top drawer, love. There's a condom or two in there, I think."

He was sweet and not so bright, and I laughed at the way that he said condom, pronouncing the second syllable to rhyme with home. We fumbled with each other's clothes, with me doing most of the work because of his arm, and there was a moment when I thought my bra was never going to come off, but in the end we managed.

And the sex?

Well, don't expect me to write any *Reginald's quivering member* or *he stroked me with his muscle of love* nonsense, because there wasn't any of that, anyway. With his arm in that big awkward cast, it was impossible for him to be on top, as he kept hitting me in the head with the heavy plaster monstrosity, which was exactly as romantic and sexy as it sounds. And so I got on top and pretty much impaled myself on him, which is an incredibly apt description of how it felt. There was no *sweet sensation of pain melting into glorious transcendent pleasure* or however the girly fuck-books describe it – it fucking *hurt!* And by the time the pain subsided, he was already done, but no one alerted me! No, I just kept bouncing up and down like a fool, completely oblivious to my objective, and all the while, he was squirming and trying to push me off of him. I looked down and saw that he was obviously uncomfortable, and began to realize that my first time was already over.

"Is that it?" I asked without thinking. In retrospect, that might not have been the best thing to say. The ego of the teenage boy might just be the most fragile thing on the whole damn planet.

His face turned red, and he called me a slag, which, given the tone of his voice, I assumed was not something complimentary, or perhaps Mancunian[7] slang for angel or goddess. I snatched up my clothes and ran to his bathroom, where I slammed the door and cried as I quickly dressed. I'd like to tell you that I was stronger than that, or that my skin was thicker. I'd like to tell you that I went back out and kicked James in the nuts. I'd like to tell you that his immature jab went in one ear and out the other. I'd like to tell you that, darlings; I am many things, but a liar is not one of them.

I stormed out of his bathroom and into his bedroom, where he was struggling to dress one-handed, and he flinched when he saw the look on my face, as if he thought I might slug him one, and that was the only satisfaction I took from that experience. Oh, and I took one other thing, too. I snatched up that strip of that fucking JAMES billboard and rolled it up under my arm and charged out his door. I earned every inch of it (the billboard, not James' tiny quivering member) and it still hangs in my studio to this day as... well, a bittersweet souvenir, I guess. I never actually ever heard the story of how he managed to get it, broken arm and all, so for that, I'm afraid you'll just have to use your imagination.

I went back to my room (where this story began) and cried for three days. I just couldn't figure out how he had changed in one split second from My Hero to The Boy Who Broke My Heart. (In retrospect, I suspect that it was only a flesh wound as the Black Knight[8] was wont to say, but that first cut is the deepest, as someone or other else said).[9]

The next time I saw James he wouldn't even look me in the eye. He was with a couple of his idiot friends, (why do all boys have

---

[7]Of or pertaining to Manchester.
[8]That would be a reference to *Monty Python and the Holy Grail*, wherein the Black Knight is hacked to bits, but proclaims, even as he lost his limbs, that it each cut is merely a flesh wound.
[9]Would you believe that this was actually Cat Stevens, who converted to Islam and became known as Yusuf Islam? See – it all comes full circle.

idiot friends – sub-question: do the girlfriends of the other boys refer to your boy as their boy's idiot friend? These are just things that keep me up at night) and when they saw me they snickered behind their hands and made some stupid suggestive comments, as idiot friends are prone to doing. I looked at James and tried to make eye contact, but he just looked at his trainers.

"Well, sod off, then!" I yelled at them, but more specifically at James. This was another term that I'd picked up, and would irritate my friends back home with upon my return.

And now, a public service announcement to any man that might be reading this – no, no, don't tune out, I'm not going to yell at you, I'm actually just trying to educate you. If you want to know why women will make generalizing statements like 'All men are assholes', here is why: All men are fucking assholes. (You'll notice that there was no exclamation point there, darlings, so do realize that I am not yelling). Now, I'm not saying that men are assholes all the time, otherwise we would have killed you all in your sleep a long time ago, and the human race would likely have never survived more than a couple of generations. But at some point, whether you were a boy, or whether you were a grown ass man, you bragged about some sexual conquest to your asshole buddies, because hey, they're not going to say anything, and some poor girl (who actually liked you) got her reputation ruined. Or else, you talked shit about some girl based on information you gathered in one of these locker-room conversations, or you made fun of or picked on some girl; called her a tease or a prude if she wouldn't put out, and then a slut or a whore or a slag (whatever local variation you used) if she did.

But don't worry, darlings – all is fair. Another time, very soon, I'll give you the skinny on just exactly why all women are crazy bitches – not always, mind you, or, you know, killing in sleep, extinction of human race, etc. etc...

For the time being, let's return again to where this story began. It began with me crying on my bunk, broken-hearted and all alone, despite the presence of my five roommates, who were right about done with my whinging. There was another thing going through my mind, and I don't know if it's completely universal, but I have spoken to a number of women and many of them have shared that they went through this, too, after their first time.

The nagging thought that kept going through my mind like a terrible mantra was: WHAT IF I'M PREGNANT?

I had never before experienced such complete and irrational panic and fear.

It was my first time for a lot of things, I guess.

an indecent proposal

"*N*ow, just hear me out," Cheyenne prefaced, sitting in my living room, the Accidental Plagiarist in tow. He'd been released from the hospital after having what can only be described as a manic/psychotic episode that resulted in him trying to ride a fire hydrant in the buff, covered head to toe in Gold Bond Medicated powder. If you have no idea what I'm talking about, you may want to go back and read all about it.[1] I'll wait, you go. Make sure you read part two, because that's where it all goes to hell, darlings.

Okay, now that you're back – the clue was: Now, just hear me out.
What are five words you should never start with when asking for a favour?
Correct!
Great, I'll take Indecent Proposals for $500, Alex.[2]

---

[1] If you somehow missed it, or forgot, go back and read And That's How the Countess Killed Bambi's Mother
[2] A reference to long running game show *Jeopardy!* and its host, fellow Canadian Alex Trebek.

I sat across from my two houseguests and wondered just where they were going with this. Cheyenne is an exotic dancer from my distant past who showed up on my doorstep a couple of months back, and I had dubbed her boyfriend the Accidental Plagiarist because of his absentminded penchant for playing songs that he fully believed, it seemed, that he wrote, but were nonetheless, quite famous songs. For example, he would be playing a four chord progression that was simple but dirty and garage-punk, and present it to us as just something he was fiddling around with, and I'd tell him that it sounded good; that I loved Iggy Pop, and that *I Wanna Be Your Dog* was one of my favourites, and he'd just give me a blank look as if he had no idea what I was talking about.

The Countess Penelope, late of Arcadia, which is somewhere in the vicinity of Dublin, was in the kitchen making Irish Car Bombs – the drink, not the incendiary device – and practicing her Irish brogue. The trick, she assured me, was lots of hard Rs and long, soft AHHs in place of the nasal 'a' that we North Americans put in the middle of words. She may have had it down in theory, but in practice, she still sounded more like the Lucky Charms leprechaun than, say, Sinéad O'Connor.[3]

"Shore an' it's not the worst ting thaht could 'appen," Penny called from the other room, having listened without interrupting once. "I mean, it's not like 'e's suggestin' that the Irish eat their babbies, is it?"

The Countess had just had occasion to read Jonathan Swift's *Modest Proposal*, in which he suggests, tongue firmly in cheek, that the Catholic Irish, who were starving, might solve two problems in one by eating their surplus children.

"It's completely out of the question, Penny," I said, and then looked at Cheyenne and the Accidental Plagiarist and repeated myself. "You'll just have to find some other way."

"I know that this is a big deal," Cheyenne said, "and don't think we haven't thought about other options..."

---

[3] Famous for her bald head, Irish brogue, cover of Prince's *Nothing Compares 2 U* and ripping up a picture of the Pope on Saturday Night Live.

"Well, keep thinking," I said sharply. Chet's face dropped in defeat. They had lived with me for several weeks, and it wasn't until I had to go see him in the hospital that I actually learned his real name.

"Chet's doing so much better now that he's got medication, Helena, but they want to send him back home, and he don't have any health insurance back there!" Cheyenne had been paying the hospital what she could, but without insurance, it wasn't feasible for him to stay. One of the things we take for granted in Canada is our health insurance. Don't let anyone tell you it's free, because we're taxed dearly for it – but no Canadian citizen ever has to worry about going to the hospital for fear of the financial implications.

Which brings us to why Cheyenne had called me up last night, and insisted that we speak face to face.

"It would only be on paper, Helena," Cheyenne insisted, trying to sell me again on the idea of marrying the Accidental Plagiarist so that he could apply for landed immigrant status. I guess that would make me Mrs. Helena Hann-Basquiat-Acccidental Plagiarist, or Helena H-BAP for short.

"It's fraud, Cheyenne," I said firmly. "And I hardly know the guy – no offense, Chet – I'm not going to convince anyone that we're together."

Chet nodded and kept silent.

"Car Bomb, anyone?" The Countess Arcade called from the kitchen.

Now, the secret to the perfect Irish Car Bomb is the Irish Mist. Some people will try to make it with just Bailey's Irish Cream and some Jameson Irish Whiskey, but if you mix a third shot each of Bailey's, Jameson and Irish Mist, and then drop that into about a 2/3 pint of Guinness, and then pound that back as quickly as you can, why, it just might be the loveliest drink on earth – like drinking chocolate malt out of the cupped hands of wee red-headed angels.

Penny and I pounded back our Car Bombs and as I was wiping my lips with the back of my hand in most ladylike fashion, another hole in their master plan occurred to me.

"You can't just marry someone and then go get a Health Card," I said. "Or else people would do this kind of thing all the time."

"Oh, I know," Cheyenne said, "the lady on the phone told us that he would have to live here for a year before he could get a Health Card."

"Well, there you go, then," I said, thinking that would settle it. "Marrying me isn't going to help you for at least a year."

"Unless...." Cheyenne prompted, but my mind just didn't go where she wanted it to go, and so she said: "Unless you were to sign a declaration that Chet's been living with you for the past year."

"No," I said flatly. "Uh uh. That's not going to happen, and I think you should leave now."

"Oh, come on, Helena," Penny said. "It's not that big a deal, is it? I mean, it's not like you're going to get married for real anytime soon."

I scowled at her and mentally projected that she should leave the room or risk my wrath, but my telepathy must have been off, because she just stood there smirking at me.

"Hey, if you won't do it, I will," Penny offered, and that was the last straw. I didn't care what I owed Cheyenne, there were just some things that you didn't ask someone to do. It's not as if Chet came from some politically volatile nation and he was begging for refugee status. And I didn't believe this 'one year' thing she was trying to sell me, either. It couldn't be that simple.

"Penny, please go to your room." I said, teeth clenched. I wasn't angry with Penny, and I realized just how ludicrous it sounded; me telling another adult to go to her room as if she were a child.

"Yes, mum," Penny sulked, and winked at me on the sly.

Once Penny left (though I'm sure she was listening – some habits never die) I told Cheyenne and Chet in no uncertain terms that they were to leave my house and never come back. Furthermore, I told them, if I found out that either of them tried to contact Penny about this, I would personally bring the police to their doorstep. I told them that I didn't give a rat's ass what they did, or how they resolved this, but that I didn't want to be involved any further. If they managed to find someone else who was willing to go along with their scam, that was their business, and as long as they didn't involve Penny or me in it, then I wouldn't feel obligated to report them.

"Helena, that's..." Cheyenne started, and I stopped her just as quickly with a pointed finger. I was trembling with the rage of a protective mama bear, and must have looked pretty scary, because she stopped talking immediately.

"Let me finish," I said, trying to maintain some semblance of sane composure. I was furious. "I will do one last thing for you, if you want it, and then you and I are through, do you understand?"

"Helena..." Cheyenne started, and the tears that welled up in her eyes only made me angrier, because when I see someone crying I can't help but cry, too, and I didn't want to look weak at that moment.

"No," I said. "You don't get to say anything else right now. I said that I would do one more thing for you, if you want me to. I will drive you back over the border – I will do that much for you. It'll be easier going over with me than trying to cross in a bus or something. You find yourself some town to settle in over there, and apply for Medicare. You'll have a hell of a lot easier time getting that – plus it's legal – than trying to defraud the Canadian healthcare system. I'll do that, but then you lose my phone number."

We sat there in silence, and I waited for her to say something. Frankly, I expected her to burst into tears and apologize, or else shower me in vitriol. I wouldn't have been surprised at either.

In the end, it was Chet who actually broke the silence.

"Thank you, Helena," he said calmly, and stood up. "I never meant to cause you any sorrow or pain."

I couldn't be absolutely sure, but wasn't that pretty damn close to the opening lyric to *Purple Rain*?[4]

I was dumbfounded, and just licked my dry lips in response.

----

[4]Yes. Yes it pretty much was.

"Can we think about it?" He asked. "Give you a call in a couple of days?"

That sounded fair. I felt my urge to kill suddenly begin to fade.

I nodded. "I'll give you a week. After that, the offer expires. And you get one phone call, so make sure you're certain about your decision when you call me."

"Fair enough," Chet said, bottom lip trembling as if he might suddenly burst into tears as well.

Chet held out his hand and offered it to Cheyenne, who pulled herself up, her glaring eyes burning holes in my skin, and accompanied the Accidental Plagiarist out my door for perhaps the last time.

I sighed as the door closed, and threw myself down on my couch and cried for a minute or two.

"You okay?" The Countess asked from behind her closed door. "Is it safe to come out?"

"Only if you tell me you were just kidding about marrying Chet."

The door opened and Penny came out, grinning at me.

"Can I tell you something, and you have to promise not to be angry with me?" She asked sheepishly.

"I'm already angry with you, so you might as well go ahead," I said, rubbing my temples. I could feel a migraine coming on. Perfect. Just perfect.

"Well," she said cautiously, "Sometimes, in order for you to, well... assert yourself..."

"Yes?" I prodded.

"Well, iss loik, The Incredibow Howk,[5] ennit?" She tried dipping into her repertoire of characters and drew out the lovable

---

[5]The Incredible Hulk for the Dickensian urchin-impaired. You wouldn't like him – or me – when we're angry.

Dickensian urchin, hoping that it would charm or disarm me, but instead, it had the opposite effect.

"Drop the bit, Penny, I'm not in the mood," I said, too harshly.

"Well, that's the point, ennit?" She said, stubbornly continuing to be the Countess Penelope of Arcadia circa 1850. "Sometimes you 'ave to get just mad enough before you do wot 'as to be done."

Was she saying what I think she was saying?

"And, loik, you ain't really concerned, beggin' yer pardon, mum, if you's the one in 'arm's way." I was beginning to realize where this was going.

"So, then, you..." I began.

"Frew meself on me own sword, mum. Thass roit, cheerio, tut tut an' such."

I should have been overjoyed that I had such a brilliant, manipulative, caring niece. Further, I should have been proud that I helped make her that way. But I was too tired. Totally knackered, as the Countess Arcade would no doubt say and all I wanted was to be alone.

"I'm going to bed," I said, and gave her a kiss on the forehead. "G'night, darling."

Penny frowned, and called after me. "Are you okay?"

"Sure," I said, and tossed her a weak smile. "I'll be fine."

charles manson
and the beatles

S o much for a long, restful weekend.

I'd forgotten about a wedding I'd promised to attend, and so spent the day trying to get myself together enough to make an appearance.

I'd woken up with the migraine to end all migraines, darlings, and would have been just as happy to spend the day in bed, but ended up drinking lots of water and regular intervals of lonelyTylenol, with a chaser of coffee in order to be semi-presentable to attend the aforementioned nuptials.

Nothing to report, darlings – pretty standard wedding fare – though I must say, the vicar or whatever had one of those long scarf-like wraps (I've no idea what they're called, but you know what I'm talking about) and I couldn't help but stifle a giggle at the thought that it reminded me so much of the kind of long scarf that football (that's soccer to you and I) supporters wear, and wouldn't it just be hilarious to go to a wedding or a funeral or a baptism or whatnot and have the vicar get up and be wearing a Manchester United scarf? Maybe it's just my recent trip down Amnesia Lane (which happened to be a cobbled street in old Halesowen most recently) lingering in my thoughts.

After spending the requisite amount of time to avoid appearing rude, I left to go home and drink copious amounts of water and retire.

When I got home, I found the Countess Penelope of Arcadia sitting in the living room, peering out the window.

"What's up?" I asked, fearing that perhaps introducing her to the films of Alfred Hitchcock recently might have been a bad idea. I almost expected her response to come in the voice of Jimmy Stewart from *Rear Window*.[1]

"Just watching the family of 'coons next door," she said absently, not turning her head from the window.

I suddenly feared that she'd developed a new faux-personality, and that Arcadia was suddenly somewhere in the heart of Mississippi.

"Uh, Penny, as amusing as I find your little eccentricities, I draw the line at Penny the racist Countess of Cornbread County."

"Oh, shut up," she retorted, eyes still glued to the window. "Come look!"

I crawled up beside her on the couch and saw what she was watching. A family of raccoons were playing on our neighbour's garage – two adults, and four cubs, wrestling with each other and crawling in and out of an air vent in the top of the garage. We watched as they poked their heads up out of their hidey-hole, and laughed with absolute pleasure. They were high enough up that no one would bother them, and so they were completely free to just hang out without human interference. I tried to take a video and cursed my iPhone for not having a zoom function in video mode. I

---

[1] Jimmy Stewart plays a man with a broken leg who is stuck in his bedroom all summer, and so starts peeping on his neighbours, and witnesses what he believes is his neighbour murdering his wife. If you haven't seen the actual movie, you've seen it spoofed on something or other; perhaps *The Simpsons*.

managed to take a couple of pictures of dubious quality, but my brain isn't so far gone that my memory won't do just fine.

The Countess was humming a tune under her breath as we watched them, smiling and enjoying the free entertainment. I recognized it as *Rocky Raccoon* by The Beatles.

"Did you know that Charles Manson said that *Rocky Raccoon* was one of The Beatles prophetic songs about the rise of the black man?" I asked conversationally.

"Shhh," the Countess shushed.

"Everybody remembers the whole *Helter Skelter* thing, but no one remembers *Rocky Raccoon*."[2] I added.

"Shhh!" Penny reiterated with great eloquence. "Just watch the raccoons, Helena. They're just... perfect. Don't ruin the moment."

She was right, of course. I put my arm around her, kissed the top of her head, and watched the raccoons. It's the moments you can't capture on video that you'll never get back. A moment like that is no time for trivialities.

She's so smart, that girl.

---

[2] Upon hearing The Beatles (White Album), Manson became obsessed with the band, and came to believe that the songs on the album were prophetic messages whose lyrics were a code that described the violence and racial tension of the time.

my parents are crying[1] - the california years (musical interlude two)

*t seemed that everywhere I went that summer, everything was Canadian – and in a good way. It was the summer of New Pornographers, and Arcade Fire; of Broken Social Scene and The Dears, and Sam Roberts. Canadian music – good Canadian music could be heard everywhere, proving what I was constantly trying to tell everyone – that even Canadians don't listen to Celine Dion, darlings – that's why we sent her to Vegas, where she belongs.

There must have been something in the air calling me back home. I was still working at Amoeba Music, trying to figure out what I was going to do about the little bundle of joy that had taken up residence inside me, and I was constantly being reminded of home – whether it be a song, or a film, or the MADE IN CANADA sticker that I found on the back of a Spoon album (*Gimme Fiction* had just come out and I was selling that disc like it came with a free hummer – which it didn't, perverts – I was just making a crude simile).

For some reason, that particular day I went home to my apartment (I was living in the Haight district of San Francisco at the time with three other roommates) and called my parents -- the last

---

[1]A reference to the lyrics of the Arcade Fire song *Neighbourhood #1 (Tunnels)*

two people that I really wanted to talk to, but for some reason needed to talk to.

Of course, they were predictably supportive and provided me with invaluable wisdom. Which is to say they cried a lot and left me to sort myself out as per usual.

the good times are killing me[1] - the california years (conclusion)

t was a summer of the mid 2000's, and all the hipsters were camped out in bookstores sipping their Americanos and reading Charles Bukowski[2] because Isaac Brock[3] had told them that he was a pretty good read, but God, who'd want to be such an asshole?

I was sitting in a Peet's Coffee reading *Ham on Rye*[4] like a good hipster and waiting to meet someone I'd contacted on Craigslist about buying the car that Robert had given me when I left LA. I'd just found out that I was pregnant, and in a rather painfully embarrassing twist, I couldn't tell you who the father was. Was it Michael, the well-meaning but weak boy who'd been pursuing me since the day he walked into Amoeba Music and couldn't form coherent sentences in my presence? Michael, the boy who assured me he understood the platonic nature of our friendship, but then took me to the most romantic spot possible, as if by seducing me

---

[1]Also the title of a song from the Modest Mouse album *Good News For People Who Love Bad News* that was so popular that year.

[2]American poet and novelist famous for his gritty poems, dirty realism, and misogyny. Also, for being an asshole.

[3]The American musician and lead singer of the band Modest Mouse, not the British General who was dubbed 'The Hero of Upper Canada' because of his valour during the War of 1812.

[4]Bukowski's semi-autobiographical novel.

he could change the fact that I just didn't love him – couldn't even respect him and his puppy dog grovelling. I couldn't love Michael because he wasn't even a real person – he was like a caricature of everything that women's psychology has been telling men that women want them to be for the last twenty years – he was sensitive, he asked me about my feelings, he listened to me and didn't get upset if I just bitched at him about nothing. He was sweet, and loyal, and playful, and everything you'd want in a Golden Retriever. See, the thing about all that women's pop psychology stuff is that it's usually just typical women wanting to fix shit stuff, and the fact of the matter is, we love men because they're men – and when they try to be everything that they're not – well, this is a perfect example of why men will make generalizations about women like 'you're all a bunch of fickle bitches!' or, 'Who could ever figure out what it is you actually want?'

Why? (And this isn't just the Bukowski speaking, darlings, though he really is a misogynist asshole). Because all women are fickle bitches and who could ever figure out what it is we actually want?!

Not all the time, of course – because, if you'll recall, if we were, we'd all be smothered in our sleep and the human race would quickly become extinct, etc…

But at some point in every woman's life, she has crushed some poor boy's heart, or made some boy jump through all kinds of hoops, or even pursued a boy just to see if she could catch him, only to find that when she got him, she didn't want him anymore.

And it's not just boys – I personally have moved Heaven and Hell to make something happen – called in favours, begged friends or lovers to do things for me in order to achieve something that, in the end, lost its glamour once I had it. On a smaller scale, I have complained about certain behaviour in boyfriends, only to complain again once they've changed it.

Sometimes I wonder that I've never been strangled in my sleep, darlings, I really do.

I just wanted to be friends with Michael, and yet, I continued going on what were essentially dates with him because I liked the attention. I didn't want a romantic relationship with Michael, but I wanted to enjoy all of the benefits of being in a romantic relationship with him. I'd like to tell you that this thought never crossed my mind. I'd love to be able to, with a clear conscience, tell you that I never worried that I was leading him on. I'd very much like to state for the record that I, Helena Hann-Basquiat, being of sound mind, do solemnly declare that I am completely innocent of using the poor boy's affection for me to my own advantage, all the while keeping him at arm's length under the guise of platonic friendship. I would very much like to be able to make those assertions, darlings, but I'm afraid that I might come across as slightly disingenuous.

But whatever – the truth is, I couldn't give Michael what he wanted, because Michael wanted so much – Michael wanted it all. I think that's why Sean was such an easy diversion – Sean didn't want anything except that moment – that stupid, irresponsible, incredibly hot, sexy and downright acrobatic moment when my baby might very well have been conceived.

But I couldn't be sure.

I hadn't even told either of them yet. I wasn't sure that I was going to. I'd been making secret plans to move back to Toronto, and I knew that the longer I stayed, the harder it would be to leave. But really, it was the only choice that made any sense to me. I had no health coverage in the US, but back in Canada, I could have my baby and not have to worry about how I was going to pay for it.

In my mind, I think that I was already gone.

The car was still in Robert's name, but I found a buyer who wasn't concerned with technicalities like filing the transfer with the DMV[5], and was able to pocket enough cash to get set up once I moved back to Toronto. Not that I couldn't have showed up on my sister's doorstep with nothing but the clothes on my back (and God knows it wouldn't have been the first time) but it was always nicer to have a pocket full of cash when I rang that fabled doorbell.

I left a letter on the bed for the guys in the now defunct band. It didn't say much. There was both too much and not enough that I could say that would ever make things right, or give anybody any kind of closure. I told them that I'd had some good times, but now

---

[5]Department of Motor Vehicles.

the good times were killing me, and that I didn't belong here anymore. I told them I was moving back to T.O. and that they were welcome to look me up if they ever made it out that way. I neglected to mention the results of my pregnancy test, because I didn't want that hanging around their necks – either of them, really. Michael would likely want to claim it for his own, do the right thing, make an honest woman of me and all that, and Sean would probably make me hate him in his aloofness. And so I carried that on my own – just as my decision to have sex with both of them had been my own.

I hopped on a plane without saying good-bye, and gave nobody any warning that I was coming. I'm like smoke that way – disappearing and reappearing without a trace or a warning. Don't get too attached to me, darlings. Dilettantes tend to come and go as we please.

My sister Cheryl opened the door nearly four years after I'd left for Los Angeles and gave me a surprised but happy smile and welcomed me in.

"You look great," I said, and then collapsed on her front steps.

When I awoke, an older, black haired version of the girl I teasingly called Penny Arcade was standing by my bed, holding my hand tightly and crying, making a complete mess of her heavy black eyeliner.

I smiled at her and tears welled up in my eyes.

"Aunt Helena!" She exclaimed, and draped herself over me, squeezing me until I thought I'd smother. I wrapped my arms around her the best I could with all the tubes coming out of one of them and held her tight.

When she stood up again, she was a frightful mess, and I couldn't help but giggle and point to the box of Kleenex on my night table. She passed it to me and I drew her to me and wiped the black mess from her cheeks, as if it was chocolate and she was four and not fourteen. She wore a black t-shirt with Emily the Strange staring out at me, and a black crinoline skirt over black and white striped leggings. She looked like what a cartoon character drawn by Robert Smith might look like.

"Nice look," I said hoarsely.

The Countess Penelope of Arcadia, as she henceforth became known to me, dropped a little curtsy, and said "Fanks, love! Drives me mum 'round the bend it does!"

This was the first appearance of the Dickensian street urchin, and I was immediately enamoured with her. I laughed weakly and agreed that her getup was likely to drive Cheryl absotively ape-shit.

"Where's your mum?" I asked, but rather than answer me, like a typical teenager, she just shouted, no matter that we were in a hospital.

"MUM! Aunt Helena's awake! She's asking for you!"

Cheryl rushed in, scolded Penny for shouting in the hospital, and then came and sat beside me and held my hand. It was obvious that she'd been crying and I realized that there wasn't going to be any good news for me that day.

I was right, of course.

The doctors figure that I was about six weeks pregnant when my fallopian tube ruptured, killing my unborn baby and nearly me.

They called it an ectopic pregnancy,[6] and asked me if I had a history of them; had I ever been pregnant before, and a lot of other clinical but essentially heartless questions. Questions that needed answers as far as they were concerned, but questions I didn't need to hear right then. Cheryl suggested that the doctors give me some more time, and asked them to leave me alone. Some habits never die – she would never let the teachers pick on me in school, either, no matter how eccentric (well, back then, it was probably just weird) I was being.

---

[6]If you don't know what this is, be thankful. An ectopic pregnancy occurs when the embryo latches on somewhere outside the actual uterus, often somewhere in the fallopian tube. They are almost never viable pregnancies as far as the baby goes, and can often be fatal to the woman.

I just lay in the hospital bed and cried, while Cheryl stroked my hair. I thought about my brush with death, and it made me dizzy and nauseous.

I thought about the last time that I was in the hospital, and how I thought that I had wanted to die. How was it, then that I so desperately clung to life now, having nearly just lost it? I had no answers for my own questions. I looked back at seventeen-year-old me with disdain and a kind of horror at what she'd almost done. Then I looked at myself as I was, and I wondered how I kept ending up in tears.

Ten years on from the lost and lonely girl on the run, and no wiser, just older, with more mistakes under my belt.

No, that's not fair – I had learned enough to know that no matter what happened, I wanted to live.

half a world away[1]
(a halesowen conclusion)

eanwhile, half a world away and around ten years earlier....

M Some stories can only be told once the wounds have closed and the scabs have healed over, until nothing is left but the silvery scars of distant memory.

It wasn't one thing that landed me in the hospital in Halesowen, but a confluence of events that made me feel helpless and alone – no, more than alone – abandoned, and by the very people that should have been looking out for me.

At seventeen, partly because I was reckless and impulsive, but also because I desperately needed to escape my tyrannical father, I followed a cute boy to England, where I found myself a part of a strange, nearly cult-like evangelical organization that destroyed any fledgling faith I might have possessed, and certainly soured my opinion of organized religion by showing me what really went on behind the Wizard's curtain. What I found there was what you'd expect: smoke and mirrors, accompanied by a smarmy sales pitch delivered by a zealous charlatan.[2] Instead of joining in the zealotry, I spent most of my time chasing English boys and discovering

---

[1] I was listening to a lot of R.E.M. at the time this happened, and *Half A World Away* was another song that could make me break down and cry.

[2] A reference to *The Wizard of Oz*, of course.

Guinness. The first of these diversions would lead to my first broken heart – the one against which all others were measured. Certainly the first boy who ever did me wrong was not the worst thing that ever happened to me, but it's that first time that stings the most – because before that, I never knew such pain was possible.

And so it was that I found myself alone even in a crowded room, and aching from my first dalliance with love or lust or whatever it is two randy teenagers feel when they first take that plunge into the adult world of sex and shame and betrayal and rejection. People there that I'd become friendly enough with tried to comfort me, but the wall that I had built brick by brick over the few months I'd been there had become solid indeed, and their congenial words of comfort fell on deaf ears.

I received a letter from my parents that day, and I remember reading and re-reading it, gripping the paper with claws of rage until the ink bled into my thumbs and some of the words had melted away with my teardrops. My sister's husband had taken a job in some tiny little town in upstate New York, and had moved there a few months previous to my departure for England, and the letter I held said that my parents had decided to move down there to be closer to their soon-to-be-born grandchild.

I hadn't even known that Cheryl was pregnant, let alone that she was far enough along that the phrase soon-to-be-born was appropriate. Communication is not exactly a virtue in my family. The news was happy, of course, but shocking. I hadn't thought much of her moving at the time, because, well, I was seventeen and self-absorbed, darlings, let's face it. But that wasn't the news that had begun to crumble my world. My parents had decided to relocate out of the country while I was abroad and the letter I was crying over was the notice that it was happening. Or at least, that's what I thought at first. Then I looked at the envelope more closely, and saw that the letter bore the postmark of the tiny and until that point, imaginary town of Arcadia, New York. It dawned suddenly on me that they weren't writing to tell me that we were moving, but rather, that it was a *fait accompli*,[3] and the letter was a mere formality to tell me that I was on my own.

---

[3] A done deal.

I turned my headphones up and listened to R.E.M.'s *Automatic for the People* again and again until the dying batteries in my Walkman transformed Michael Stipe's voice into something drawling and creepy.[4] In the end, he sounded like a demon lamenting his own inescapable predicament.

Nothing is going my way...[5]

It was a very confusing moment, and to be honest, what I most recall was a feeling of helplessness; of being adrift. I tried to focus on the moment – on where I was, and what I was doing, but I was never very good at that, and I was particularly reckless at seventeen, in a way that scares me now that I am more than twice that age. As I listened to the droning, depressing music, my sense of sorrow and loss and abandonment turned to anger, and I set out to call my sister and demand to talk to my parents and have it all out over transatlantic phone lines.

I had just gotten through to the operator to make a collect call when one of the administrators, a kind and friendly Irishman who'd never done me any specific wrong stepped into the office where I'd secreted myself away to make my furious phone call, and told me that he needed to speak to me; that it was urgent.

His name was Declan, and his accent put me at ease with its familiar hard 'R's that almost mimicked the Continental accent of most of North America. He brought me into his office and had me sit across from him while he pulled out a file that contained my application and financial information.

"How are you doing, Helena?" He asked, seeming genuinely concerned. I would just like to point out that, for the record, many of the people there were absolutely wonderful human beings, and no matter how I may have felt about the whole situation, or their tactics or whatever, this wasn't a compound populated by fascistic types. Now that I am much further removed from it, I can honestly

---

[4]For those of you who don't remember cassette Walkmans, just because the batteries were dying, it didn't mean that you had *no* music. Instead, the machine simply *slowed down*, resulting in the demonic sounds I describe.
[5]A reference to *Find the River* by R.E.M.

say that Declan was one of the good ones, and that he truly never meant to hurt me. In all honesty, what I ended up doing probably hurt him, because he likely felt somewhat responsible for me.

I shrugged – the best answer I had available to me at the time. I couldn't very well tell this nice man about how some boy that I'd taken a passing fancy to had taken my virginity and then rejected me all because of an ill-timed comment from me, and how I couldn't show my face in town around any of his friends because of how they'd ostracized me. I certainly couldn't tell him how I thought that what we (and I say we, because it wasn't fair for me to exclude myself) were doing every day was wrong, and fucked up, and how I didn't want anything to do with it anymore, and that I just wanted to go home, except that my home was gone. I couldn't tell him that my parents were such big proponents of Thomas Wolfe's[6] theory that you can't go home again that they actually stole my home right out from under me while I was sleeping uneasily in some godforsaken town in the middle of nowhere, England whose only claim to fame is being the childhood home of Robert Plant.

I couldn't tell him that I was absolutely miserable, and that each escape plan that I'd worked out in my head only led to more misery. I couldn't admit to being that trapped, or that short-sighted. Even then, I had my pride, darlings.

It didn't matter that I had no answer. He did most of the talking, anyway. He explained that I had run out of funding, and that I had to make a decision about whether to drop out of the program, or else stay and end up owing the organization roughly $5000 when I returned at the end of the year. At seventeen, that seemed like a lot of money, and I remember feeling like my stomach had just dropped to the floor. All the spit in my mouth dried up, and had to clench my jaw to stop my teeth from chattering.

My parents had been kind enough to put up the initial fee to send me to England, but I was supposed to be sending fund-raising letters in order to come up with the rest. I remember that I almost didn't go because of this, but then Andrew's dad (remember

---

[6]Famous American novelist of the early Twentieth Century and author of *You Can't Go Home Again*.

Andrew? He was the reason that I ended up in Halesowen in the first place) had encouraged me to trust the Lord or some other admonition, but in practical terms, he never mentioned what might happen if for some reason the Lord didn't come through.

By the time it came up, and one of the counsellors there asked me if I'd been sending letters, I had already determined that there was no way that I was going to ask anyone to contribute to what I was a reluctant part of, and I put it out of my mind. And now, because of that, I had run out of money, and had to make a decision to stay and go into what seemed monumental debt to seventeen year old me, or else go home. But then, home, that four letter word – that was the problem. I had no home to go to. There was nothing for me in Arcadia – at that time, I hadn't yet applied for my dual citizenship, and so what was I going to do in some tiny little burg in the Catskills?[7] I wouldn't be able to go to school, I wouldn't be able to work – I would be trapped. And if I chose, instead, to go back to Canada – well what then? All alone at seventeen; left to fend for myself? It terrified me. I honestly felt like my life was over, and I was in such a terrified panic that I wasn't able to conceive of anything outside of that mindset. I felt torn apart at the seams, quite literally being pulled in directions that I didn't want to go, and I felt that if the cosmic thread-puller kept pulling, that very soon, I would end up naked, like that poor character in that Weezer song.[8] (In fairness, my sweater was already bordering on the brink of frayed-edge chaos, and this was just the last thread pulled that caused me to unravel completely).

Perhaps that metaphor was on my mind as I sat by myself in the corner of the common room, picking apart a homemade sweater I'd found in the Lost and Found and fallen in love with. It was far too big for me, and was the non-colour of dusk during a rainstorm, and I wore it like a security blanket. I tore at one string in the wrist and watched as it snaked its way up my arm. I wore the thousand-yard stare of the traumatized, somehow outside myself. With one hand I tore at my sweater, unraveling and destroying it, while I kept my other hand hidden up my sleeve. In that hand, I

---

[7]Mountain range in New York State.
[8]*Undone – The Sweater Song*, which had come out right around that time, if I remember correctly, and I always do.

had a bottle of pills, and when I was sure no one was watching me, I'd palm a pill and pop it into my mouth.

I think there is something to be said about the fact that I did this first bit in public. I think that part of me wanted to see if anyone would stop me, but after about eight pills, no one had noticed (or so I had thought) and so I quietly and calmly stood up and retired to my room, where I downed the rest of the pills in one shot, and lay down on my bed to die.

For the first time in my life (but not the last) I lost consciousness only to wake up in a hospital bed.

I was starving – like I hadn't eaten in weeks. They had pumped my stomach and saved my life – and I hated them for it. I refused to speak to anyone for days, and after the second day, they just stopped sending people in except for the hospital staff, who were professionally polite and dutiful. Finally, on the fourth day, the last person I wanted to see came to see me.

Bill, the teacher who had warned me of the dangers of Muslim boys and chastised me for being flirtatious came in with a sombre, sober and serious visage that tried to evoke concern but instead projected disappointment of the kind usually only parents are capable of. So of course, my back was immediately up, like a cat protecting its territory, and had I been a little more feline I do believe I would have hissed at him, and maybe given his nose a swipe with my retractable claws.

Instead, I glared at him and told him that I was fine, that it was a mistake, that I'd begged Jesus for forgiveness and just wanted to put it all behind me. I didn't ask him if he'd come there to play Jesus to the lepers in his head, although I'd really wanted to. I'd had that U2 song *One* [9] playing in my head as my own private entertainment for the two days I spent in silence, and while I really wanted to say that and sound clever doing it, in the end, I decided that my cleverness would be lost on him anyway, and so I told him

---

[9] R.E.M.'s *Automatic For the People* and U2's *Achtung Baby* were two of the most popular albums at the time, and the song *One*, with its admonition that we're all the same and that we have to carry each other was a sentiment that resounded with a lot of people, certainly it did with me. Incidentally, in 1993, at an MTV Concert for then Inaugural President Bill Clinton, Michael Stipe and Mike Mills from R.E.M. and Adam Clayton and Larry Mullen Jr. from U2 performed the song, and billed themselves as Automatic Baby.

what he wanted to hear, because it was easier that way. What I didn't tell him was that I didn't know for sure if I had really wanted to die, or if I had just wanted to see the looks on their faces when they found me. I didn't tell him that I had just wanted them to see how much they were hurting me. Him, Claire – the whole self-righteous lot of them. James, my parents, all of the people who had let me down when I had still wanted to believe that people could be trusted, that people were good, and love was possible, and that when you get sucked away into the maelstrom, you simply have to put your feet on the ground and remember that there's no place like home, there's no place like home, there's no place like home, and everything will be okay. Your parents will always be there waiting for you to return.

Instead, I landed in some nightmare land that was about as much like Oz as I am Judy Garland, and there's some part of me, I think, that was lost there forever, and has never returned.

When I called my sister after my release from the hospital to let her know I'd be coming home, my mother answered the phone. She sounded like she'd been running, and I hardly got to say anything at all.

"Mum," I said, having to shout to speak and hold my hand over my free ear just to hear her and be heard. "What's going on?"

"Oh, it's so exciting, dear!" She said, not really wanting to talk to me, just at me, as per usual. "Your sister's had her baby! You've got a little niece!"

Suddenly, I didn't have the heart to tell her where I'd been and what I'd done. And so, not for the last time in my life, I bore the pain alone, and have never told her what happened to me, or about what my medical chart called self-harm and what the hospital psychiatrist called a wakeup call, and what more than one person in the evangelical school called a cry for attention under their breath, or sometimes not so far under.

Instead, I found it in my heart to be happy for her and my dad, and for Cheryl and my brother-in-law Ted (really not a bad guy, in retrospect), and lastly, I found it in my heart to be happy for myself. Whatever lay ahead, it had to be better than this. I would figure out what to do with myself, even if it did require a few months of exile in the vast wasteland of Arcadia, where it was decided by all parties other than me as the best place for me to go. Besides, I had a little niece, now. Imagine, me – Auntie Helena.

"That's great, Mum," I said, swallowing my bitter tears. "What's the little nipper's name?"

"Penelope," Mum said, laughing. "Isn't that just the cutest?"

And so was born the future Countess of Arcadia, who would only get seventeen years with her parents before they were senselessly taken away by a drunk driver driving with a suspended license. I feel like a bit of a monster saying this, darlings, but I miss my sister dreadfully, while I am strangely indifferent to my parents' continued existence. After England, I spent around four months in what felt like an insane asylum, but was, in fact, Arcadia, and after that, I moved back up to Canada. Since then, I've been pretty much lost to my parents, and they to me, and I have never been able to truly reconcile with them. For this and other reasons I won't get into right now, my parents have been dead to me for nearly twenty years.

In retrospect, what I went through at seventeen pales in comparison to what Penny has had to live with. But we were both of us orphaned – me figuratively, and Penny literally. I can't tell you if one is harder than the other, or if it's just different.

Whatever the case, in our grief for my sister Cheryl, we are united, and we are never alone as long as we have each other.

We're one, but we're not the same.

We carry each other.

bonus materials: cutting floor, leftovers, and assorted miscellany

got nuffink

"So what you're saying is you're not going to write a story this week?" The Countess Penelope of Arcadia asked, disappointed.

I looked at the picture again, but nothing came.

"Everyone's going to write about the dancing girl, and I'm drawing a blank." I said finally.

"What about a crazy tale anthropomorphizing the fire hydrant? I bet fire hydrants see all kinds of crazy stuff, Helena."

"Hey, that's not a bad idea! The fire hydrant, whose secret name was Hank, liked to…"

"What?" Penny asked. "Why did you stop?"

I sighed. "Well, I've run out of words now, haven't I?"

This is the first of three "banter pieces" that I slipped into the weekly Flash Fiction challenge I participate in when I wasn't feeling particularly inspired to write something traditionally fictional. I confess it was also a shameless way to introduce and possibly seduce new readers to come and read more of Penny and my misadventures.

Did it work?

It certainly did, darlings.

observations on writing
eco-conscious
sci-fi/fantasy

"**W**hat about an eco-conscious sci-fi tale?" Penny suggested. "Sentient trees take their revenge on evil humans who pollute the air and water. What better target for their ire than the automobile, symbol of all things technological?"

"Didn't we do this bit last week?" I asked dubiously.

"Yeah, but people didn't seem to mind."

"I just don't want it to wear thin. But I like your idea, even if it is just a transparent rip-off of Tolkien's Ents." I replied cautiously, wary of the rage of rabid Tolkienites.

"Fuck Tolkien," the Countess Penelope of Acadia replied eloquently. "Yeah, you heard me."

Sometimes the photos in these prompts just scream for the obvious story – in this case, a tree branch fallen on a crashed car – and all you can do is to attempt to brainstorm something slightly less literal. Sometimes the brainstorming itself is far more interesting that anything you come up with.

isn 't it ionic?

" **T**hey're Doric columns, I'm telling you, Helena -- I just took a class in Greek History." The Countess Penelope of Arcadia (which is apparently in the area of Athens or perhaps Peloponnesia) proclaimed.

"And I insist they're Ionic," I insisted insistently.

(Allow me an indulgence, darlings, as I absolutely adore alliteration).

As we admired the Greek-inspired decor, the Countess and I found ourselves in disagreement.

"Excuse me, miss," I said demurely to the cashier, who looked remarkably like Alanis Morissette, "but what would you say is the style of these Greek columns?"

"Isn't it Ionic?" She replied without missing a beat.

Give me a picture of something with Greek columns in it, darlings, and this is the joke I'm going to make every time. Every. Single. Time.

This tale is special to me in that it has what may be my favourite, most self-indulgent line ever. I'm sure you'll be able to pick up on what it might be. In fact, I insist that you will.

charming:
a modern fairy tale

Had she really thought that they would live happily ever after, having just met him?

With a dashing smile, sparkling eyes, and an enchanting singing voice, it was no wonder they called him Charming.

He liked playing games, the first one called *Dreams of Escape*.

He liked watching her face wilt as she reached the telephone only to find it broken and dead.

His seven compatriots dragged her back to him, an apple in her mouth, her mascara staining her snow-white cheeks.

"Come here, you silly bitch," he leered. "Let's play a game called *Hide the Broken Telephone Receiver*."

As promised, I'm including this piece of Flash Fiction that I contributed to a weekly online community, the idea being to write a 100-word story inspired by a photo prompt. I'd been thinking about women making stupid decisions about men, and wondered how fairy tales would look if written by a darkly cynical person. This particular photo was of graffiti littered phone booth, with the receiver broken.

dress rehearsal
for a dilettante

When I first started writing the memoirs, I had no real plan — hard to believe, darlings, I know, but it's true. As such, my very first entry feels like something of a dress rehearsal of sorts, and while it doesn't necessarily work very well as the beginning of something bigger, the fact is, this was me cutting my teeth. It's my indictment of social media culture and the exchange of cheap shots rather than enlightening discourse.

the internet has made
assholes of us all

Iwas at a coffee shop the other day when I ran into a friend I hadn't seen for a while. I asked him to join me, and we got into discussing new music. I said that I quite enjoyed the new David Bowie album "The Next Day", and had he heard it, but before he could answer, a voice from a nearby table blurted out "It sucks. Nothing Bowie has done since Scary Monsters has been any good." To which I replied that the new album actually kind of had a Scary Monsters vibe to me, and 14 people "Liked" my comment. My friend said that he hadn't heard it yet, but hadn't been overly impressed by the singles that had been released so far. Three people "Liked" his comment and someone from another table spoke up and added"I don't know why they chose those two songs as singles to promote the album -- they're totally not representative of the album as a whole. They're really safe, radio-friendly choices, but the rest of the album is pretty cool -- there's even saxophone on there -- and when's the last time you heard Bowie play sax, I mean, really?"

At this, the first voice, let's call him SuperCreep1980, reasserted that "Bowie lost his imagination after he discovered Buddhism", and the barista, some thirtysomething hipster with a -- swear to God -- waxed handlebar moustache -- yelled "Bullshit!", and 5 people "Liked" this comment.

"I'm sorry,"SuperCreep1980 replied,"I just prefer his '70s output. Scary Monsters was the last album I really liked of his."

"Bullshit!" SBuxBarista1476 spat. Apparently it can be bullshit to state a personal preference.

"I love Skrillex!" BellaNEdward4ever piped in, and 2 people "Liked" this.

"Your an idiot," BengalsFan1133 said, and rolled his eyes.
"That's you're, fucktard," MikalDbois added self-righteously. (Though how they could distinguish a dropped apostrophe from the spoken word is quite beyond me).

At this point, my friend and I left the coffee shop, but I have it on good authority that the conversation went on for days after we left, and when I popped my head in this morning, I overheard someone declare that anyone who likes Skrillex deserves to have their ears melted and their tongue ripped out.

Not wanting to seem presumptuous, I asked the barista for a transcript of the conversation, so I could scroll through it and "Like" or comment on the responses.

After all, you are all entitled to my opinion.

jessica b. bell

*J*essica B. Bell is the name I go by when I'm writing strange, dark fiction -- the kind that people just wouldn't take seriously coming from a smartass by the name of Helena Hann-Basquiat. Jessica's story *The Best Medicine* was published in Off the KUF Volume One, as well as All Hail the New Flesh, an anthology of short fiction on the theme of Technology Gone Wrong by Dagda Publishing. I'm including a preview of it here as a tease, darlings, so you can see what Penny was so upset about.

the best medicine

$\mathcal{J}$udy's last memory of Helena was a bloody handprint on the train window as it sped away. It was somewhat larger than the painted handprint that hung in a square frame on the wall of her office, but she would never see that treasured handprint ever again, whereas this horrible red one would linger by her side until...

Until I die, Judy thought grimly. The familiar loops and whorls of Helena's bloody fingerprints on the glass as the world rushed by outside were something for Judy to focus on, but they were poor comfort – her daughter was gone. Left behind, and only 12 years old.

"Quickly!" Judy whispered in a panic, grabbing Helena by the arm and pulling her out of bed. "We've got to go! Now!"

Helena woke immediately and followed her mother out of her room into the upstairs hallway. They had all taken to sleeping in their clothes, never wanting to be caught off-guard, but Helena's feet were still bare. Judy bit her lip in a kind of annoyance with her daughter that was almost akin to contempt, but brushed away the ugly feelings as quickly as they surfaced. She knew that they stemmed from fear, and that she wasn't really angry, she was...

Something smashed against a wall somewhere else in the house, and Helena let out a startled cry.

"Shhh!" Judy hushed her, holding a hand firmly over Helena's mouth. The older woman's heart was trembling in her chest, and her mouth was dry and cottony. She licked her lips and whispered: "We've got to get out of the house."

Helena nodded and pointed to the stairs, and as she looked down, her eyes paused for a moment at her bare feet, and she jerked up her head in panic. A silent apology passed between them, and Judy reached out and cupped her daughter's face with one hand, her thumb caressing Helena's tear-streaked cheek. She was so young and so beautiful.

What have we done to her world? What have I done? Judy thought. It wasn't supposed to be like this. They promised that we would be safe.

Judy's contract stipulated that she and her family were to be exempt from the Acclimation, as they were calling it. All the families of employees were supposed to be safe.

Somebody at PharmaCon obviously had other plans, Judy reflected, miserably.

Helena quietly crept back to her room and pulled her well-worn Chuck Taylors out from under her bed, then made her way back to the stairs. Each step threatened discovery, so Helena tried to avoid the creaky boards. Once the disease progressed to the third and fatal stage, the Infected were faster than anyone would have believed.

Downstairs, the television clicked on, suddenly perforating the silence with the disorienting din of static. Helena bolted from her room and leapt into her mother's arms.

"Come on," Judy whispered. "I don't know where your father is."

"He's not my father," Helena said petulantly, tears welling up.

"Yes he is," Judy said, wanting with all her heart for that to be true, but knowing that it wasn't. Like a good mother, she lied to her daughter. "He's just sick. And a lot of really smart people are trying to make a cure, okay? But right now…"

"Right now, he might hurt me," Helena whispered almost inaudibly.

"Yes," she agreed, nodding, thinking of what the first outbreak patients had done to each other in the lab and shuddering. "Yes, he might hurt you."

Read the whole story! E-book now available on Amazon's Kindle store.

acknowledgements

There are several people that I would like to thank, for their encouragement and inspiration. These are people I only met because of sharing these stories, and after a while, they became some of the reason I kept writing them. Thank you Katie for your tireless promotion and praise. Thank you Andra for your advice, commiseration and the lovely fridge calendar. Thank you Jennie for urging me to write what was in my heart, even if it was dark or painful. Thank you Jex for voraciously devouring everything there was to read and then forcing me to show you all the stuff I'd been hiding. Thank you Marie for making me feel brilliant.

My friend and editor, Hannah Sears -- I cannot thank you enough for being a sounding board, and for all the behind-the-scenes banter (which could fill another whole volume, I think) that helped shape and inspire a lot of this writing. Thank you for your friendship; your many helpful suggestions, and all your hard work in editing.

Thank you to everyone who dropped by to read, whether it was all the time or even once.

Thank you to my long time friend Jim for the editing, the advice, and most of all for pestering me to write because I enjoyed it, and for assuring me that the rest would come in time. Still waiting for that...

And of course, thank you to Penny... and Penny... and Penny... always Penny. Thank you.

The portraits in the dramatis personae, as well as the cover, were drawn by Ros Webb. You can check out more of her work at www.roswebbart.com

about the author

The enigmatic Helena Hann-Basquiat dabbles in whatever she can get her hands into just to say that she has.

She's written cookbooks, ten volumes of horrible poetry that she then bound herself in leather she tanned poorly from cows she raised herself and then slaughtered because she was bored with farming.

She has an entire portfolio of macaroni art that she's never shown anyone, because she doesn't think that the general populous or, "the great unwashed masses" as she calls them, would understand the statement she was trying to make with them.

Some people attribute the invention of the Ampersand to her, but she has never made that claim herself.

Helena also writes strange, dark fiction under the name Jessica B. Bell Find more of her writing at www.helenahb.com, www.whoisjessica.com, or connect with her via Twitter @HHBasquiat

www.ingramcontent.com/pod-product-compliance
Lightning Source LLC
Chambersburg PA
CBHW022145170626
46807CB00005B/2076